I0653704

TILTED

BONDED BILLIONAIRE SHAPESHIFTERS
BOOK 3

DG IRELAND

ARTISTIC ORIGINS

MY BOOKS

Nonfiction	
The Puppy Baby Book	Mastering Your Money (2022)
Puppy Adoption and Beyond	Writers Preparation Handbook
Mastering Your Money (2008)	What's Breaking Your Budget
Online Classes	
Writers Preparation Handbook	How to Format Word Docs Like A Pro
Cozy Mysteries	**Sci-Fi-Fantasy**
The Alcott Family Adventures	**The Thol Series**
Hot Chocolate	Prophecy of Thol
Bitter Chocolate	Gifts From Thol
Spicy Chocolate	Love of Thol
Nutty Chocolate	King of Thol
Katz' Cat Series	Earth Calling Thol
Katz' Cat	**Sci-Fi Romance Adventure**
Bill Hill's Pills	Forced Dreams
The Detectives	**Dystopian**
The Pact	The Last Dog
	Texmexzona
Books by my Alter Ego ~ DG Ireland	
Bonded Shapeshifter Billionaire Series	
Bonded	
Tothars	
Tilted	
Unforeseen	
Connected	
Need A Notebook?	
See my 54 themed notebooks on my website	
www.degreenfield.com/notebooks	
Screenplays formatted as books	
Plan B (Dark Comedy)	Where's Ralphie? (Family Comedy)
The God Child (Action Adventure)	Standing Dead (Drama/Tragedy)
The Far Corner (Sci-Fi/Psychological/Creatures)	
Screenplays as TV Episodes	
Hot Chocolate ~ Episode 1	Prophecy of Thol ~ Episode 1
Bonded ~ Episode 1	
See my screenplays and awards on my website: degreenfield.com	
Filmfreeway, ISA Network	

Tilted by DG Ireland

Published by Artistic Origins Inc.

Copyright © 2019 Dawn Greenfield Ireland All rights reserved.

Cover design Marcha Fox / Kalliope Rising Press

Interior layout by Yours Truly (me); corrections made 1/2024, 5/2024, 4/2026

Pendulum cover image from Pixabay.com

Pendulum scene break icon by Carlos Salgado from the Noun Project

Pendulum "swish" by AskOrbin with Fiverr.

ISBN 978-1-940385-24-2 (eBook)

ISBN 978-1-940385-25-9 (paperback)

All rights reserved. No part of this publication may be reproduced, distributed or transmitted in any form or by any means, including information storage and retrieval systems, without written permission from the author and/or publisher, except for the use of brief quotations in a book review.

Dawn Greenfield Ireland

Artistic Origins Inc.

http://www.degreenfield.com/

Publisher's Note: This is a work of fiction. Names, characters, places, and incidents are a product of the author's imagination. Locales and public names are sometimes used for atmospheric purposes. Any resemblance to actual people, living or dead, or to businesses, companies, events, institutions, or locales is completely coincidental.

This book may contain references to specific commercial products, process or service by trade name, trademark, manufacturer, or otherwise, specific brand-name products and/or trade names of products, which are trademarks or registered trademarks and/or trade names, and these are property of their respective owners. Dawn Greenfield Ireland or her associates, have no association with any specific commercial products, process, or service by trade name, trademark, manufacturer, or otherwise, specific brand-name products and/or trade names of products.

The scanning, uploading, and distribution of this book via the Internet or any other means without the permission of the publisher is illegal and punishable by law.

Please purchase only authorized electronic editions, and do not participate in or encourage electronic piracy of copyrighted materials. Your support of the author's rights is appreciated.

Please visit my website: http://www.degreenfield.com/ and sign up for my newsletter to get the latest news before the public.

Be kind = leave a review!

TO ALL MY READERS... if you discover bloopers in this book (or any of my books), PLEASE send me an email and tell me what the blooper is so I can fix it! dawn@degreenfield.com

ACKNOWLEDGMENTS

Many thanks to the Noun Project for their fabulous collection of icons, specifically Carlos Salgado for the pendulum icon I have used between scenes.

The beautiful cover pendulum image came from Pixabay.com. Thanks to AskOrbin of Fiverr for the pendulum "swish".

Many thanks to Brandon White for his help with IT wiring descriptions. I had it totally wrong.

A great cover says it all. Once again, Marcha Fox of Kalliope Rising Press delivered the goods.

To my beta readers who poked and prodded me with suggestions, you're the best.

Secret weapon: Jeff Gonyea, my proofreader with eyes like lasers—you've done it again—kept me out of trouble! Thanks, cuz!

And, finally, Grasshopper (Richard Stone) who caught last minute blunders. The student teaches the teacher a thing or two.

ADULT CONTENT

This book contains sexually explicit material that may offend some readers and is intended **for adult audiences only**.

That means if you're under 18, it's scorching enough to burn your eyes out, so stay away. Everything in this book is purely fictional (make-believe), and none of the people in it are real. They exist only in my wild imagination.

All sexually active characters are over 18 and none are related by real or imaginary blood.

TO ALL MY READERS... if you discover bloopers in this book (or any of my books), PLEASE send me an email and tell me what the blooper is so I can fix it! dawn@degreenfield.com

CHAPTER ONE

Gage Stryker pawed the deflated airbag out of the way, then opened the driver's door of his Mercedes, dazed. His sandy blond hair stood on end in places.

He ran a hand through his hair, blinked and looked around. Gage didn't recognize where he was.

The brand-new white Camaro, which now had a buckled hood, grill, and fender, hit the passenger side of the black car.

A young man in a red polo shirt with an office supply logo, black slacks and clunky black shoes, got out of the white car. He stared at the damage in dismay.

Gage swiped a hand down his *4 Non Blondes* collector's t-shirt that sported Linda Perry on the front, then pulled himself out of the Mercedes. He swayed slightly, slammed his hand onto the side of the car to steady himself, then walked around his damaged car to where the other driver stood.

"You okay?" Gage didn't see any blood, but the kid's face was red and welted where the airbag smashed into him.

The young driver's eyes flicked up to the blood on the side of Gage's head. "You're hurt."

Gage touched his head at the hairline on his left temple and stared at the blood on his fingers. "Just a superficial scratch." He wiped his fingers on his denim shorts.

The young driver fretted. "My father is going to kill me! The car still has paper tags!"

"You didn't see that stop sign?" Gage pointed to the unobstructed sign the kid plowed through.

The driver shook his head.

"Better call a tow truck," Gage suggested.

Several motorcycles barreled down the street. Gage stared after the bikes. He patted his pockets and found a cellphone. He scrolled through his contacts and placed a call.

ML

Under five minutes later, a taxi pulled up. Gage got into the back of the cab, and the taxi drove away without a backward glance at the kid. He didn't even take down the kid's information.

Panther Industries Security Division was a hive of activity. Sherman (Sherm) Foo's fingers flew over one of his keyboards as he stared at a wall of monitors. He barked out questions and orders to his team via the office phone's PA system.

"Travis, any luck on that paint chip?"

"Close," Travis yelled back.

"Kevin, any visuals from the cameras in the vicinity of the accident?" Sherm shouted.

Kevin bellowed back, "Lonnie and I are looking at footage on three other cameras, trying to determine the time of the accident."

"Let me know when you find visuals."

Roman Davenport paced in front of Sherm's desk. He ran both hands through his black, shoulder-length hair.

Nothing yet, Ari. I promise to tell you the second anyone has anything solid to report, Roman sent to Ari in mind talk.

Shifters had that advantage over humans. No texting required. They had to remember that their human pals didn't have that ability and couldn't hear them.

Roman's panther slept out this crisis in a corner of his mind. As a shapeshifter, Roman had the face and body of a forty-five-year-old man, but he was closing in on one hundred years old. He had regained the weight he had lost when he had been abducted and starved by the maniac Tothar king in Italy.

Now, Roman and Ari's life partner, Gage, was missing. They determined he was probably suffering from a concussion after the auto accident and was confused. He hadn't answered calls or texts from Roman, Ari, Sherm, Leander, the boys, or anyone else. No one knew the exact time of the accident.

Lonnie started his camera search from the approximate time Gage left the penthouse. Kevin started his search backwards from the time Leander called Ari asking about Gage's where-abouts, which was two to three hours later.

The door to Sherm's domain opened, and Jason entered. "Any news?"

Roman shook his head.

Jason muttered under his breath. "I can't believe this is happening again." He watched his brother and his team working in their cubicles through the glass wall of Sherm's office. He twitched as Ari, his mother, asked him again for an update.

No, Mom, there's no point in coming down here. Let the guys do their work.

Jason and Kevin recently discovered their own strange heritage. When their mother was abducted by the serial killer, they freaked out when they discovered Roman and Gage were shapeshifters. Then, when the Italians captured Roman, their mother transformed into a huge liger. She battled the Italian Tothar king's saber-toothed tiger to the death. That transformation sparked Jason and Kevin to shift into their animals, a tiger and a lion, respectively.

"I'd better go back upstairs," Roman said.

Sherm stood and stretched. "I'll ride up with you. Right now, Ari needs our support, and Eddie probably needs a distraction."

The three men left Sherm's domain. Jason returned to his office on the thirtieth floor. Sherm and Roman rode the elevator up to the penthouse.

Ari jettisoned off the sofa and rushed across the room to the foyer. "Anything at all?"

Worry creased her flawless face. She looked twenty-five years younger than her actual age and joked that she was catching up with her sons. Jason and Kevin were in their forties.

A little girl's screech sounded, and tiny feet pattered down the hallway. Eddie slammed into Sherm's legs. "Sherm! You came to visit me!"

"I sure did, cupcake," Sherm said as he picked her up. "Are you helping Ari stay calm while we look for Gage?"

"Where did Daddy Gage go to?" Eddie asked.

"We don't know," Sherm said. "He bumped his head and doesn't remember anything."

Roman pulled Ari into a full-body contact hug. His arms wrapped around her, and he kissed her long, waist-length white hair at the side of her head. "We'll find him."

Sherm's phone beeped an alert. He set Eddie on the floor, then pulled his cellphone out of his pocket and read the screen. "We've got visuals!"

Roman kissed Ari, then Eddie. "I'll send pictures." Sherm and Roman rode the elevator down to Panther Security on the twenty-eighth floor. As soon as they were through the door to the security division, Sherm bellowed out questions.

"What do we have? Put it up on the screens."

"Daddy will not be forgiving," Lonnie said. He shared his monitor, which showed the crumbled, brand-new Camaro.

Another view showed the kid out of the car talking with Gage.

"Zoom in. Is that blood on Gage's head?" Sherm barked. The picture zoomed. They saw the trickle of blood on Gage's head.

"Check out the kid's shirt. Looks like a work outfit. See if you can read the store logo, then get someone over there with a picture to ID him," Sherm said.

Sherm turned to Roman. "We should have the full picture within the next half-hour. Once we have the kids' ID, we'll go talk to him.

🏋ML🏋

Sherm pulled the heavy-duty Navigator SUV up to a magnificent mansion on Reading Boulevard in Wyomissing, Pennsylvania, a wealthy town west of Reading. He turned to Roman in the passenger seat. "Remember, do not get riled up."

Roman huffed out an angry snort. "I promise."

They got out of the SUV in the wide circular driveway and approached the front door. Sherm rang the doorbell. They heard the deep tones through the door. Moments later, the door opened.

A man in a three-piece bespoke suit glanced them over. "May I help you?"

"We hope so," Sherm said, as he held up a Panther Securities Division badge. "I'm Sherman Foo, the head of Panther Industries Security Division, and this is Roman Davenport, the CEO of Panther Industries."

"Panther Industries? Did something happen at my company that I'm not aware of?" the man asked. He pulled his cellphone out of an inside suit pocket and checked for alerts.

"No, you're good," Sherm said. "We're here on a different matter." He pulled out his phone and thumbed up a picture.

He turned the phone screen toward the man. "Is this your son?"

The man stared at the iPhone screen. "Yes, what happened?"

"Is he here?" Roman asked.

Sherm thumbed the screen and showed pictures of the accident.

"That goddamn, irresponsible twit..." the man spat out. "Was anyone hurt?"

"My business partner is missing," Roman said. "We can't find him."

"We need to speak with your son and see if he can give us any information," Sherm said.

"Come in," the man said. He opened the door wider, stepped aside and guided them into a sitting room to the left of the entryway. He held out his hand. "Jack Sprat."

Roman's eyebrow quirked as he accepted the hand. "Sprat?"

"Yes, like the nursery rhyme. Be thankful you didn't have my parents," Jack grumbled.

They all shook hands.

"Let me see if Cody is home," Jack said. He walked to the bottom of the enormous staircase and hollered. "Cody?" He listened for a moment, then yelled again.

A door opened upstairs, and a disheveled teenager came to the upstairs railing. "What?"

"Get down here. You've got some explaining to do," Jack said.

Cody thumped down the stairs and stood before his father, his face bruised. He looked the visitors over and noticed Sherm's corporate shirt with the logo. He swallowed. Everyone in Reading knew Panther Industries. Their security division protected his dad's company.

"Do you have something to tell me?" Jack asked his son.

Cody was as nervous as a piece of popcorn in a microwave. "I had a little fender-bender, that's all."

"Little? You totaled the Camaro," Jack said, in a raised voice.

Sherm provided his phone screen to refresh Cody's memory.

"You think it's totaled?" Cody asked. His voice rose to a squeaky panic.

"Look, that's for your private discussion," Roman said. "We need to know if you can tell us where the driver of the Mercedes went."

Cody's wild eyes focused on Roman. "He told me to call a tow truck, then he called a cab, and just left."

"What was the name of the taxi, did you notice?" Sherm asked.

"Yeah, the Wyomissing taxi company," Cody said.

"Okay, thanks," Sherm said. He and Roman headed toward the front door. Sherm commanded orders on his phone. "Pull up Gage's phone records. He called the Wyomissing Cab Company. When you have the time, he placed the call, get them on the phone and find out where they took him."

Roman and Sherm had already exited the mansion when Cody ran outside to catch them. "Hold up a sec!"

"Is there more we should know?" Roman asked.

"Yeah. He didn't seem to know where he was. That's all," Cody said.

Roman and Sherm shared a concerned glance. "Thanks, we appreciate your help," Sherm said.

ML

They hurried to the Navigator, got in, and the SUV shot out of the circular driveway onto the street.

As Sherm drove the SUV back to Reading, Lonnie called. "We've got two things. He took a cab to the Harley dealership in Leesport. Travis got a ping alert for a large cash withdrawal on his bank account and two purchases at the Harley dealership on his American Express Centurion card."

Sherm and Roman exchanged a curious glance.

"We'll head over to the dealership," Sherm said. He disconnected the call, made a wide U-turn and sped off.

"What the hell is going on?" Roman said. "This is not like Gage at all."

"He's got a head injury," Sherm said.

ML

Fifteen minutes later, they pulled into the dealership and got out of the truck.

A salesman approached them. "What can I help you with today?" He eyed Roman. "You look like a Sportster kind of guy."

"We need to speak with your manager," Roman said, all businesslike.

The guy quirked his eyebrow. "Is there a problem?"

"Are you the manager?" Sherm asked, with a hint of warning in his voice.

"No..." the salesman said.

Sherm pulled the front door open, and he and Roman stepped inside. The salesman tailed them inside and skirted around them. He disappeared into an office.

The place was hopping. People were buying motorcycles and accessories.

The salesman exited the office with a big, burly man in his wake. They approached Sherm and Roman.

"This is Buzz, the manager," the sales guy said.

"What could I help you gentlemen with?" Buzz asked.

"A taxi dropped our business partner off here a few hours ago," Roman said.

Sherm worked his phone and pulled up a picture of Gage. He held the screen for the manager to see. The salesman peeked over his boss' shoulder.

"He was in an accident and has a head injury. We're trying to locate him," Sherm said.

The manager's face became guarded when he heard *head injury*. He looked at the phone screen and recognized the man. Cash sale. Fully loaded bike. Clothing and accessories.

"Why don't we go into my office where we can discuss this," Buzz said. He turned to the salesman, dismissing him. "I'll handle it from here."

Roman and Sherm followed the manager to his office. Buzz closed the door after them, then walked around his desk and sat.

"Have a seat. What name would he have used? I'll look up the sales tickets," Buzz said.

"Gage Stryker," Roman said. "That's Stryker with a "y"."

Buzz's fingers clacked on the keyboard. He pulled up the sales order and printed a copy. "I had no idea he had a head injury, but it was a rather odd sale."

"What do you mean?" Sherm asked. "Odd, how?"

"He was just so matter of fact. He didn't express the excitement you would expect of someone buying a top of the line Harley," Buzz said. "He acted rather clinically. Same with the clothes and accessories he picked out. All clearly functional choices."

"Did he mention where he was going when he left here?" Roman asked.

Buzz shook his head. "Not much of a conversationalist. Signed the papers, grabbed the keys, slipped into his new clothes, then he was out of here."

Buzz gathered the papers from the printer and stapled them together. He handed them to Sherm. "I wish I could tell you more."

"Do you have a picture of the bike?" Sherm asked.

Buzz stretched over to the wall and pulled a brochure out of a rack, and handed it to Sherm. "This is the bike Mr. Stryker drove off the lot."

Sherm set the brochure on the desk and snapped a picture with his phone. "Thanks."

Roman and Sherm stood.

"Thanks for your time," Sherm said.

"I hope Mr. Stryker is going to be okay," Buzz said.

Sherm grabbed the door handle, and he and Roman left the dealership.

CHAPTER TWO

"He could be anywhere," Roman said, as he got into the passenger side of the Navigator.

Sherm settled into the driver's seat. He worked his phone with his thumbs. "I'm sending the picture to the team. They can look at the cameras around the dealership and try to catch up with him. At the very least, we can find the direction he's heading."

"That business about him acting odd and clinical has me thinking he might have a touch of amnesia," Roman said. "I'll have Ari check in with Mr. Tran and Dr. Tanner. They need to be on call for when we catch up with Gage." He sent a mind-message to Ari.

I'm on it! Ari sent back.

Sherm started the SUV and pulled out of the dealership parking lot and headed back to Reading. "Maybe you should blast out the picture of the motorcycle to the community. At the very least, call Atsa so he knows Gage wasn't kidnapped."

"Good idea," Roman said. He clicked on the database of shifters on his iPhone and sent the motorcycle picture to everyone with a note. Then he pulled up Atsa's information.

ML

Four days later, Gage pulled the motorcycle up to Butch's Biker Bar in Little Rock, Arkansas. The place needed a fresh coat of red paint around five years ago, but the lot held more than a dozen bikes and one trike. Gage dismounted and headed for the door. He entered the low-light bar and removed his sunglasses, and pocketed them. He headed toward the bar and settled on a stool.

A fifty-something man with long, stringy hair, multiple face and ear piercings ambled up to him behind the bar. "What can I get you?"

"Cold beer," Gage said. He slapped a five-dollar bill on the counter. "Where's the restroom?"

The bartender pointed to the left of the bar. "Over there."

Gage removed his leather jacket and hung it on the back of the bar stool. The bikers noticed the stunning, full-color eagle tattoos on his biceps. He meandered to the restroom and went inside. He looked around the messy bathroom. Gage rested his hands on the counter and stared at his reflection. He sprang back when the face of an eagle appeared in a flash, momentarily blocking his human facial features.

A stall door opened at that moment. Tommy, a twenty-two-year-old shifter with dark brown hair, straight as a board, startled at who and what he saw.

Gage shook his head, ran his hands down his face, then turned the water faucet on and splashed cold water on his face to clear his head.

Tommy bent and scrutinized the other three stalls. They were empty. He straightened and approached the sinks. "King Gage?" Tommy whispered. "Are you all right?"

Gage jumped when he noticed the kid. "Who are you? What'd you call me?"

Tommy screwed up his face. "My name's Tommy Littlefield, King Gage. What are you doing here? Is King Roman or Queen Ari with you?"

Gage stared at the boy. "King? I don't think so. I'm going to drink my beer and get something to eat." He pushed away from the counter, left the restroom and returned to his seat at the bar where a cold beer sat waiting for him.

Tommy entered the bar and sat on the stool next to Gage. He recalled the email from King Roman, and the blast he received about Gage's accident. He looked over the Tothar king. There was a knot on his temple.

"I'll be right back. Save my seat, okay?" Tommy asked Gage.

Gage looked the kid over. "Sure."

Tommy hurried out the front door to his pickup truck and ducked inside. He found Roman's email, but couldn't find a telephone number. He sat there thinking for a moment, then he decided to just blast out a local message.

This is an emergency! I need King Roman's phone number!

A nervous, silent moment passed, then several local shifters pinged Tommy.

What's wrong? Who is this?

Where are you?

It's Tommy. I'm over at Butch's. King Gage is here, and he doesn't know who he is, he sent back.

We'll be there in a little while.

A shifter sent Roman's phone number. Tommy plugged the number into his phone and placed the call. It rang four times, then someone answered.

"Roman."

🏰 **ML** 🗻

"King Roman! This is Tommy Littlefield. King Gage is here!" Tommy sputtered. "I don't think he realizes he's a shifter." He shared the mind picture from the bathroom mirror with Roman.

Roman bolted to his feet, practically knocking the coffee table over. He shoved his feet into his loafers and headed down the hallway, phone to his ear. "Where are you, Tommy?"

Tommy gave Roman the information.

"Okay. We'll be there in a couple of hours. Try to stay with Gage at all costs. Call in reinforcements from the community, if you have to—just make sure you don't lose him. We're pretty sure he has a concussion."

"I'll do the best I can," Tommy said.

Roman disconnected the call. He called Sherm, told him where Gage was. The panther shifter rushed to Ari's suite and found her napping on the sofa in her sitting room. Roman slid to the floor in front of her and kissed her forehead. "Honey, wake up!"

Ari started awake. Her eyes were unfocused from the sudden disturbance. Then, she sprang to a sitting position when her full faculties returned. "What... have you found Gage?"

"Call just came in from Little Rock. Get Eddie. I'll be downstairs with Sherm," Roman said.

Roman rushed to the elevator and rode down to Sherm's domain on the twenty-eighth floor. He found Sherm gearing up, switching from office clothes to his commando uniform.

"Figured if we're going to a biker bar, I'd better be prepared," Sherm said. He picked up a satchel that looked like a doctor's black bag. "Dr. Tanner provided a tranquilizer syringe the other day. I told him we wouldn't use it unless it was absolutely necessary."

"Good thinking. We don't know what the hell to expect," Roman said. "This guy, Tommy, will let us know if there're any problems he can't handle. Sounds young."

"I don't understand what he's doing in Arkansas, of all places," Sherm said. "Big Bear Muchisky is meeting us at the jet. Figured his presence alone will stave off any problems once we get there."

"Not necessarily," Roman said. "They could see him as a challenge."

The office door opened and Ari rushed in, an excited Eddie running toward the men.

"Are we going to bring daddy Gage home?" Eddie asked.

"We sure are," Sherm said. "You ready to fly on the airplane?"

Eddie jumped and squealed. "I love to fly! Daddy Gage can *really* fly!"

ML

Gage dug into a plate of chicken-fried steak smothered in gravy, mashed potatoes and steamed carrots. Tommy sat on the barstool beside him with a plate of food in front of him.

"How long did it take you to drive from Reading?" Tommy asked.

Gage paused, his fork in the air as he thought about Tommy's question. "Where exactly is Reading? I'm not familiar with that name."

Tommy stared at Gage, thoughts racing through his head. "Pennsylvania, where you live with King Roman and Queen Ari."

"I'm pretty sure I'd remember if I lived in a palace," Gage chortled.

Tommy huffed out an exasperated sigh. "You don't live in a palace! The three of you live in a high-rise. You don't remember?"

Gage shook his head. "Two kings and a queen? I don't think so, kid."

"You're Tothars, King Gage. Did you see your eagle in the mirror?" Tommy asked.

The front door of the bar slammed open. A big, burly guy who must have weighed at least four-hundred pounds, sporting long hair and a scraggly beard, entered. He looked mean and dangerous. The patrons all stopped what they were doing when they noticed who entered.

"Oh, no," Tommy whispered. "It's Earl."

Gage turned on the stool and looked the guy over. He returned to his plate of food.

"Try to ignore him," Tommy said.

Earl strolled over to the bar and clamped a beefy hand down on Gage's shoulder. "You're sittin' in my place."

"You'd better get your hand off me if you plan to keep it," Gage said. He calmly set the fork down on his plate and pushed the plate back.

Tommy seemed to shrink beside Gage.

"Oh! I'm scared!" Earl asked. "Get off my fucking barstool."

"Earl, back off and leave the man to his meal," the bartender warned. "There's plenty of empty stools."

"You mind your own fucking business," Earl said. He shot the bartender a look of pure evil.

Gage pushed the barstool back, grabbed Earl's hand and squeezed.

Bones cracked.

Earl screamed. Then rage covered his face.

Tommy was on his feet, distancing himself from the fight to come.

Gage turned to face Earl. He was coldly calm.

The front door opened and three men came inside. They scanned the room with their eyes and followed the tension of the patrons stares to the bar.

At that moment, Gage grabbed Earl by the neck with one hand and lifted him clear off the floor without any effort—a seemingly impossible feat because of Earl's size.

A couple of bikers stood, posturing. The three men rushed to the bar.

"King Gage, you'd better put the guy down before you hurt him," one man said.

"King Gage, this isn't exactly keeping a low profile," the second man said.

"Tommy, you'd better call King Roman!" the third man said.

Tommy's phone was to his ear in a split second. "King Roman! King Gage is out of control! I think there's going to be a fight!" He listened. "Okay. We'll try to diffuse the situation. My friends are here."

He turned to his shifter friends. "They should be here within half an hour."

Everyone faced Gage.

Earl's face was turning purple with rage and lack of oxygen. His hand gripped Gage's. He tried to pull it off his neck, but he couldn't even budge a finger.

One of the bikers approached. "Put Earl down, man!"

Gage appeared scary-calm and cold. His eagle talons dug into Earl's neck. "If you want this piece of shit to live, I'd advise you to back off and leave me the fuck alone."

The look in Gage's eyes had the bikers inching away a few feet. They suddenly busied themselves.

The shifters hovered around Gage's side opposite the bikers.

Tommy placed a hand on Gage's free arm. "You might want to put him down, or someone's going to call the cops."

Gage glanced at Tommy. After several long moments, he nodded. He let go of Earl's neck.

The biker landed on his butt on the floor, gasping. He held his bloody, sore neck with his good hand while he stared at Gage in fear and wonderment.

Gage returned to his barstool as if nothing happened.

The bartender approached him. "Why don't I reheat that for you?"

"Appreciate it," Gage said.

The bartender took both their plates.

The three shifters huddled around Tommy and Gage. "You don't want to call attention to yourself, King Gage," one of them said.

"These people are going to wonder how you could do that," another man whispered to Gage.

A biker guy walked up to Earl. He reached out a hand and dragged Earl to his feet. Earl staggered over to a table and crashed down into a chair.

The front door opened. Big Bear Muchisky lumbered inside. He was the Paul Bunyan of lumberjacks without ever working in the lumber industry. His six-foot-five frame was solid muscle. Not a roll of flab in sight. Big

Bear stopped just inside the doorway and took in the scene.

Sherm and Lonnie followed the bear shifter inside.

Every biker in the joint stared at the enormous man and the two obvious commandos loaded with weapons. Adam's apples bobbed as the men swallowed, wondering if there was going to be a fight. All eyes swung back to Big Bear.

Earl shoved his chair back and stood. "Who the fuck are you and what are you doing here?"

Sherm and Lonnie approached the bar.

Big Bear advanced over to Earl. He towered over the biker. "You want to discuss this problem outside, sweetie?"

A friend grabbed Earl's arm and pulled him back into his chair. "Haven't you had enough for one day, Earl?"

"Obviously not," Big Bear said.

Sherm nodded to the four shifters. "Everything okay here?"

"Not really," Tommy said.

Roman and Ari entered the bar. Eddie dangled on Roman's hip with her arms around his neck.

Eddie saw Gage. "Daddy Gage!" She squirmed to get down.

Roman tapped her on the hip with two fingers. "Not yet, pumpkin. Gage might not know who you are. He hurt his head, remember?"

Eddie digested his words. "It's okay. Gage loves me. He'll remember me."

"Let Roman hold you for now," Ari said. She warily looked at Gage's face in the bar mirror. There was no recognition in his features as he stared at them through the mirror.

Roman and Ari walked to the bar. Roman laid his hand gently on Gage's shoulder. He sent him a friendly pulse of warmth. "You doing okay, Gage? We've missed you."

Gage stared hard at Roman in the mirror. "Who the fuck are you?"

Ari stood beside Roman. She cleared her throat. "Language!" She nodded in Eddie's direction.

Tommy stood and tapped Roman on the shoulder. "King Gage doesn't know who he is or what he's saying."

Roman stared at the young man. "Tommy?"

"Yes, sire." Tommy bowed, along with the three local shifters.

Gage took in Ari's waist-long white hair and her beautiful, flawless face. Fitted cropped pants and a scooped-neck shirt hugged her body, and purple painted toenails peeked out of sandals. His face was plastered with lust.

He stood and walked around Roman, bumping him intentionally—not in a friendly way. Gage slipped an arm around Ari's shoulders and pulled her against his body.

"Hello, gorgeous. What say we slip out of here and I slip inside you?"

Ari's eyes widened. She looked from Gage to Roman, then to Sherm and Lonnie.

"What the fuck did you say to her?" Roman exploded. "Do you know who you're fucking talking to?"

Gage's eyes wandered over Ari's body. "No, but I hope to find out."

Roman handed Eddie over to Tommy. "This may get violent. Can you take Eddie outside?"

Tommy gripped Eddie and balanced her in his arms. "Sure. Hi Eddie. I'm Tommy. We'd better let the adults figure things out."

"I want Daddy Gage," Eddie said. She rubbed her little fist against her eye as she pouted her quivering lips.

"Don't worry. Everything will be okay," Tommy said. "Daddy Gage is having problems remembering everyone. Adults have a difficult time with this stuff. Let's get out of their way and let them talk."

Tommy and the shifters left the bar with Eddie.

Big Bear finished staring down Earl and lumbered up to the group at the bar.

Roman grabbed Gage's shirt with his left hand and pulled back his right fist.

Sherm stepped in between the two men. He pushed Roman back. "You're not thinking rationally, Roman. Knock it off."

Lonnie extracted Ari from Gage and pulled her aside. Sherm appraised Gage. "We're taking you back home, Gage."

"Who the fuck are you?" Gage spat the words at Sherm.

"Sherm. One of your best friends, and the head of your security business."

All the while, the bartender watched the drama play out. He clutched his baseball bat in one hand, out of sight, behind the bar. The bartender had cleared most of the glassware out of the way in case there was a struggle or an outright fight. He eyed the huge man in the flannel shirt who towered over everyone.

"I don't know who the fuck you think you are, but you're no friend of mine, and I'm not going anywhere with you people," Gage said.

"You can either come willingly, or we'll use force," Sherm said.

"You and what army?" Gage said.

Big Bear stepped directly in front of Gage. "Me!" He grabbed Gage in a bear hug and lifted him off the floor as if he were as light as Eddie, and walked him outside.

Roman turned to the bartender. "I'm sorry for the tension this caused. Our business partner was in an accident. He has temporary amnesia." Roman dug into his wallet and pulled out a fifty-dollar bill. He left it by Gage's plate.

"No harm done," the bartender said, as he eyed the bill on the bar.

Roman gathered Ari to him, and they all walked out of the bar.

A Sikorsky S-92 helicopter sat in the parking lot. Lonnie walked ahead of everyone and opened the doors. He entered the cockpit and waited for the rest of the party to climb aboard.

Big Bear Muchisky hauled a struggling Gage into the bird, followed by Sherm. "Where should I put him?"

Sherm pointed. "This is good." He stared down Gage. "You can either come willingly, or I'll tranq you. Which is it going to be?"

Gage tried to headbutt Big Bear.

"Okay, that's the way it's going to be?" Sherm pulled the black medical bag out from under a seat. He extracted the syringe, prepped it, and plunged it into Gage's neck. "Nighty-night. Sleepy time."

Ari approached Tommy and his friends. Eddie reached out to her, and Tommy turned her over to Ari. Roman joined them.

"Thanks for keeping our little girl safe, and keeping Gage out of trouble," Ari said.

"There were more than a few scary moments," Tommy said. "He lifted that bruiser Earl off the floor as if he didn't weigh chicken scratch. I'm pretty sure people will talk about that for years to come."

Roman saw Gage's Harley with the paper license plates.

He turned to Tommy. "Do you have family here? A pack?"

Tommy shook his head, sad. "No, I left home a long time ago. I don't have any bonds or ties here. I'm pretty much on my own."

"Think you can get the motorcycle to Reading, Pennsylvania?" Roman asked.

Sherm and Big Bear joined them in the parking lot. "He's out. I had to tranq him," Sherm said.

Roman nodded.

Ari let go of a breath. "I'm just glad we have him back."

Roman turned his focus back to Tommy. "What are you driving?"

Tommy pointed to his battered pickup. "That's my truck. It may not look like much, but it's in great shape. I rebuilt the engine and transmission, and it runs real smooth."

Roman dug his wallet out of his pants. He pulled out a thick wad of money and handed it to Tommy. "This should cover all your expenses."

Ari laid a hand gently on Tommy's arm. "Do you have an apartment here? A job?"

"I work at a repair shop," Tommy said. "I can fix anything, not just cars, and I bunk over the shop in the attic. Haven't been able to get into an apartment yet."

"Gather your things. We will find a place for you to live, and we'll find you work," Ari said. She shared a silent look with Roman and Sherm. They nodded.

"Do you have anything in the truck to strap the motorcycle down?" Sherm asked.

"Yes, I do. I'm not sure how to get it up in the truck's bed, though." Tommy looked around. "We need a board long enough to roll it up there."

Big Bear let out a long, hearty laugh. "No need for a board, kid. Get into the bed." He walked over to the motorcycle, sat astride it, and released the stand. He walked the bike over to the back of the pickup.

Tommy and Sherm jumped into the bed of the truck.

The huge man got off the bike, hefted it up and placed it in the back of the truck without even breathing hard.

Sherm and Tommy grabbed the bike to steady it and pulled it to the front of the bed.

Tommy opened the passenger side door of his pickup truck, then rummaged through a box behind the back seat. He pulled out a ratcheting come-along attached to some hefty-looking nylon tie-downs. He and Sherm went about working the cable through the openings on the bike and attaching the ends to hooks alongside the truck bed. Tommy then used the attached ratchet handle to take the slack out of the cable until the motorcycle was snugly anchored down. When Sherm determined that the bike was secure, they jumped down to the pavement.

Tommy's friends joined the circle.

"So, you're leaving Little Rock?" One of the guys asked.

Tommy nodded. "Yeah, looks like it. Better life ahead. Thanks for helping in there." He nodded to the bar.

Roman shook their hands. "Thanks for helping diffuse the situation."

The three shifters bowed to the royals, then went on their way.

"It's a pretty straightforward drive," Sherm said. "About eleven-hundred twenty-five miles. Take I-40 east, then I-81 north."

"Make sure you take plenty of breaks. There's no hurry. Stop for the night," Ari said. She looked at Roman. "Did you give him enough for hotels, food and gas?"

Tommy pulled the wad of cash out of his pocket. He unfolded it and counted. "There's almost two-grand here!" He started peeling bills off the stack.

Roman stayed his hand. "Keep it. You don't know what lies ahead, or if you'll have any problems with the truck."

"Go to the bank and get some ones and quarters in case there're tolls along the way," Sherm said.

"You've got my number. Call day or night if you have any problems whatsoever," Roman said. "You're doing us a big favor."

Eddie squirmed in Ari's arms. "Can I ride in the truck with Tommy?"

Ari smirked. "No, honey. You're going to ride in the helicopter, then the jet. You'll see Tommy in a few days."

Eddie reached out to Tommy. She kissed his cheek.

"Should I be jealous?" Sherm asked. He snickered.

Ari bashed his bicep. "Honestly, Sherm!"

A lightbulb went off in Sherm's head. He dashed over to the helicopter and hopped inside. He rummaged through Gage's pockets until he found the key to the bike, then returned to the group.

"Figured it would be best if you had the key. The paperwork is probably on the bike somewhere," Sherm said. He handed the key over to Tommy.

"Okay. I'd better let you get on your way," Tommy said. "I've only got a few things to gather, then I'll hit the road."

The bartender ran out the door, Gage's jacket in his hands. "Almost didn't notice your friend's jacket."

Sherm took the jacket. "Thanks. It's only four days old."

Roman stuck out his hand. He and Tommy shook. "Thanks, man. Call when you get to Reading so I can direct you to the building."

"Will do." Tommy walked to the cab of his pickup and got in.

Ari handed Eddie to Roman.

Roman, Ari, Sherm and Big Bear walked to the helicopter.

Tommy drove out of the lot as the rotors began to turn, churning up dust.

The bar door opened and the gaping bikers emerged. They stood around, dumbfounded as they watched the Sikorsky take to the air.

"That kid called the guy a king. Guess he is," one of the bikers said.

Earl scowled.

CHAPTER THREE

With Gage out cold, the transfer to the jet went seamlessly. They all buckled down, and Lonnie brought them home. When they reached their building in downtown Reading, Big Bear hauled Gage out of the Navigator, into the elevator, then into Gage's bedroom in the penthouse.

Roman got Big Bear aside and handed him two hundred dollars. "Thanks for all your help. Couldn't have done it without you."

"You don't owe me anything, Roman," Big Bear sputtered. He tried to hand the money back to the king.

"Go buy your wife some flowers and take her out to dinner. Just know we appreciate everything you do for us," Roman said.

Big Bear hung his head, embarrassed. "It's an honor that you called me to help." Big Bear left, and the others retired to the living room.

"I could use a drink right about now," Roman said. He walked to the bar and pulled the bottle of *Blade and Bow 22-year aged Kentucky Straight Bourbon* from the shelf. He raised the bottle to the group.

Ari, Sherm, and Lonnie nodded. Roman poured half an inch into Ari's glass and handed it to her, then he poured a more liberal amount into the remaining three glasses.

"To a successful extraction," Sherm said. They clinked their glasses together.

"What are you going to do when he comes to?" Lonnie asked.

"He won't be able to leave the penthouse," Roman said. "I've got his phone."

Ari appeared nervous. "I hope you don't have to fight him!"

Sherm let out a snort. "We know for a fact you can put a stop to that."

"Let's not freak him out by any of us shifting," Ari said. "He probably doesn't realize he has an animal inside."

"When he comes to, we'll get Dr. Tanner and Mr. Tran up here to help determine how to proceed," Roman said. "Until we fully understand what he does and doesn't remember, we're going to have to wing it."

"I'll help!" Eddie said. "Daddy Gage loves me."

"Yes, he does, pumpkin, but he doesn't even know he's Daddy Gage right now," Sherm said.

Five hours later, Gage rolled to his side. The movement jarred him awake. He slowly opened his eyes. He didn't recognize the room.

Where the hell am I? Doesn't look like a hotel.

Then a fuzzy memory tried to surface.

Strangers. A bunch of strangers.

He stayed on his side as his mind strayed. The bed was comfortable. The room looked like a man's domain. He could see an attached bathroom through the door that was slightly ajar.

Gage swung his legs over the side of the bed, then pulled himself up to a sitting position. The room spun. He gripped the bedding to hold himself steady. Gage looked around again—he didn't know where he was. He stood and lurched his way to the bathroom. The door slammed against the wall. He winced at the noise. His head pounded.

The outer door opened, and he heard the tinkling of chimes. "Gage? Are you okay? Do you need help?" a guy called out.

He heard soft footsteps enter the room. A face stared at him through the bathroom mirror. He had seen that face before; he was sure of it.

"Who're you? Where am I?" Gage asked.

"I'm your best friend and business partner, Roman Davenport. You and I are Ari Davis' life partners," Roman said. "This is your suite. We live in the penthouse of our building."

"Life partners? Penthouse?" Gage asked, dazed.

"Are you hungry? Ari's cooking dinner," Roman said. "Do you want to shower first?"

Gage glanced at himself in the mirror. He felt dirty. "Yeah, shower."

Roman opened the linen closet and pulled out a thick, gold-colored Egyptian cotton towel and a washcloth. "Want me to pull out a change of clothes for you, or do you want to get those yourself?"

"Where's the clothes?" Gage asked.

Roman pointed back into the bedroom at a chest of drawers. "Your underwear, socks, T-shirts." He pointed to a door. "Your shirts, pants, jeans, suits, jackets, shoes."

"Okay. I'll figure it out." Gage turned back to the mirror.

"When you're ready, go to the end of the hall and turn to the right. That leads to my suite, which is the hall to the right. If you go straight through, you'll see the living room, dining room and the kitchen," Roman said. He did not want to mention where Ari's or Eddie's suites were located.

Roman turned and left the suite.

Gage heard the snick of the outer door closing and the tinkle of chimes. He looked over the bathroom. He figured it was upscale. The shower could easily fit two people, maybe more. There was a freestanding tub that looked good for a soak. The farmer's sink offered ample space for his large hands and for his head if he ducked it under the faucet.

He explored the medicine cabinet, the drawers, and the cabinets. He discovered shaving tools, a brush, a comb, a toothbrush and toothpaste. There was a bottle of cologne. He removed the cap and took a whiff. It smelled good.

Gage undressed slowly. There was a hamper against the wall. He pulled a wallet out of his pocket and placed it on the counter. Gage stared at it a moment, then picked it up and opened it. He extracted the driver's license and read all the information, then studied the picture. He glanced up at the mirror. The name said he was Gage Stryker. The picture matched the face staring back at him in the mirror.

He dug through the wallet and found pictures. There was one of himself and the dark-haired man—Roman—with his arm draped across his shoulders in a best-friend sort of way. He turned the picture over and started when he read the date.

This can't be right. I'm positive this picture is at least fifty-years old. What year is it right now?

There were two other pictures. One of the three of them—himself, the woman—Ari, and Roman three years ago, and another one of a little girl in a fancy dress. He placed the pictures showing himself with the man and woman side by side on the counter. Besides different hairstyles, their faces were exactly the same.

His head reeled. He was on the brink of freaking out over the bizarre discovery. He just didn't know what it meant.

How could Roman and I look the same? It's not possible!

Gage returned everything to the wallet, glanced at the credit cards and some store cards, then checked other pockets in his pants. He found a handful of folded money on a clip and some loose change. He placed that on the counter, then dumped the dirty clothes into the white wicker hamper.

Gage turned the faucet handle in the shower. He stared at his body in the full-length mirror. He decided he must be obsessed with eagles. Each bicep had an eagle tattoo. He twisted to see his back. An eagle in flight was tattooed across his entire back. It was magnificent. He stared at it.

He noticed the steam filling the room. Gage stepped into the shower and let the spray from multiple shower heads rain down on him. He studied the bottles on the shelf in the wall. He pumped shampoo into his hand and washed his hair. Then he cleaned his body.

A strange vision of an eagle in flight flew through his head. Gage slammed his hand against the wet shower wall as dizziness followed the image. He shut off the water, grabbed the towel and wrapped it around his waist. He stepped out onto the bath mat. He stumbled to the counter and gripped the edge.

"Fuck."

Eagle. There's that eagle again. What's going on? Eagle tattoos. Daydreams...

He grabbed a hand towel and wiped down his sandy-colored hair. Gage ran a hand across the stubble on his face. He pulled out the shaving cream and the razor and went about shaving his five o'clock shadow. He splashed some cologne on his face.

Gage thoroughly dried himself, then stared at the damp towel. He looked around and decided it wouldn't be a good idea to dump it in the hamper. He hung it on the towel rod to dry. He found deodorant—some weird natural brand he couldn't remember ever seeing before—and applied it to his armpits.

Gage wandered into the bedroom and walked over to the chest of drawers.

He said this was my stuff.

He pulled open drawers to see what they contained. He returned to the second drawer, where he found an assortment of men's briefs. There were boxer shorts, short briefs and thongs.

I wear thongs?

He held up a thong and studied it. He replaced it in the drawer. Most of the briefs were black. He chose a pair of short briefs and stepped into them.

Comfortable.

The next drawer had an assortment of neatly folded T-shirts. A dark gold one caught his eye, so he extracted it and pulled it over his head. He opened the next drawer and found socks—all neatly paired, all black. He picked up a pair of socks, closed the drawer and went to the closet to find a pair of jeans and some shoes.

Gage stared at the contents of the immense closet. He blinked, taking it all in. There was a rack of belts, a rack of ties, and a rack of shoes. More T-shirts with pictures on the fronts or backs, hung on a rod, arranged by color. On another rod were long-sleeved dress shirts hanging on a rod, and more folded on a shelf from the laundry. The other rods held suit jackets, vests, dress pants, jeans, slacks, and casual jackets.

He stared at the choices, his mind whirling. He grabbed a pair of jeans and stepped into them, pulled them up, fastened the top button, and drew up the zipper. Gage turned to the assortment of shoes and chose a pair of black loafers. He sat on the bench and pulled on the socks, then slipped his feet into the shoes.

They fit.

These must be mine.

Gage looked over the belts and chose one. He threaded it through the belt loops and fastened it. As he looked around, he spotted a jewelry case and walked over to it. He found cufflinks, chains, wristbands and watches.

There were several watches.

He chose a sporty watch which he thought looked like chrome, and fastened it to his right wrist.

Gage left the closet, shut the door, and stood in the middle of the room. He saw another door and opened it. There was a large flat-screen TV on the wall, a sofa, chairs, and a desk with a laptop.

I must live here. It looks like I'm wealthy. Is all this my stuff?

After a few minutes ruminating, he returned to the bathroom, shoved the wallet into his rear pocket, then placed the money into his front pocket. He returned to the bedroom and opened the door. The chimes on the door handle caught his attention. He stared at them for a long moment, then he closed the door and went down the hall and turned to his right. He didn't know what to expect, but the view from the wall of windows took him by surprise.

The city sprawled out in front of him, lit by streetlights. Mountains and a forest were off in the distance. He wondered how he could see it all so well. It was dark outside. Nighttime.

He drew in his gaze at the mountains to study the living room. He heard noises to his left and saw the woman in the kitchen.

Is she mine?

Do the three of us live together?

Is she my wife—what's our relationship?

The woman startled as if she heard him. She turned in his direction.

"Gage, we're ready to eat. Are you hungry?" she asked. Ari saw the confused look on his face. "I'm Ari. You and Roman are my life partners."

"Life partners," he said, getting a feel for the word. He wasn't quite sure he understood what that meant.

A door opened down the hall and moments later, Roman entered the room. He gave Gage a hard look, then smoothed his features and looked the man over. "Looks like you found everything you needed."

Tiny feet thundered down the long hall. Eddie ran into the room. "Daddy Gage!" she squealed. She ran into his legs and hugged them. "I'm so glad you're home. I missed you!"

A smile spread across his face. He scooped the little girl into his arms. "What's your name?"

Eddie cocked her head to the side, trying to understand his question.

Daddy Gage doesn't remember us. He banged his head in the accident and all his memories are gone, Ari sent.

Eddie stuck a finger in her mouth, shy. "I'm Edris, but you can call me Eddie."

"Edris is a pretty name. How old are you, blondie?" Gage asked.

Eddie held up three fingers. "I'm three!"

"Everyone sit. We're ready to eat," Ari said.

"What can I help you with?" Roman asked.

"Can you cut up Eddie's food? Make sure you give her at least one bite of chicken and a mushroom," Ari said.

"I don't want a mushed room," Eddie grumbled.

"Mushroom. You get one mushroom cut into pieces, and a little chicken," Ari said.

"Can I help with something?" Gage asked. He was nervous that he couldn't remember his life here in this place with these people.

"Why don't you get the water on the table," Ari said. "There's a pitcher of berry water in the fridge, and the glasses are in that cabinet." She pointed to a cabinet close to the refrigerator. "There are little glasses for Eddie."

Gage pulled out glasses, then the water pitcher. He stared, fascinated, at the blueberries at the bottom of the pitcher of bluish-colored water.

Ari glanced his way. "Swirl it around before you pour."

Gage swirled the water in the pitcher, then poured three medium-sized clear glasses and one little juice glass of the beverage. He returned the pitcher to the refrigerator and picked up two of the glasses. He looked at Eddie. "Where do you sit?"

She scooted up onto her booster chair. "Right here!"

Gage placed the small glass at her place setting, then sat the second glass on the table at another place setting. He retrieved the other glasses and set them to the right of each plate, above the knife.

"Where should I sit?" Gage asked.

Eddie pointed to the end of the table. "You sit there." She pointed to the other end of the table. "Daddy Roman sits there, and Mommy Ari sits there."

Gage sat in *his* place.

None of this feels familiar. I don't know these people. I should go to a hotel.

Roman and Ari stole a quick glance at Gage.

He noticed.

Ari carried two plates to the table. She set one in front of him, and the other at Roman's designated place.

Gage stared at the plate. Some kind of chicken in a light cream sauce with baby portobello mushrooms, mashed potatoes and Italian broccoli. It smelled heavenly.

Roman placed a plate in front of Eddie. It contained cut-up pieces of hot dog, two tiny pieces of chicken, a tablespoon of mashed potatoes, and a "mushed room" cut in pieces. One broccoli floret lit up the plate with its steamed green color.

Ari carried her plate to the table and sat.

"This looks delicious," Gage said. He watched as Ari and Roman placed their napkins in their laps. He mimicked them.

Eddie stabbed a piece of hot dog with her child's fork.

Ari cleared her throat.

Eddie glanced across the table.

"Don't forget your napkin, honey."

Eddie put the fork down and snatched up her napkin and put it in her lap.

Ari noticed Gage's questioning expression. "Kids form good habits at a young age."

They ate quietly. Gage felt tension wafting off Roman. He knew he was the reason for that tension. He was a stranger in his own residence. Gage felt it was normal to talk during a meal and wondered what they typically discussed. He also sensed they were not telling him something.

He chewed a piece of delicious, tender chicken. He tasted the delicate cream sauce. If this was the way they ate all the time, he thought they must be wealthy.

Roman quirked an eyebrow, but kept quiet.

"This is where I live? I'm rich?" Gage asked. "What do I do?"

Roman laid his fork on his plate. He stared at the man at the other end of the table. "Yes, this is where the four of us live. We are very wealthy from the electronics and security businesses you and I built over the years."

"So, we've known each other for a long time, then?" Gage asked.

Roman glanced at Ari.

Gage noticed they stared at each other quietly, longer than what he thought was normal.

How do I explain this? Roman sent to Ari.

Tell him you've known each other for a long time, Ari sent.

"You and I have known each other for a very long time," Roman said.

Gage nodded, looking from one to the other. He knew there was something off about what Roman said.

They finished the meal in relative silence. Ari and Roman cleared the table. He offered to help, but they waved him off, as if he were a guest. He watched the little girl run down the hall to what he supposed was her room.

After they finished the clean-up, Roman invited him to the living room.

"Come, make yourself at home. You live here," he said.

They walked into the living room. Gage looked around at the sofas, chairs, tables, artwork, fireplace, and the bar.

"Remind me how we can afford all this," Gage asked, sweeping his arm out.

"When we met, we each had our own electronics business. You had just moved to Reading from Boston," Roman said. "We built up the business, and we formed a security company. We have teams that go across the globe on security projects."

Gage thought for a moment. "Like those guys in the bar? Those were our people?"

"Yes. That was Sherm and Lonnie," Roman said.

"Sherm is one of our best friends," Ari said, as she joined them in the living room.

"Who was that big guy?" Gage asked.

How do I explain that? Roman asked.

Just tell him his name. A lot of people have nicknames, Ari sent.

"That was Big Bear Muchisky," Roman said, after the short delay.

Big Bear.

"Why's he called that?" Gage asked.

"You saw how big he was," Ari said. "Evidently, he was a big kid, and the kids at school gave him that nickname."

Gage sat quietly, taking it all in.

I think that's a line of shit.

He saw Roman and Ari's eyes flinch. He couldn't figure out what was going on.

"What do we typically do?" Gage asked.

"We read, watch movies, go out to eat, take care of business during the day—normal things," Ari said.

The elevator dinged. Company. The doors opened and Jason and Kevin entered.

Go easy. He doesn't remember anything. Keep everything under control, Roman sent.

Jason and Kevin's eyes flicked from Gage to Roman, then to their mother.

Nothing at all? Kevin sent.

Roman gave a slight shake of his head.

"Hi, Mom," Kevin said.

Ari stood. She hugged each of them and kissed them on the

cheek. She put her arms through her boys' arms and focused on Gage.

"Gage, these are my sons, Jason and Kevin," she said.

Gage stood. He shook their hands. Then he thought quietly. "Are you my sons?"

"Nope, you and Roman are our chosen fathers, but not our biological fathers," Jason said.

"The little girl?" Gage asked. He tried to force memories to come through.

"No, we adopted her after her mother was murdered," Roman said.

There was another awkward silence.

"What do you do for work?" Gage asked. He turned to Jason, then Kevin.

"I work in finance on the thirtieth floor," Jason said.

"You work for our company?" Gage asked.

"Yes, we both do. Kevin works for the security division," Jason said.

"What's the name of our company?"

"Panther Industries and Panther Industries Security Division," Roman said.

"Why's it called that?" Gage asked. "Seems odd."

Roman rolled up his T-shirt sleeve. He showed Gage the tattoo of his panther on his bicep. "I love black cats."

Gage stared at the tattoo. He touched one of his own tattoos.

This is like a fucking altered reality.

He noticed everyone seemed uncomfortable.

It's like they can read my fucking mind. I've got to get the hell out of here. Is this some kind of cult?

Gage stood. "I think I'm going to leave now."

"Leave?" Ari squeaked out. "You can't leave! You live here. You're not well."

Suddenly, they were all on their feet.

Gage looked from Roman to Kevin to Jason, then finally to Ari.

Eddie ran down the hall. Her face was crinkled with worry, and her lower lip quivered. "Daddy Gage! Don't leave! I love you!" She flung herself at his legs.

Ari flinched, worried about her child being in the middle of what could prove to get ugly in a split second.

Gage stood, frozen in his spot. Uncertain what he should do.

Ari darted forward and grabbed Eddie. She talked inside her head. *I want you to go back to your room and close your door, Eddie. Daddy Gage is having a lot of problems because he can't remember us. I want you to stay safe in case there's a fight.*

Eddie cried as if her heart was broken. She rubbed her tiny fists into her eyes. "Okay."

Gage jerked his head in Ari's direction. He knew he missed some kind of silent communication. He couldn't figure it out.

Ari lowered Eddie to the floor.

Eddie ran back to her room and slammed the door shut.

Gage walked around the sofa to the foyer. He pressed the elevator button. The door opened. He entered the elevator car. He pressed L for Lobby. Nothing happened.

Roman walked to within several feet of the elevator. "It's programmed for security. No one can come or go unless they use a code."

"What's the code?" Gage asked. His voice was lethally cold.

Call Sherm. Have him bring up a tranq, Roman sent to Kevin.

Kevin worked his phone with his thumbs.

"Can't give you the code," Roman said. "You need to stay here until you recover your memories."

Gage lunged himself out of the elevator car and plowed into Roman, swinging his fists.

Kevin and Jason tried to intervene. Everyone shouted.

"Don't shift!" Ari screamed.

The elevator doors closed. Moments later, a ding announced Sherm. He took in the scene: Gage and Roman duking it out, while Jason and Kevin tried, unsuccessfully, to pry them apart.

Ari rushed over to Sherm, frantic. "Do something!"

Sherm pulled a syringe out of his pocket, uncapped it and rushed into the melee. He jammed the needle into Gage's bicep.

Gage turned, swung at Sherm as if in slow motion. He grazed the man's chin, but his fist slid off into the air.

Everything seemed fuzzy. The shouts sounded distant.

Multiple hands grabbed him just before he hit the floor.

Ari sobbed into her hands.

"Help me put him into his bed," Roman said.

Kevin and Jason brushed Roman out of the way. They hauled Gage to his feet and balanced his arms across their shoulders. They half-dragged him down the hall to his bedroom, Sherm on their heels.

Roman slid his arms around Ari. "I'm sorry, but I didn't know what else to do."

"Not your fault," Ari sobbed out.

He held her for a few minutes, then brought her to the sofa. They settled onto the cushions.

Sherm, Kevin, and Jason returned to the living room. "Everyone okay?" Sherm asked. He looked around the room at the tight faces.

"You need to sue that goddamn kid," Jason said. "Who knows how long this amnesia will last."

"What if he never gets his memories back?" Kevin asked.

Ari sobbed louder.

"He'll remember everything!" Roman was furious about the turn of events. "Tomorrow we'll get Dr. Tanner over here and see what he can do to help. He and Mr. Tran will work together as they did for me. Everything will be okay."

"Man, I hope so," Sherm said. "Pour me some bourbon, will you?"

Roman got up and walked to the bar. He grabbed their favorite bourbon and set up the glasses. This time, he didn't cheat on Ari's portion. She got the full two fingers' worth.

The guys wandered over to the bar and picked up their glasses. Roman brought his and Ari's glass over to the sofa. They all sat.

Roman downed his drink in one throw. His nerves were shot. These had been a challenging couple of years. First, Ari's kidnapping, torture, and coma. Then his own abduction by that crazed fuck in Italy. Now this. He blocked his rambling, caustic thoughts. He realized that everyone else most likely had the same crap zooming around in their brains.

Ari sipped her drink. She forced soothing thoughts and visions through her mind.

The boys and Sherm finished their drinks.

"What if he wakes in the middle of the night?" Jason asked.

"He should sleep until morning," Sherm said.

"God, I hope so," Kevin said. "Want me to sleep over?"

"Nah, it should be okay," Roman said.

Sherm stood. "I'm leaving you to it."

Jason and Kevin stood.

"Call out if you need us," Kevin said.

"Go home. Get some sleep," Roman said.

"I'll get Eddie ready for bed," Ari said.

The boys kissed Ari on the cheek, then she walked down the hallway.

CHAPTER FOUR

Ari woke early, showered, dressed, and sauntered to the kitchen. She made a pot of coffee, prepared her cup, and sat at the table, lost in thought. She wondered if Gage would regain his memories. Ari wracked her brain for ways to help him through this ordeal. She imagined what it might be like for him to be here among people he perceived as strangers.

She caught a sob and hid her face behind her hands. They were forcing him to stay in the penthouse against his will. She wondered if they should let him go to a hotel until his memories were restored. She sobbed at the contemplation of him taking up with another woman... or women.

Roman heard her meandering thoughts. *For safety's sake, he needs to stay here. He remembers nothing of his life, and that makes him vulnerable. People could take advantage of him, or worse. Try to calm down, honey.*

Ari sensed Roman in the shower. She stood, considered checking in on Gage, but was leery about going to his room.

She didn't know how he would react. Instead, she headed toward the refrigerator and began pulling breakfast fixings onto the counter.

For now, don't be alone with him. I'll make sure someone is here with you at all times if I have to go downstairs. We don't know how he will react to anything Roman sent.

We sort of figured that out last night, Ari sent back.

Roman wandered to the kitchen, barefoot. He kissed Ari on the neck. "Morning, honey. What can I do to help?"

"Why don't you go see if Eddie is awake," Ari said.

"Will do," Roman said. He went down the hall to Eddie's room. He opened the door and stuck his head inside. Her bed was empty. He came fully into the room and headed to her playroom. She wasn't there. He stood and rocked on his heels a moment, then left Eddie's suite.

He headed down the hall to Ari's room. Sometimes Eddie got into Ari's closet to play dress-up. He checked the closet and the bathroom, but Eddie wasn't there. Roman returned to the main living areas and looked around the living room, then the dining room.

"Where is she?" he asked out loud.

Ari looked up. "She wasn't in her room?"

They shared a frightened expression and rushed to Gage's room. They discovered Eddie, curled up on the bed with Gage looking at photo albums.

Roman and Ari entered the room.

"What a smart little girl you are," Ari praised.

Roman met Gage's eyes. "Do any of the pictures stir a memory?"

Gage shook his head. "Nice pictures, but I get nothing. We must have had a lot of good times."

Ari's eyes glistened. "We did, and we will have many more." She sniffed the air. "Oh! The bacon!" She fled from the room, Roman on her heels.

"Do you like bacon?" Eddie asked. "I love bacon!"

"I guess we'd better get ready for breakfast. Thank you for showing me the pictures," Gage said.

Eddie scooted off the bed. She grabbed the photo albums. "I'd better put these away." She scurried to the door and slipped outside.

Gage sat on the bed for a moment, cataloging the pictures he saw with the little girl. He wondered about this mysterious life. He wondered about the experiences he had shared with these people. Nothing surfaced. A giant void remained in his head.

He slipped out of bed and headed to the bathroom. Now that he knew where everything was, he took a shower and got ready for the day. That brought another puzzled thought his way. What was he getting ready for, exactly?

Roman was monitoring Gage's thoughts in the kitchen while he helped Ari get breakfast ready. "We'd better let Gage know that Dr. Tanner and Mr. Tran will be here after breakfast. He's wondering what he's supposed to do here."

"He should be okay with seeing them, right?" Ari asked. She wasn't sure what to expect since Gage's behavior and responses were so far off.

"I would assume seeing a doctor or herbalist would be safe," Roman said. "I expect he wants to get this problem sorted just as much as we do."

They heard his bedroom door open and returned to concentrating on preparing breakfast.

Gage walked down the hall and entered the kitchen and breakfast area. He shyly watched Roman and Ari organize breakfast. "What can I do to help?"

"Why don't you get the juice poured, get the bowl of fruit, then help Roman prepare the toast," Ari said.

He remembered where the glasses were and retrieved three medium and one small glass from the cabinet. Then he grabbed the pitcher of orange juice and the bowl of fruit from the refrigerator. Once he had that taken care of and the glasses were on the table, he stepped up to the toaster while Roman turned the bacon over in the pan.

Two cut slices of buttered toast were on a plate. He placed four more slices in the toaster. "How many slices of toast do you usually make?"

"We're big breakfast eaters," Roman said. "Make four more slices after these."

The toast popped. Gage swapped the toast for four more slices of bread. After he finished up, he placed the plate on the table. By that time, Ari had finished up with the scrambled eggs, and Roman had the bacon patted free of extra grease and on a clean plate.

"Eddie!" Ari hollered. "Breakfast is ready."

"Coming! Save me some bacon!" Eddie yelled.

They heard her little feet running down the hallway.

"She really likes bacon, doesn't she?" Gage asked. He grinned.

"Yeah, she's a little carnivore," Roman said.

Ari shot him a questioning glare.

Eddie climbed up into her booster chair and plopped her napkin into her lap.

Ari gave her one of those mother's stares. "Come on, Eddie. Open the napkin and lay it across your lap, like I taught you. Your napkin keeps your clothes clean in case a piece of food drops in your lap."

"O K A Y," Eddie said, exasperated.

"Is it time for a nap already?" Ari asked. "What side of the bed did you get up on?"

Eddie huffed. "I'm super-duper hungry."

"Well, we'd better feed you so you don't try to eat us!" Roman said.

Again, Gage noticed the irritated glance Ari slid toward Roman. He repeated the words Roman used inside his head. He couldn't find anything wrong with what he said.

The adults settled into their chairs and passed the bowls between them. Ari dropped a spoonful of scrambled eggs on Eddie's plate, while Roman gave her one piece of bacon.

"What fruit do you want this morning?" Ari asked.

Eddie studied the fruit bowl. "Grapes and strawberries."

Ari dished the fruit onto Eddie's plate, while Roman slid half a slice of toast to the edge of it.

"All set?" Ari asked.

Eddie looked over her plate. "I want more bacon!"

"Eat what's on your plate first. There's plenty," Roman said.

Eddie picked up her fork and started eating.

Gage had watched the interchange. He wondered how he fit into the mix. Did he help with the child at mealtimes?

Roman and Ari heard his thoughts.

"Meals are always a challenge with a child," Roman said. "Anytime you want to jump in and help with the munchkin, be my guest."

"I don't know anything about raising a child," Gage said.

"Me neither," Roman said. "Ari's the only one with experience. She has two grown sons."

"Kevin and Jason," Gage said.

"That's right," Roman said.

They ate in silence for a while.

"After breakfast, Dr. Tanner and Mr. Tran are coming up to check you out," Ari said.

"A doctor who still makes house calls?" Gage asked.

"We have a very special group of friends," Ari said. "Including Dr. Tanner and Mr. Tran, the herbalist."

"Mr. Tran helped me get my life back on track," Roman said.

Gage quirked an eyebrow. "What happened?"

"Several months ago, a distant relative who was more than a little crazy, had me kidnapped," Roman said.

Relative? How are you going to explain this? Ari sent.

Can't very well explain what a Tothar is, can I? Roman snapped back.

"Kidnapped?" Gage asked. That intrigued him.

"We have a house in the woods, and I had been walking through the woods when they jumped me," Roman said. "They tranquilized me, hauled me onto a helicopter, then a jet, and brought me to his palazzo in Italy, outside of Rome."

"Sure went to a lot of trouble," Gage said. "What brought this on?"

"Never knew this relative existed," Roman said. "He was a lunatic through and through. Tossed me into a cell and practically starved me to death before our people rescued me."

"We almost lost him," Ari said. "His ribs were sticking out; he couldn't eat, and he was out of it for days. Mr. Tran came to the rescue with several herbal teas and potions. We trust that man with our lives."

"How do you suppose he'll help me with a bunch of herbs?" Gage asked.

"We hope he can help restore your memory," Ari said. "I need you back, Gage. All of you, not this stranger." She upset herself, pushed her chair back, and hurried from the room.

Roman and Gage watched her departure.

"It's okay," Eddie said. "Mommy is just a little upset." She looked the men over. "Can I have more bacon?"

"Nice try," Roman said. "There're still eggs and fruit on your plate. You'd better eat up, or Gage and I are eating all the bacon and toast." He grabbed a piece of bacon and chomped it into his mouth.

ML

Ari stood in Roman's bathroom and gripped the counter. *I can't take anymore crisis'. What do we have to do to get through the rest of our lives without this trauma?*

Honey, it will be okay, Roman sent. *I'll ask Mr. Tran if he can give you something for your stress.*

Why can't everything be back to where it was two years ago? Ari sent.

Things happen. We can't control our environment outside of this penthouse, and we can't let these experiences cripple us to the point where we become reclusive.

The elevator dinged visitors. Ari gathered her wits and went to the foyer to greet Dr. Tanner and Mr. Tran. Gage and Roman cleared the table and filled the dishwasher.

"Hi, Dr. Tanner. Hi, Mr. Tran," Ari said. "Come in. Would you like some coffee? We have French roast this morning."

"I'll take a cup," Dr. Tanner said. He carried his black bag to the kitchen and placed it on the floor by a chair.

"Me, too," Mr. Tran said. He carried a bulging satchel and placed his bag by the chair he sat in.

Ari introduced Gage to the guests while Roman poured coffee. After everyone sat at the table enjoying their coffee, the silence became awkward. Dr. Tanner jumped in and steered the visit to the medical problem.

"Gage, does your head hurt anywhere?"

He thought about that. "Not really. I get a little headachy every once in a while."

"Where exactly does it hurt?" Dr. Tanner asked.

Gage pointed to his temple. "Right around here, but sometimes I have these flashes of pain behind my eyes."

Mr. Tran studied him. "What type of pain behind your eyes? Is it a slow pain, hammering pain—can you describe it?"

Gage stared at the Asian man, contemplating his question. "It sort of slides across both eyes. Sometimes it feels like my eyes are going to explode."

"Why don't I set up an MRI? I'd like to eliminate the possibility of lesions or a brain tumor," Dr. Tanner said. He worked on his cell phone.

Ari's hand flew to cover her mouth.

"You think he might have a brain tumor from the accident?" Roman asked.

"It's a far fetch, but what bothers me is there could be internal bleeding from a lesion. He hit his head hard enough to crack the window," Dr. Tanner said.

Gage sat there, taking it all in. "My head cracked the window?"

Roman pulled up pictures on his phone. He pointed the screen to show Gage the picture of him with blood dripping down the side of his head at his temple, and the cracked driver's window.

He touched the side of his head. "I don't even remember this happening."

"It will come back," Mr. Tran said.

"When can you have the MRI set up?" Ari asked.

"I texted Vanessa to schedule it for as soon as there's an opening," Dr. Tanner said.

"In the meantime, I have some remedies for you to start on immediately," Mr. Tran said. "Roman can tell you that they might not taste that pleasant, but they are effective."

Mr. Tran opened his satchel and pulled out a dropper bottle and a baggie of chopped herbs. He glanced up at Ari and Roman. "You still have the tea-bag cases?"

Ari jumped up and scrambled to the kitchen counter and dug into a drawer. She retrieved the plastic bag that contained two silk tea-bag cases. "Yes. We have two."

Mr. Tran tapped the dropper bottle. "Four drops under your tongue in the morning, then at bedtime. Roman can show you tonight." He picked up the baggie. "This is a special tea. Much stronger than what I prescribed for Roman."

"Boy, are you in for a treat," Roman said, with a grimace.

He turned to Ari. "Do we have plenty of honey?"

"I'll add it to the list. If I remember correctly, our supply is low," Ari said.

"Drink this tea at least four times a day," Mr. Tran said. "It is best fifteen minutes before you eat anything."

Dr. Tanner's phone chirped a text. He read the screen.

"There's an opening at three this afternoon at Reading Hospital. Is that a good time?"

Gage nodded as he looked over at Ari and Roman. "Let's get this over with. I don't want this cluttering up my life."

"Okay, I'll have Vanessa set it up," Dr. Tanner said.

"Start on the formulas after the MRI," Mr. Tran said, then he turned to Ari. "Roman texted me. I have something that will soothe your nerves."

He dug a dropper bottle out of his bag and handed it to her. "Six drops at breakfast. You can start now."

"Thanks, Mr. Tran," Ari said as she clutched the bottle. Mr. Tran and the doctor stood.

"Thank you so much for coming," Ari said. "I'll call Vanessa in a little while and get the instructions so we know where we need to go."

Roman walked them to the elevator, and they said goodbye. He returned to the kitchen and plopped down in his chair. He smirked at Gage. "The tea tastes like crap, but it worked miracles for me. Ask Ari."

"Jesus, I hope I don't have internal bleeding or a tumor," Gage said. "It's bad enough feeling out of place... like a stranger here."

"Luckily, we heal quickly," Roman said. Ari kicked him under the table.

"What do you mean?" Gage asked.

Roman squirmed. "I mean, you're in great shape. You've never had any major illnesses."

Eddie clomped down the hall in a pair of Ari's shoes with a handbag over her arm that was half her size. She wore a long string of costume pearls that dangled to her waist. They noticed she had experimented with lipstick and blusher.

"Who is this stranger? Are you a movie star?" Ari asked.

"Miss Piggy!" Eddie squealed in delight.

"Did you make a mess in Ari's bathroom?" Roman asked.

Eddie twisted her body back and forth. "No..."

"I'd better check for damage control," Ari said.

Roman stood. "I'm going to go down to see Sherm." He turned to Gage. "Want to come with me?"

"Ask him if they can babysit Eddie when we go to the hospital," Ari asked.

"Will do," Roman said.

Gage stood and followed Roman to the elevator. He was glad to be going somewhere, even if it was still in the building. The doors opened on the twenty-eighth floor.

"Only people with clearance can stop at this floor," Roman explained. "It's all programmed in the phone app or the employee badges."

Roman opened the door to the security division. Several pairs of eyes looked up from computer systems.

Sherm stood. He glanced at Gage, wary. "How's it going?"

Kevin stood up in his cubicle and made his way over to Sherm's office, with Lonnie close behind.

"Hey, Gage," Kevin said. "Any memories?"

Gage stared at Kevin as if he were trying to remember. "No."

"Dr. Tanner's scheduled an MRI this afternoon at three," Roman said. "Ari wanted to know if you guys could keep an eye on Eddie while we're gone."

"Sure, bring her down when you're ready to leave," Sherm said.

"Do you think we can move up our meeting with Donatello and Marco?" Roman asked. "It should be a simple update." Roman tried to figure out how he could explain things while keeping the whole shifter business under wraps. He silently sent a message to Kevin to make sure no one mentioned anything about shifters while Gage was in the room. Kevin nodded ever so slightly and excused himself to go back to his desk.

Roman turned to Gage. "We recently opened a new Panther Industries division in Italy, outside of Rome. Mr. Tran, who you just met this morning, is our translator and historian. He's in charge of a huge project we're still hiring translators for."

Sherm sat at his desk. "Let me see if they're available for an update." He pulled up their online meeting source on the big monitor on the wall and placed the call.

The strange ringtone sounded, and they answered the call on the third ring.

"Panther Industries, Donatello speaking." Then, "Oh!" when Donatello saw Sherm, Roman, Gage and Lonnie.

"Hello Panther USA!" Donatello said. He looked to the side and hollered. "Marco!" Then he picked up his phone and clumsily thumbed a text. "He'll be here in a moment."

Donatello stared at the screen. "I hope you're feeling better, Gage."

Gage stared at the Italian on the monitor. "Not really."

"Oh! I'm sorry to hear that. Hopefully everything will sort itself out soon," Donatello said.

Marco entered the room and waved at the screen. "Hi, everyone."

"Roman, the mayor is throwing a gala next month, and he's sending you an invitation," Donatello said. "We're sure he's using this to distract the public from his association with your cousin and the mess that he and the police chief were involved in."

"That, and if you're here endorsing him, he's sure to build up his chances for a profitable consulting business down the road," Marco said. "This will probably be his last term in office."

"How are things going in the library?" Roman asked.

"That Janina is a sharp woman. She has all the shelves labeled already," Donatello said. "She's very organized and doesn't sit around waiting for someone to hold her hand or tell her what to do."

"Alan and the new translator, Mr. Benston, will be here tomorrow for two weeks," Marco said. "Mr. Tran was supposed to come with them, but he said there was an emergency back home. We hope he's okay."

"His emergency is Gage's predicament," Roman said. "Once Gage has his memory back, Mr. Tran will head your way. Abbot Benston was one of Mr. Tran's colleagues. He should be able to coach Alan and Janina until Mr. Tran can step in."

"We all know first-hand how good Mr. Tran is with his herbs and teas," Marco said. "He had his hands full with you, Roman, and look how well you turned out." Marco chuckled at his own joke.

"Can you pull in the IT team?" Sherm asked. "I want an update from them."

The call continued for another forty-five minutes while the men discussed servers, European connections, and the new service they were establishing in Russia and Ukraine.

Roman and Gage rode the elevator back upstairs to the penthouse.

"I feel like I'm holding things up with your business dealings," Gage said.

Roman stared at him. "Gage, it's OUR business, not mine exclusively. I'm the CEO and you're the president. We merged our businesses and created the security division. This is a minor setback. It will get sorted."

CHAPTER FIVE

They stepped out of the elevator into the penthouse. Eddie was on the sofa in the living room, surrounded by photo albums.

"Daddy Gage, look what I found," she called out.

Gage walked over to the sofa and joined Eddie. She plopped an album onto his lap while Roman looked over her shoulder. The photo she was excited about was Gage in his eagle form.

"This is you!" Eddie said.

Gage looked at the picture, smiling goofily. "That's me, huh? Can I fly?"

"Yes! I wish I could fly, but I'm a tiger." Eddie made a growling noise while she stretched her little hand out in front of her.

Gage tussled her hair. "You look like a little tiger." He played along with what he took to be a joke, or a child's game of make-believe.

Eddie! Don't talk about shifters with Gage. He doesn't remember and won't understand, Roman sent.

Eddie looked over her shoulder, a grumpy expression on her face. *It's okay.*

No, it isn't okay, Roman said, somewhat sternly.

Ari heard the conversation and left her study. *Eddie, we talked about this. Roman and I explained Gage's head injury from the car crash. It's too soon to talk about shifters.*

Eddie turned a page in the album. She jammed her finger on the picture of Gage with his eagle face peeking out of his human form. "See? You're an eagle!" She looked over her shoulder at Roman and Ari in defiance.

Gage stared at the picture. He glanced back at Roman and Ari. "How'd you do that, Photoshop?"

"Yeah, Ari's great with Photoshop," Roman said. In his mind, he glared at Eddie.

"Young lady, put the photo albums away right now," Ari said. "Gage is probably tired and might like a nap."

Eddie slid off the sofa and stacked up the photo albums. She put them in a cabinet, then returned to the sofa. She pointed to the other sofa. "That's where you take a nap every day."

"Is that my favorite sofa?" Gage asked her.

She nodded. "Don't worry, you don't snore."

Gage chuckled while he stood. He turned to Roman and Ari. "Do you mind? I don't have very much energy."

"Not at all, that sofa has your name on it," Roman said. "I'll be in my suite if you need anything."

Ari pulled a sofa throw out of an end table. "In case you feel a chill."

ML

Gage dropped onto the other sofa, removed his shoes and settled his head on a throw pillow. He lay there for a moment, then shook the sofa throw over his body. A soft sigh escaped as he closed his eyes.

Bizarre scenes flashed through Gage's head as he napped on the sofa. The eagle face that stared back at him in the mirror in that restroom in the bar. He had a glimpse of the eagle viciously attacking a man in the woods. His mind's eye studied the eagle. It recognized that the eagle was large. Very large, unusually so.

Sexual scenes of a *ménage à trois* in explicit detail with the three of them—Roman, Ari and himself—in an extra-large bed. Gage immediately experienced himself getting hard. He started at a flash of Roman shifting to a panther in the bed. He fought Roman in his human form.

The words *human form* echoed in his head.

ML

Roman crept down the hall to Ari's study. "Should we wake him?"

Ari looked concerned. "No, we should let that run its course. Evidently our little girl knows better what to do than we do."

"Well, we can't tiptoe around him forever," Roman said. "Perhaps showing him those pictures nudged something in his memory. Eventually, a conversation will bring up shifters. He's just going to have to deal with it, regardless of whether he believes he's not one-hundred percent human."

Roman sank onto the sofa and pulled Ari into his arms. He lowered his mouth to hers and ran his tongue along her lips. Her fingers ran through his silky pitch-black hair.

"That image of the three of us making love turned me on," he said.

"We don't have to wait, you know," Ari said. She slipped out of his arms, crossed to the door and locked it so Eddie wouldn't walk in on them. She returned to the sofa and straddled Roman.

His hands were all over her as his mouth seared her lips with their passion. He pinched her nipples, then lowered one of his hands to her mound. Her heat blazed through the material of her crop pants. He worked at the button and zipper and slipped a hand inside her panties. His thumb and index finger pulled on her clit.

Ari felt the flood of her juices as Roman's fingers stroked her. She fumbled with his belt. It seemed to take forever to unlatch it and pull it from his pants. She managed to unbutton his slacks and struggled to get the zipper down. She reached in a hand and pulled out his cock.

"Oh, Roman. Now! Please get inside me now!"

Roman lifted her off the sofa and yanked her pants and panties down. She stepped out of them and he grabbed her by the waist and settled her over his cock.

Ari positioned herself over his shaft and lowered herself in one fast stroke. She stayed there for a second, then she started moving, rocking back and forth, while he pumped up. She ducked her mouth to his.

Their kiss was hot. All tongue.

Entwined.

Nipping each other's lips.

She pumped onto him faster. She was on the edge of an orgasm that built like lava rising to crest the volcano.

Roman's eyes glazed over as he watched the passion on her face. Her muscles tightened on his cock. She made the little noises that told him she was close to exploding. He rammed up inside her, and she let loose, her vaginal muscles gripping his shaft and pulsing out a powerful orgasm. She did her best not to scream out. His hand pushed the back of her head to his face, and his lips and tongue absorbed her moans.

The chimes on the door handle jingled. They started.

"The door's stuck," Eddie called out.

Ari jumped to her feet. She held her hand between her legs, grabbed her clothes and rushed to her bathroom.

Roman stood, grabbed his belt, rethreaded it through the loops, straightened his shirt, ran his hands through his hair, and rushed to the door. He made a great display of unlocking it, opened the door, then pretended to study the door-locking mechanism.

"That's strange. The door seemed to lock itself," he said.

Eddie studied the door with him. She pressed the door latch

several times. After she lost interest in the door assembly, she looked around the room. "Where's Ari?"

"She's in the bathroom," Roman said.

Hide my panties! Ari called out.

We're over at the door, he sent back.

"Can I have mac and cheese for lunch?" Eddie asked.

The bathroom door opened, and Ari stepped out. She walked swiftly over to the sofa, saw her black lace panties on the floor, and kicked them under the sofa. "We're having BLTs."

Eddie clapped her hands together. "Bacon!"

"I knew you'd like that for lunch," Ari said. "We made a lot of bacon at breakfast time. I'll let you know when lunch is ready. We should let Gage nap a little longer. He was really tired."

"Okay. I'll go play," Eddie said. She skipped to the door and ran back to her room at the end of the hall.

Roman's hands pulled Ari against his body. They melted together in a smoldering kiss. He kissed her neck down to her collarbone.

"That was some hot sex, woman," Roman said.

She chuckled. "It was pretty hot, mister." She nipped his bottom lip.

Roman grinned. "Seems like you're commando right now." He slid his hand into her crop pants.

Ari grabbed his hand. "Don't you dare!"

"Why not? Eddie's playing. Gage is sleeping. You're wet and ready."

Her face flushed with heat as his fingers rubbed her most sensitive ball of fire. She grabbed his shirt. "Roman! I'm going to come!"

He worked two fingers inside her and stroked her clit with his thumb. She grabbed his hard cock through his slacks and squeezed. Then she came undone.

Roman wrapped an arm around her waist as her legs started to give out. He whispered against her mouth. "I want to suck you dry."

Ari melted against him. When her body calmed, she smoothed his shirt where she had clutched it.

"Do you suppose Gage would want to sleep with us tonight?" she asked.

Roman shook his head. "I don't think that's a good idea. He doesn't know his place in our relationship yet, or how we came together in the beginning. I wouldn't want him to demean our lovemaking to debauchery."

Ari nodded. "You're right. I just feel bad about leaving him out. I want him in our bed."

"It's no worse than the two of you waiting for me when I was out of it after Italy," Roman said.

"This is worse, don't you think? At least you knew what happened to you. He doesn't have a clue, except for what people have told him," Ari said. "I hope the MRI doesn't present us with more horror."

"I'm sure he's going to be cleared of any internal problems," Roman said. "The sooner he can start on the tea and drops, the better."

Ari grabbed his hand. "Come on, let's go start lunch. Gage should be okay."

They left the room and returned to the kitchen. Roman washed his hands, then pulled out the plate of bacon. He retrieved the jar of mayonnaise, the bag of washed romaine leaves, and two ripe red tomatoes.

Ari set the oven warmer drawer to start. She placed the plate of bacon on the rack and shut the drawer. Next, she pulled the loaf of organic, non-GMO, stone-ground wheat bread out of the breadbox. She opened a drawer and got out a table knife and grabbed the jar of mayo.

Roman pulled plates out of the cabinet, spread them out in front of him, then chose a cutting board and a sharp knife.

Gage stirred on the sofa. He pulled himself up to a sitting position and rubbed his eyes. He noticed Roman and Ari in the kitchen. They had a little assembly line going, creating sandwiches.

"Did you sleep well?" Ari asked.

Gage walked to the kitchen and slipped onto a barstool. "I had strange dreams."

"Perhaps some of your memories are trying to return," Roman said.

"Not unless I can fly as an eagle," Gage joked.

"All things are possible," Roman said. He shrugged.

"That'd be awesome, wouldn't it? I can't imagine being able to fly," Gage said. He didn't offer to help, as it appeared they were finished building the BLTs.

"We should leave here no later than two-fifteen," Ari said. "Hospitals have all these checks and balances. It's amazing they get anything done for all the hoops people have to jump through, even when they have a scheduled appointment."

"Lunch is ready," Roman called out.

Eddie's feet thundered down the hallway. She climbed up on her booster chair.

"Have you washed your hands, young lady?" Roman asked.

Eddie pouted. She climbed down, ran to the half-bath, and washed her hands. She returned to the table, held her hands up for all to see, then climbed up onto her seat.

The adults carried their plates and sat at the table. Roman placed Eddie's dish in front of her.

She dug into the small pile of potato chips. Then she bit a chunk out of the dill pickle spear. "I love these pickles."

"They are good. Nice and tart," Ari said.

Eddie turned to Gage. "These are your favorite pickles."

Gage stared at his plate. "They are? You sure?"

Eddie nodded. "You love little jerks and big dills."

Ari chuckled. "Jerkins are sweet pickles. They're not little jerks."

"Maybe the other pickles think they're little jerks!" Eddie proclaimed.

"I'll bet they do," Gage said. He bit into his dill spear and winked at Eddie.

"This afternoon, Gage has to go to the hospital for some tests," Ari said. "You won't be able to come with us, but... you can go downstairs and stay with Sherm, Kevin, Lonnie and Travis while we're gone!"

Eddie clapped her hands together. She turned to Gage. "Sherm and I are going to get married when I grow up!"

"I guess I'll have plenty of time to buy you a wedding present," Gage joked.

After lunch, Ari pulled Eddie's backpack down from the top shelf. "What do you want to bring downstairs with you?"

Eddie stood in the middle of the room, planning her trip downstairs. "I want my tiger kitty, my coloring book, and Elmo!"

"Okay, I'm going to pack them now, so you play with something else," Ari said.

"When are we leaving?" Eddie asked.

"You have plenty of time to take a nap," Ari said. "It's twelve-thirty this very minute. We're leaving here at two-fifteen. That's an hour and forty-five minutes! A long time!"

Eddie yawned, then hopped around like a bunny. "I don't need a nap right now."

"What was that big yawn all about?" Ari asked. "Let's get you all snuggly and warm in your bed. I'll bet you dream about Elmo riding your tiger kitten."

Eddie snatched her stuffed toys out of the backpack and climbed onto her bed. Ari pulled up the throw and covered Eddie. She tiptoed out of the room.

Eddie screeched into Sherm's domain and ran up to him.

Sherm scooped her up. "Hey, munchkin. You ready to go to work?"

"I'm too little to work!" Eddie said.

"Ha! When Ari, Roman, and Gage return, you'll be a pro!" Sherm joked. He set Eddie down in his chair.

Ari handed over the backpack. She unzipped a pocket and pulled out the little glass that fit Eddie's hand. "No soda!"

"What, you don't want a hyped-up sugar-buzz who stays up all night?" Sherm asked.

"That's fine, but you'll be on babysitting duty," Roman said.

Ari kneeled in front of Eddie. "You be a good girl. Remember, Sherm is at work, and if he needs you to be quiet, you button your lips."

"I promise," Eddie said.

Ari stood. "See you later."

"Text me when you know anything," Sherm said.

CHAPTER SIX

Gage stared at the MRI machine, keenly aware of a cool breeze on his backside. He knew hospital gowns had their purpose, but the things sure didn't instill confidence in patients when their asses hung out for all to see.

"Maybe I shouldn't have taken that nap this morning," Gage said.

"You'll be okay. Just stay still," Roman said.

"You ready to begin?" the technician asked.

"Do you have to go to the bathroom?" Ari asked.

"I'm good to go," Gage said.

"Just lie down," the technician said.

Gage lay down on the table with his head on the low pillow.

When the technician was satisfied with his position, she began the test. The table slid into the MRI tube.

Gage's eyes were wide open as he stared at the ceiling of the tunnel. He didn't think he had an issue with claustrophobia, but the ceiling of the tube was only inches from his face. He decided he'd be better off keeping his eyes closed so he wouldn't panic in the tight enclosure.

Through all the tapping, pounding, and other loud sounds of the machine, Gage managed to doze off. A storybook of events passed through his mind. He saw himself when he was about twenty years old. At least he thought it was him. He saw a woman he thought was his mother, and a man he resembled who must have been his father.

He remembered walking in the woods behind their family home, when he shifted into his eagle the very first time. It freaked him out into a full-blown panic attack until his eagle took flight. Then the experience was so joyous that he flew for hours.

Gage recalled moving to Reading after his father passed away. His mother had died two years previously, and there was nothing to keep him in Boston. He wanted to stay on the East Coast, but he wanted a smaller city with more freedom.

Pain flooded his brain as he recalled getting shot out of the sky with an arrow in his wing. Then he remembered being rescued by Roman.

Roman and Ari watched Gage's memories unfold. Roman had never seen the memories of Gage's younger days back home with his parents.

Maybe he'll remember more of his past, Ari sent.

It looks like the amnesia has lifted, Roman sent.

What the fuck! Where am I? Gage sent.

Roman and Ari jolted in their chairs when Gage joined their silent communication.

Stay still! You're having an MRI, Roman sent.

What the hell for? Gage asked.

You were in an accident and had amnesia, Ari sent.

Accident? Amnesia? Gage asked, confused.

It's almost over. Give it a few more minutes. Just stay still, Roman sent.

When did this happen? This accident? Gage asked.

About two weeks ago, Ari sent.

I don't recall any accident, Gage said.

Maybe you're not one-hundred percent in the clear, Roman sent.

The test concluded, and the table slid out of the tube.

Gage sat up. "Christ! Who the fuck designed these things?"

"He's back," Roman declared, all smiles.

"Where's my clothes?" Gage asked. He shed the hospital gown and looked around, naked.

The technician squeaked out instructions. "Mr. Stryker! Your clothes are in the dressing room. Please cover up..."

Gage stomped to the dressing room. He donned his clothes and stepped outside the curtained enclosure. He studied Roman and Ari. "Did I do anything you'll hold against me?"

"Nothing unforgivable," Roman said. "Still not sure if you're all there."

Ari laid her hand on Gage's arm. "You can't remember the accident?"

He shook his head. "Which vehicle?"

"The Mercedes," Roman said.

"Mercedes... I don't even remember what a Mercedes looks like," Gage said.

"Come on, let's get out of here," Ari said. "Mr. Tran wants you to begin drinking his special tea and taking his drops."

"I don't know anyone named Mr. Tran," Gage said.

"Yes, you do. He pulled me out of some bad places after the Italian debacle," Roman said. "Do you remember any of that?"

Gage thought. "Yeah... that king kept you in a tower. It's fuzzy."

"What about Eddie or Sherm? Do you remember them?" Roman asked.

They left the room and walked to an elevator.

"Eddie's our little girl," Gage said. "Sherm—I know that name."

"It looks like you'll be able to piece things together," Roman said.

The elevator doors opened, and they rode down to the ground floor, went outside to the surface parking and piled into the Navigator.

Ari pulled out her phone. "I'll check in with Dr. Tanner." She made the call. "Hi Vanessa. We just left the hospital. Gage has some of his memories back. We're headed home. He'll begin Mr. Trans herbal formulas."

She listened to Dr. Tanner's wife for several moments. "Okay, thanks."

"We think Eddie triggered your memories this morning. She was adamant to show you pictures of you and your eagle," Roman said.

Roman's phone rang. He didn't recognize the number, so he answered it formally. "Roman Davenport."

"King Roman, this is Tommy Littlefield. I'm in downtown Reading. Where should I go?" Tommy said.

"Tommy! Everything went okay?" Roman asked.

"Had a flat tire, and I didn't realize my spare was missing," Tommy said. "Had to wait for Triple-A to tow me to a tire store, but it's all good now."

Tommy told them where he was, and Roman drove to his location and found him.

"Who's Tommy Littlefield?" Gage asked.

"He's a young shifter from Little Rock. He hauled your motorcycle back here," Roman said.

"Motorcycle? I don't recall owning a motorcycle," Gage said, somewhat confused.

"Evidently, you left the scene of the accident here in Reading, took a cab to the Harley dealer in Wyomissing, where you bought the motorcycle and clothes. Then you drove to Little Rock, Arkansas," Ari explained. "You were MIA for four days. We didn't know where you were."

"Are you serious?" Gage asked, bewildered.

"Tommy found you in the bar," Roman said.

"I didn't stir up anything, did I?" Gage asked.

Roman snorted. "Not you."

They drove to the high-rise and entered the garage. Roman stuck his hand out the window and pointed to where Tommy could park in the row just past their personal vehicles and several Panther Industries vehicles.

The young shifter got out of his pickup and stretched. He met Roman, Gage, and Ari halfway across the row of vehicles. He stared at Gage. "How are you doing, King Gage?"

"I've probably been better, but I don't remember everything," Gage said. "That's my bike?"

Tommy turned to look back at his truck and the motorcycle in the bed. "Yup. It's a beauty."

"We'll call Big Bear to get it out of there later," Ari said. "You must be tired. Come upstairs and have dinner with us. You can bunk on a sofa tonight. We'll get you sorted tomorrow."

They all walked to the door that led to the lobby.

Ari invited Sherm, Kevin, Jason, Leander, and Trisha to dinner. They gathered in the dining room, and Eddie climbed into her booster chair. Roman, Ari, and Gage brought bowls and platters of food to the table.

They discovered that Tommy's animal was a jaguar. Since

Trisha was the alpha of the big cats, she took him under her wing.

"Tommy, why don't you stay in my spare bedroom tonight? Tomorrow I'll show you around Reading, and we can see what's available for work," Trisha said.

"Another kitty!" Eddie squealed. She clasped her little hands to her heart.

"I recall you saying you could fix anything," Sherm said. "What exactly do you like to do the most? Are you more mechanical, or do you have computer skills?"

Tommy was not used to having a lot of attention focused on him. He felt his face heat up and his ears burn. He had never been able to control those things, and it frustrated him in new situations when he wanted to appear cool.

"Well, I seem to have great intuition troubleshooting anything. I've fixed toasters, generators, computers, vehicles—and everything in-between," the young man said. "A few months ago, this company called me to fix a glitch in their gas turbine they were shipping overseas."

"We have a database of all the shifters in our community, so we can share each other's services," Roman said. "I'll bet you'll have plenty of work, including Panther Industries. Our manufacturing facility could use someone with your skills."

Tommy's eyes widened and his head spun as he thought of his options. "Wow! I should have moved here a long time ago."

"We'll get you set up in your own place within the next few days," Ari said. She met Trisha's eyes. "Can you show him what's available so he can find a place? We'll cover the deposits and all that."

"Where's your family?" Leander asked.

"North Carolina. My dad's not a good leader, and my mom is a little too devoted to him. She practically grovels at his feet for attention. I left when I was seventeen," Tommy explained.

"I've seen a lot of people like that," Trisha said. "Spouses, parents, boyfriends and girlfriends can get a little desperate for affection."

"Not in this household," Ari said. "We're all pretty much independent-minded."

Roman's phone dinged. He pulled it out and glanced at the screen. "It's Dr. Tanner." He connected the call. "Hi, Dr. Tanner." He listened to the doctor. "That's good news. I'll tell everyone."

He ended the call and turned to Gage. "Dr. Tanner said they didn't find any internal bleeding, lesions, tumors, or anything else out of the ordinary."

Ari stood. "That's good. You can start on Mr. Tran's potions tonight." She picked up her plate and silverware and walked to the kitchen. "Why don't we get comfortable in the living room?"

Roman grabbed plates. When Trisha, Sherm, Leander, and Gage started stacking dirty dishes, Roman stopped them. "Leave them. Ari and I will clean up. Sherm, you man the bar."

"I should help," Gage said. "I live here too."

"If you insist," Roman said. "But you're still pretty much a guest until your memories return in full. Then it's no holds barred."

"Grab the napkins and put them in the hamper in the butler's pantry," Ari told Gage. She nodded at the door.

"Eddie, brush your teeth! Bedtime in thirty-minutes," Roman hollered.

Gage grabbed all the napkins and dumped them in the hamper. He returned to the kitchen and watched the way Roman and Ari worked together.

Sherm was getting everyone settled with drinks. Gin and tonic for Leander and Trisha, rum and coke for Kevin, beer for Jason and Tommy, and four rocks glasses of bourbon. "Come, sit down. You're not going to die if the kitchen isn't a hundred percent."

"I can't believe you take care of this place by yourself," Trisha said, as Ari walked over to the bar.

"I have help," Ari said. "The building housekeeping people help with the bathrooms and floors. I do the rest." She noticed Jason manning his phone continuously. "Who are you talking to?"

Jason flushed. "Just a friend."

Kevin leaned over and spied Jason's screen, then he snorted. "You'd better pray Janina doesn't hear you say that."

"You two getting serious?" Roman asked. Gage raised his eyebrows.

Jason scowled.

"How's it feel?" Kevin asked. "Remember the *Amanda* incident?"

"That was the girl we never met," Gage said. He started, as if his words surprised him.

"Things are coming back to you!" Ari said. She glanced over at Jason. "Payback is tough, isn't it, son?"

The evening wound down and everyone left. Ari went to the kitchen and pulled the bag of herbal tea out of the drawer, along with one of the silk pouches. She put the kettle on to boil, then got out the dropper bottle.

"Roman, show Gage how to do the drops." She handed the bottle to Roman.

He and Gage went to the half-bath. Roman instructed him to tap the bottom of the bottle several times to activate the formula. Next, he told him to hold up his tongue and allow the drops to fall under it.

"This doesn't even have a taste," Gage said. "I thought you said it tasted horrible."

"Nah, it's the tea. Stuff tastes like horse piss," Roman said. "Just wait."

They returned to the kitchen where a covered cup of tea sat on the counter.

"The tea needs to steep for at least ten more minutes," Ari said.

Gage walked over to the cabinet where he had seen Eddie store the photo albums. "I'm going to look at more pictures. Maybe I'll remember more about my life here."

They sat on the sofa with Gage in the middle and flipped through pages in a photo album. He remembered the house in the woods, Silver Wolf and Gloria. He didn't recognize Atsa or any of the Navajos.

"Atsa's an eagle, but much smaller than your Tothar eagle," Roman said.

"You don't remember Yiska or the elders?" Ari asked.

Gage shook his head. "Drawing a blank."

They kept leafing through the pictures. Gage remembered their first anniversary and their fifth. He remembered Ari being in a coma, but couldn't recall the man who abducted her or the boy who worked with him. His memory was like hopscotch.

The timer on the stove dinged. Ari retrieved the hot tea and gave the cup to Gage. He took a sip.

"What the hell is this shit?" Gage ranted.

"Told you," Roman smirked.

"Just drink it! Mr. Tran's teas and potions work," Ari said, as she grilled him with stern eyes.

Gage took a healthy swallow. "God almighty! Can I add honey or something?"

"There's honey in there already," Ari said. "Just man up and drink it. Don't be such a baby."

Gage tipped the cup to his mouth and sipped. He shuddered. "How many times do I have to drink this stuff?" He set it on the coffee table to cool down.

"Four times a day," Ari said.

"You'll be able to drink bleach when you're finished with this stuff," Roman snorted.

Ari bent forward on the sofa and scowled at Roman. "I'm going to bed!" She got up and headed to Roman's room.

Gage and Roman exchanged a questioning glance. Roman shrugged.

They looked at more pictures. Gage rubbed his face as odd things filtered down into his memory banks. He picked up the cup and swigged the rest of the cooled tea.

"It's late," Roman said. "Let's call it a night."

Gage closed the photo album, stood and returned it to the cabinet. He followed Roman to his bedroom. Ari was curled up in the middle of the bed.

Roman climbed onto the bed. "I'm sorry I made you mad."

Gage stripped off his shirt, pants, and socks. He climbed onto the bed in his briefs, in his regular place on one side of Ari. "Don't be mad at us, honey."

She harrumphed. "This has been a long day. Go to sleep."

Roman undressed down to his briefs. He slipped into bed, kissed Ari on the temple, then turned onto his side. "Goodnight."

"Goodnight," Gage said. He draped an arm across Ari as he typically did.

CHAPTER SEVEN

A few minutes before four o'clock in the morning, Ari awakened to Gage's advancements. She felt his erection through her nighty while his finger massaged the hood of her clit. She turned on her side to face him, pulling him into a steaming kiss, all tongue and teeth. It had been over two weeks since they had made love, and she wanted him.

"Oh, Gage," she moaned.

"I want to be inside you," he whispered against her lips. His head ducked to her right nipple. He was boiling with need.

Roman stirred. Instinct kicked in. He turned toward Ari, his hand brushing her left nipple. He leaned in and ran his tongue across her lips. She turned her head toward him, and their mouths fused together in a passionate kiss.

Gage slid down the mattress, positioned his head between her legs, and wrapped his arms around her hips. He latched onto her sensitive peak.

Ari could barely stay still. She let out a cry as Gage sucked on her clit, then slid two fingers into her wet, hot core.

Roman sucked on one nipple while tweaking the other. "I'm going to come!" Ari tensed. Her knees tightened around Gage's shoulders as her body spasmed and the orgasm swept through her. She clutched his hair with both hands and held his head in place as the shudders continued.

As the orgasm weakened to a dull throb, she lowered her legs and let go of his hair. Gage climbed her body. He forcefully shoved Roman out of the way as he readied himself to enter Ari.

Roman rammed into Gage's shoulder. His panther face snarled at his life partner.

Suddenly, Gage shifted. His large eagle screeched. He focused his eyes on Roman, as prey.

Ari barely had the chance to get out from under Gage when his large wing slammed down on the bed where she had lain. The wing bashed Roman.

In a split second, Roman shifted to his panther. He dove at the bird and grabbed one of the eagle's legs.

Ari was off the bed in an instant. She shifted to her liger.

STOP!

Neither animal obeyed her.

Gage clawed Roman with his sharp talons.

Roman pulled feathers out of Gage's eagle where he had bitten him in several places.

Ari's liger grabbed Roman's panther by the scruff and hauled him off the bed.

Shift back, right now, Ari sent to the men. She shook the panther by the scruff, then dropped him on the floor. She darted to the bed and grabbed the eagle, none too gently by one of his wings, and shook him. She dropped him on the floor.

Both men shifted to their human forms. The fight didn't stop there. They were at each other with fists, pounding full-force.

Ari's liger roared. The sound was deafening.

Roman and Gage sprung apart at the loud roar. They stared at Ari's animal, both of them panting.

Ari shifted to her human form. She was burning with rage. "What the hell is wrong with you two? You made me shred my favorite nightie! I'm going to my room!"

She grabbed her robe from the hook on the inside of the closet door, slipped into it and stormed out of the bedroom. The thought of Eddie sleeping kept her from slamming the door.

"I ought to beat the shit out of you for starting this shit," Roman said.

"I don't know what came over me," Gage said, remorseful. "I'm sorry."

"Until you get everything in your head straight, and know your place in our relationship, stay away from Ari," Roman snarled. His body bore claw marks from Gage's sharp eagle talons, and the beginning of bruising on his face.

Gage's shoulder, thigh, and arm sported bite and claw marks. The beginning of a black eye and a bruise on his chin smarted.

He sat on the edge of the bed, looking forlorn. "Did you go through this when you were recovering from Italy?"

Roman sat on the opposite corner of the bed. "Yeah. I guess I did. I don't know how you and Ari put up with me. None of us had sex for a long time."

"Let's get some sleep," Gage said. He slipped under the covers, his back facing the middle of the bed.

Roman slid onto his side of the bed.

ML

When Ari woke, she smelled coffee and food. She washed her face, brushed her teeth, slipped into her robe and headed to the kitchen.

Roman and Gage had everything ready. Eddie sat on her booster seat at the table. She was unusually quiet.

"Morning," Roman said in an even tone.

"Morning," Gage said. He didn't meet her eyes. He swigged the last mouthful of the disgusting tea, then rinsed the cup.

"Morning," Ari said, with a hint of attitude.

She's pissed! Roman sent to Gage, blocking Ari and Eddie.

My fault. What should I do? Gage sent.

Act like nothing happened. Have to take her lead, Roman sent.

Okay, Gage sent.

Eddie looked from one to the other of her adopted parents. She saw Gage's black eye and bruised chin, then the black and blue marks on Roman's face. Ari didn't have any bruises; she just looked mad. "I dreamed I heard a loud kitty roar last night."

They all looked at her.

"We had a little scuffle," Roman said.

"Mommy shifted and put us in our places," Gage said.

Ari walked over to Eddie and kissed her forehead. "I'm sorry I disturbed your sleep. Your fathers were having a disagreement, and I had to be the boss, but everything is okay now."

She noticed they had made French toast. Ari figured they were trying to get on her good side.

Gage poured coffee and prepared the three cups.

Roman grabbed the heaping plate of French toast and the spatula. He served the three adults two slices of toast each and Eddie half a slice. He sat the serving plate on the table, grabbed Eddie's plate and prepared her breakfast. Roman buttered, cut, and drizzled syrup over her toast.

Ari sat at the table and let them wait on her. She ate in silence —it made them uncomfortable, but she was still processing the fight. When she finished, she pushed back her chair, stood and announced she was going to shower and dress. It definitely wasn't an invitation.

Roman turned to Eddie. "Let's get you dressed, pumpkin."

Gage stacked the dishes.

The elevator dinged Kevin and Jason's arrival.

"Are we too late for breakfast?" Jason called out as he and his brother walked to the kitchen.

"You made it right on time," Gage said. "I'll reheat the French toast."

Kevin stopped in his tracks when he saw Gage's black eye. "You okay?"

Gage shrugged it off. "We had a misunderstanding."

The boys stared at Gage.

"Where is everyone?" Jason asked.

Roman came down the hall. "Your mom's getting dressed. I just got Eddie ready for the day."

The boys looked Roman over. His face was a mess of bruises. They waited for him to say something, but an explanation never came.

"Want coffee with breakfast?" Roman said.

"Sure..." Kevin said.

Roman got out two cups and made their coffee as they typically liked it. He brought the cups to the table.

Ari entered the kitchen, dressed and reserved. "Good morning, Jason... Kev." She busied herself with loading the dishwasher and cleaning up the kitchen.

The boys drank their coffee and ate their breakfast in silence, eyeing everyone through the emotional blizzard.

Eddie trotted down the hall in one of her cute outfits.

She looked like a little ragamuffin in a mismatched outfit.

"Hey, Edris-Eddie," Jason said. "Who dressed you this morning?"

Ari turned away from the sink and took in the green shirt with the red crop pants on the little girl. She glared at Roman. "There's a white T-shirt with red and blue splotches in the bureau. Think you can find it?"

Everyone stared at Ari. The men could tell she was seething below the surface.

Roman stood. "Sure, I'll go find it." He hurried out of the room.

Gage followed. "I'll help you."

Kevin and Jason followed Roman and Gage.

"What the hell's going on?" Jason whispered. "Did you two get in a fight?"

"Why's Mom so mad?" Kevin asked. He kept his voice low, but he knew his mother could probably hear them with her sensitive liger hearing.

"Yeah, I started something I shouldn't have," Gage said. "Roman and I shifted, and we started fighting in our animal forms. Your mom shifted and pulled us apart, but we were stupid. We shifted and kept duking it out."

"You'd better lie low today," Jason said. "I don't think I've ever seen her so mad."

Roman rummaged through the chest of drawers for the shirt. He pulled one out of the neatly folded stack and held it up. "Is this the right one?"

Kevin grabbed the shirt. "That will do. It goes with the red pants." He left Eddie's room and returned to the kitchen with the shirt. "Eddie, let's change your shirt so you don't look like a Christmas tree."

"But I like my green shirt," Eddie said.

Eddie, Mommy wants you to wear this shirt. We need to make her happy right now, okay? Kevin sent.

Eddie pouted. *Oh, all right.* She let Kevin change her shirt. He draped the green shirt over the back of a kitchen chair.

"If all of you are through with your *meeting*, finish your breakfast and get to work," Ari said. With frost.

"We're finished," Kevin said. He turned and hurried down the hall to where his brother and stepfathers were. He closed the door behind him. "Man, is she pissed. Come on, Jason. Mom made a remark about us getting to work."

"Maybe we'd better go downstairs and visit with Sherm," Roman said.

"Yeah, we'd better let her have her space," Gage said. All four men headed back to the kitchen.

"Call if you need anything," Roman said. He approached Ari for a quick smooch, but she turned her back on him. He backed away, and they went to the foyer and called the elevator.

When they were safely ensconced in the steel car, Jason turned to Roman and Gage. "Man, you two are in deep shit. You might consider a shopping expedition."

"Yeah, chocolates, flowers **and** jewelry," Kevin said. "Maybe even a new purse and shoes. Mom loves books. Pull out all the stops."

Jason exited the elevator on the thirtieth floor. Kevin rode down to Panther Industries Security Division on the twenty-eighth floor with his two dad-friends.

When they entered Sherm's office, the Asian head of the division looked up and stopped mid-stroke on the keyboard. He stared at Gage and Roman's bruised faces.

"I'll bet there's a good story behind those faces," Sherm said. He stood and walked around his desk to inspect their faces up close.

"You'd freeze to death in Mom's presence right now," Kevin said, as he passed through Sherm's office to his cubicle.

"So, you going to tell me what brought on your faces in their present condition?" Sherm asked.

Gage shook his head. "Better to let it drop."

"I get it—must be something in the bedroom," Sherm said.

Roman scowled at his best friend. "Christ, I wish you were a shifter, Sherm. It would be so much easier for you to understand some of this."

"Wouldn't that be interesting," Sherm said. "Lowly human here. Sorry to disappoint."

"You do pretty damn good for a human," Roman said. "Anything interesting going on?"

Sherm smirked. "You're going to love this. Janina accidentally sent me something that was meant for Jason's eyes only. She tried to recall the email through Outlook when she saw my email address, but I'd already opened it."

"It's not nude pictures, is it?" Gage asked, slightly disturbed.

"Not quite. Let's just say *scantily clad* doesn't do them justice," Sherm said. He snorted, then shook his head in disbelief. "I could have fun with Jason from here to the end of the world with this stuff. Evidently, they like to role-play."

Roman and Gage raised their eyebrows. They weren't sure they wanted to know details about Jason and Janina's sex life.

"Why don't we go to Pomodoro's and get a dozen of their cannoli?" Roman said to Gage. "Ari loves them."

"Good idea," Gage said. They bumped fists with Sherm and left his domain.

ML

Roman and Gage sat at the bar of Pomodoro's drinking bourbon. They had a silent conversation going, so the human lunch crowd couldn't overhear them. They each nodded and made physical movements with their heads and hands.

The bartender walked to their side of the bar. He leaned toward them. "King Roman, King Gage, you might want to reconsider what you're doing. You look pretty strange to people who can clearly see you're not having a conversation out loud."

Roman started. He stole a look around and noticed some people staring at them and whispering behind their hands. "Oh! Didn't think about that."

Gage coughed. "Great. More chaos. Just what we need right now."

The bartender looked them over. "Might want to wait until your healing kicks in before you venture out."

Roman stood. "We can't win this round, Gage. Might as well go home and face the wrath of our mate."

Gage grabbed the box of cannoli and stood. "At least we'll be bearing gifts... the edible kind are always appreciated."

"Good luck with that," the bartender said.

They parked the car, entered the building and crossed the lobby to the elevator. They rode up to the penthouse and stepped into the foyer. The place was quiet. They went to Ari's suite and found her reading on her iPad.

Gage held the box out as a peace offering. Ari's fingers were inches away when Gage's world tilted. He dropped to the floor in a dead faint, the box falling upside down.

"Gage!" Ari was on her knees in a split second beside him.

Roman dropped to the floor. His finger searched for a pulse on Gage's neck. "Should we call Dr. Tanner or Mr. Tran?"

"Mr. Tran is closer," Ari said, as she fretted. She raised Gage's head onto her lap.

Roman pulled his phone out and called the Asian herbalist, historian and translator. He explained the problem and listened. "Ari, does Gage's forehead feel sweaty? Mr. Tran's on his way up. He wanted to know if he was warm or cold to the touch."

Ari brushed the hair off Gage's forehead, then touched the skin. "He feels clammy."

Roman called Sherm. "Gage passed out. Need your help!"

The elevator dinged Mr. Tran and Sherm's arrival.

Roman was on his feet to fetch the men. They returned to Ari's suite.

"What happened?" Sherm asked.

"He just dropped," Ari said, fretting.

The herbalist sank to the floor and observed the eagle shifter. He lifted his eyelids and felt his skin. He made eye contact with Roman. "You didn't hit him in his temple during your squabble, did you?"

Roman's eyes widened as he stared at the herbalist. "No! I'm positive I didn't go anywhere near his temple!"

Ari glared at him. "Of all the stupid things you two could have done, so soon after his amnesia seemed to have lifted! Honestly, Roman, what were you thinking?"

He glared right back at her. "I can't undo what's been done, Ari. Can you just let it go?"

They scowled at each other for another few moments, then turned their full attention to Mr. Tran and Gage.

"Let's get him to his bed," Mr. Tran said. "We will have to see if there are any setbacks when he wakes."

Roman and Sherm pulled Gage to his feet and shuffled his dead weight down the hall.

Eddie came out of her room and screamed when she saw Gage. "Daddy Gage!" She looked frantically from Ari to Roman to Gage, then to Sherm, and finally, Mr. Tran, waiting for an explanation.

"Daddy Gage fainted," Ari said. "Everything is going to be

okay, Eddie." She scooped up the distraught girl and held her tightly, patting her back.

Sherm and Roman got Gage settled onto his bed. Roman removed Gage's shoes.

"Should we cover him?" Ari asked.

Mr. Tran shook his head. "No, best to let his body temperature adjust." He opened his satchel and withdrew a tiny bag that contained little balls of compressed herbs. He slipped on a sterile glove, opened Gage's mouth and stuffed one ball up against the inside of his cheek.

"Don't worry, he won't choke on this," Mr. Tran said. "Has he been taking the drops and drinking the tea?"

"Yes, he's been faithful to the schedule, while complaining loudly every time," Roman said.

Mr. Tran nodded. "Let's determine where he is mentally when he regains consciousness. It's difficult to say what caused this episode. If you want to have Dr. Tanner to examine him, give him a call."

Ari bounced Eddie from side to side. "No, I think we should wait to see how he is when he wakes up."

"Yeah, let's wait," Roman said.

Sherm headed for the door of Gage's room. "Call me if you need help."

CHAPTER EIGHT

An hour and a half later, Gage stirred on his bed. Roman sat up straight in the chair and looked his partner over. Gage opened his eyes and blinked. He chewed something disgusting in his mouth and made a face.

Gage saw Roman. "What happened?"

"We're not sure. One minute you were handing the box of cannolis to Ari, and the next you were on the floor," Roman said. "Mr. Tran put some herbs in your mouth."

He's awake! Roman sent to Ari.

Moments later, Ari rushed into the room and practically launched herself onto the bed. "Are you okay? Do you hurt anywhere?"

"Let me sit up. I'll let you know if the room spins," Gage said. He swung his legs over the side of the bed and sat still for a minute to assess himself. "Everything seems to be okay. No headache."

"Do you want to try to stand?" Ari nervously hovered.

Gage stood. He swayed a little.

Roman jumped up and steadied him. "Are you sure you want to be up?"

"I think I'm fine," Gage said.

"You're not *fine* if you drop to the floor, out cold," Ari said. "Something triggered that."

"Did you eat all the cannoli?" Gage asked, sidestepping the issue.

"You want a cannoli?" Ari asked, stunned.

Gage shrugged. "Is that okay? And coffee?"

"Guess everything is okay," Roman said. "He remembers that much at least."

Ari looked from one to the other. "Honestly, I sometimes wonder whether you two are even adults at times." She turned and left the room.

Roman walked beside Gage as they headed to the kitchen. Ari was making coffee, so they figured she wasn't that upset with Gage's request.

The home phone rang. Ari grabbed the handset. "Hello?"

"Ms. Davis, a certified letter just arrived for you," the lobby guard announced.

"A certified letter—for me?" Ari asked.

"It's addressed to Arianna Davis," he said.

"Okay, thanks. I'll be down in a minute," Ari said, and hung up the phone.

"That sounds urgent," Roman said.

"I'd better go get it. I can't imagine who would be sending me something so urgent," she said. She wiped her hands on a dish-towel and headed toward the elevator.

Ari practically sprinted into the penthouse, the envelope in hand. She headed to the kitchen table where Roman and Gage drank coffee and ate cannoli.

"Who's it from?" Gage asked.

She looked stricken. "It's from an attorney! I hope I'm not being sued by someone!"

"You haven't opened it yet?" Roman asked.

Ari shook her head, then she sat at the table. She slid her finger under the flap and opened the envelope. She pulled out the single sheet of paper and read it—twice.

"I think they have the wrong person. This attorney was contracted by an attorney in Texas to contact Arianna Davis to inform her that her uncle, Charles, had passed away. I don't have an Uncle Charles," Ari said.

"Well, at least you aren't being sued," Gage said.

"I'll contact him and get it straightened out," Roman said. One of his degrees was in law, and he kept the license up with the continuing education courses that were required, and paid his annual bar dues.

Ari got up and opened the refrigerator. She grabbed the jug of almond chocolate milk and gave it a good shake. "Anyone want some chocolate milk?"

Tiny feet ran to the kitchen. "I do!" Eddie squealed. "I love our chocolate milk."

"Me too!" Ari said. She looked to the men.

"None for me," Roman said. He stood. "I'll be in my office." He held up the letter.

"I'll take a little," Gage said. "I can't remember whether I like it or not."

"You love our chocolate milk!" Eddie said.

Gage tickled Eddie. "I'm so glad you remind me what I like and don't like."

Eddie snuck a glance at Ari. "We don't like liver." She made an alarming face.

"You don't? I was going to cook liver and onions for supper tonight!" Ari said, with a straight face.

"I'm not hungry," Eddie said. She ran off to her bedroom to play.

🏯**ML**🗾

Roman sat at his desk in his office suite off his bedroom. A legal tablet and a pen sat on the desk before him, with Ari's letter beside it. He picked up his desk phone receiver and made the call. The phone was answered on the third ring.

"Mr. Thompson, please," Roman said. He listened. "Roman Davenport for Arianna Davis." They put him on hold and he tolerated the music.

"Mr. Davenport, Jordi Thompson here," the man announced.

"Jordi, call me Roman. We received your letter, but Ari informed me she doesn't have an uncle Charles, or any uncles, for that matter, so you contacted the wrong Ari Davis."

"The estate attorney in Texas was a long-standing attorney to Charles O'Briain. He mentioned that Ms. Davis might not know of her family connections. I can assure you that your client is the correct party," Jordi said. "When do you think she would be available to meet with me?"

"Might as well sort this out as soon as possible. Are you available this afternoon?" Roman asked. He heard keyboard clicks and determined the lawyer must be accessing his electronic calendar.

"Four-o'clock is open," Jordi said.

"We'll see you then," Roman said, and disconnected the call. He stood and returned to the kitchen. He sat in his chair, folded his hands on the table, and met Ari's eyes. "The attorney said there was no mistake. We're meeting him this afternoon at four."

"I don't understand," Ari said.

"He mentioned there are family connections you may not be aware of," Roman said. "We need to go and find out how this affects you. I don't know if he died with huge debts, or if you're due an inheritance."

Ari was stunning in a dark blue sheath dress that came to her knees, along with matching flats and a purse as she walked between Roman and Gage. They walked through the glass-etched doors to the reception desk of the attorney's office. The color of her dress matched her eyes. The long, silver necklace gleamed, and her rings made her beautiful hands stand out.

"We have an appointment to see Jordi," Roman announced.

"Mr. Davenport?" the receptionist asked.

"Yes, with Ms. Davis and our partner, Gage Stryker."

The receptionist sent an inner-office message to the attorney. He responded immediately. She stood and came around the desk. "This way, please." She escorted them to an office, opened the door, and stood out of the way.

Jordi Thompson stood, came around his desk, and introduced himself. The attorney was approaching sixty, but his hair remained dark and there were no wrinkles on his smooth, handsome face. The Black attorney stood a few inches shorter than Roman and Gage in a three-piece suit and tie.

He took Ari's hand in both of his. "I'm sorry for your loss, Ms. Davis. Especially since you weren't aware, you even had an uncle. It's a tragic loss."

"I don't understand how this could happen," Ari said. "My mother told me she had a sister, but I've never met her. There must have been a rift in the family, but no matter how many times I tried to get information, she refused to talk about her relatives."

Jordi nodded. He motioned them to a small conference table. "Won't you sit down?"

They settled in the chairs with Ari in between her men. "Your uncle, Charles O'Briain, left you his entire estate in San

Marcos, Texas, which is substantial," Jordi began. He grabbed two file folders from his desk, along with his pen, and joined them at the table.

Ari's mouth fell open. "This is just bizarre. I don't understand why someone I never knew would leave me his estate."

"There are some private documents he left for you, but we'll get to those later. I'm sure there are explanations in those pages," Jordi said. He slid a thick file folder that was at least an inch thick across to Roman. "Since you're an attorney, I figured we'd go through the paperwork together."

Jordi and Roman both opened their folders.

"Are there debts Ari will be responsible for?" Roman asked.

"On the contrary," Jordi said.

They spent the next two hours going through the contents of the folder, with Gage perusing all the financials that were presented and Ari signing documents. By the time they finished, her head was spinning.

Jordi returned to his desk and retrieved three envelopes. One letter-sized envelope, one large clasp-type envelope, and a smaller clasp envelope that jingled. All of them were sealed with wax and a custom stamp of CoB. He presented them to Ari. "Your uncle instructed that these two should be opened in private. I have no idea what they contain. The smaller envelope contains keys to the property and vehicles."

Ari accepted the envelopes. She ran her finger across the wax seal of the smaller envelope. "Thank you. I can't imagine what else could shock me more than what you've told me already."

"Hopefully, you'll discover some family information," Jordi said. They all stood and shook hands.

"If we have any questions, I'll get in touch," Roman said.

They left the office and rode the elevator to the ground floor, keeping their thoughts to themselves, then exited the building. They walked in silence to the surface parking lot and got in the Navigator.

Gage turned in his seat. "Atsa's going to be happy. He always said we should move closer."

"You remember Atsa?" Roman asked.

"Huh, guess I do," Gage said.

"We're not moving!" Ari said. "We don't know anything about this place. It's probably a piece of property out in the middle of nowhere."

"Honey, from the figures I saw, your holdings are substantial," Gage said.

"You're a wealthy woman," Roman said.

They drove the few blocks back to their building. Roman and Gage stopped off at Sherm's office to pick up Eddie, then they rode the elevator upstairs. They found Ari at the table with the envelopes and a letter opener.

"I couldn't bring myself to ruin the seals," she said. "I don't recall ever receiving anything with wax seals. They're beautiful."

Ari pulled the document out of the white, letter-sized envelope. She unfolded it to discover a letter from her uncle. It was typed on letterhead, printed double-sided, and signed with a strong signature. She wondered if he had written it prior to his health deterioration. She began to read.

Dear Ari,

I realize this may come as quite a shock—to discover you had a maternal uncle your mother hid from you. Alannah—your mother's real first name, would not admit to the true nature of our family so she chose to live estranged from us. She changed her name to keep that distance. Fortunately, I had the resources to follow her life as Susan Murphy, and yours.

When I discovered my health was taking a turn for the worst two years ago, I started to put my estate in order. I wanted to make sure that you and your sons would never want for anything. While I realize your two life partners take care of you, my great nephews shall now enjoy knowing they are, and will always be cared for.

Up until now, I have seen no sign of any physical changes in your person. So, what I am going to tell you may sound like the rantings of a crazy man. But I assure you, what I am about to disclose to you is not a fairytale.

My great grandfather—your great- great-grandfather, Emeril Ó'Briain, was a world traveler. While on a safari in Africa when he was in his early twenties, a lion attacked him. The natives said it was a were-cat that had been in its lion form for many years, having given up its human life for that of its cat. Evidently, Emeril stumbled upon its lair, which contained some human possessions. The cat attacked him, but did not kill him.

Upon arriving home in Ireland, Emeril became very sick. After several days of delusions and ranting about the lion while in this fugue with a high fever, he overcame the sickness. He married his sweetheart shortly thereafter. After his second child was born, Emeril came down with a fever and was violently ill for several days.

Our relatives said that one night he thrashed in his bed, then staggered out of the house and ran into the woods. His brother-in-law witnessed him fall to the ground, thrash around and change into a lion. It shocked both of them. The lion did not attack his wife's brother. He seemed to understand that anyone with family blood was protected.

All of his children, except one daughter, inherited the gene of the were-lion. Moving forward, your mother did not get the gene, but I did. My were-cat is a tiger. I do not know why my cat deviated from the lion to a tiger, but I discovered that our family has a number of both cats.

At this time, my only sibling in the States remaining alive is my elder sister Aileen. I urge you to contact her. She can tell you more about our family history.

I tell you all this so you can make your sons aware that they may carry this gene. Any of you could shapeshift at any time. Your grandchildren, if your sons were to have children, may carry the gene as well. This is no secret you should keep from your family. Your mother made a grave mistake in hiding your true nature from you.

You will find Aileen's contact information among the paperwork you receive from my attorney, along with access codes to all my accounts. I have amassed a fortune, a beautiful home, and hold-ings in Texas. Please go to my home in San Marcos as soon as possible. Mrs. Peña, my housekeeper of twenty years, will look after the house until which time you can make the trip west.

I hope you fall in love with the area and make it your new home. The house is surrounded by the Spring Lake Preserve, and I own land further west which is more forested. We big cats need room to roam.

I'm so sorry that we did not meet face to face, but understand that I have loved you from afar.

Uncle Charles

Ari broke down and cried when she finished reading the letter. She pushed the pages across the table to her men, got up and rushed to the half-bath in the butler's pantry.

When she returned to the kitchen, Roman and Gage had finished reading the letter. They stood.

Roman encased her in his arms. "I'm so sorry they withheld this information from you."

Gage's arms wrapped around them. He kissed her neck. "This is truly tragic. To think that you could have shifted at any time! What was your mother thinking?"

"There's probably an entire clan of relatives over in Ireland that don't know of your existence," Roman said. "It sounds like you come from wealth, seeing that your great-great-grandfather was a world traveler."

"We should ask Mr. Tran to do some genealogy to find out who they are," Gage said.

Ari pulled herself gently out of their embrace and sat at the table. She pulled the larger clasp envelope to her and emptied it onto the table. She sifted through the paperwork until she found what she needed. A piece of paper with her aunt's address. Ari stared at the address in Pearland, Texas.

Gage and Roman looked over her shoulder.

"Let's look up the place where your aunt lives. We can search for her on the Internet and see what we can find out about her," Gage said. They followed him to his suite, to his home office beyond his bedroom. He sank into his desk chair and woke his computer.

He did an online search for the address on Countryside Estates Boulevard and discovered it was an over fifty-five community. Then he clicked on the website and they looked the place over. It was a gated community with tennis courts, a pool, a decent exercise room with basic equipment and free-weights, a clubhouse with a large banquet room, and walking paths. The big draw was the golf course.

They searched online for Ari's aunt. Not much came up, so Roman dinged Sherm so he could do a thorough search. It took longer than they expected, but half an hour later, Sherm sent a profile sheet with pictures, locations, and background information. His note caught their interest.

It appears that Ari's aunt is very old. We found information with photos of her in different locations, most likely to hide the fact that she hadn't aged. She's used several aliases that changed every twenty-five to forty years. That prompted me to search for her late uncle, and I discovered the same pattern. Which brings me to Ari's mother. She obviously did not have the gene. She aged normally, like a human, and passed away because of normal circumstances.

Ari, Roman and Gage scrolled through the document to see the pictures and to read the information. Aileen could have been Ari's sister, and no more than five years older.

"Looks like you have some great genetics," Roman said as he perused the photos of Aileen.

"Should I call her, or should we just go there?" Ari asked.

"Let's make the trip. We can check out San Marcos while we're in Texas," Gage said.

Ari pulled two envelopes out of the pile of documents. One was addressed to the housekeeper, Mrs. Peña, and the other was for the gardener, Mr. Fuentes. She needed to assure them that they did not have to worry about their positions. Ari replaced her uncle's letter in the envelope and stuffed it into the large clasp envelope, followed by the other documents and the keys.

"I should sit down with Jason and Kevin. They need to make this trip with us," Ari said. "I still can't get my head around this. I want to connect with my aunt as soon as possible. I don't want to lose another relative that I never had the chance to meet."

"Get the boys up here," Roman said. "Gage and I can go down to Sherm's and make arrangements to fly out whenever you're ready."

CHAPTER NINE

Ari mentally sent her sons a message. *Can you please come upstairs right now? There's something very important I need to tell you.*

Jason mind-pinged her back. *No one's fighting, are they? Be right up.*

Kevin sent, *On my way. Everything okay? Should I bring help?*

Ari told them both that all was well; she had to tell them something.

Roman and Gage took off downstairs. Five minutes later, the elevator dinged Jason and Kevin's arrival.

"I'm in my study," Ari called out.

The boys entered the room and sat on the sofa opposite her. Eddie skipped into the room and hopped onto the sofa next to Ari. Once everyone had settled, Ari started the conversation.

"I just found out that my uncle Charles died," she said.

"You had an uncle?" Jason asked. He stole a glance at his brother.

"How come we never met him?" Kevin asked.

"Because I never knew he existed," Ari said. She explained about the letter from the attorney, the meeting, then pulled her uncle's letter out and handed it to Jason. She waited while they read the letter together.

When Jason folded the letter and stuffed it back into its envelope, he handed it back to his mother. "We need to find this Aunt Aileen!"

Ari handed them the profile Sherm put together. "We have her address. We're all going there to meet her, then we'll fly to San Marcos and see this estate. Do either of you have any pressing plans?"

"I was going to go to Italy..." Jason said.

"You'll have to postpone the trip. Janina will understand when you explain the circumstances," Ari said. "There's no telling how old my aunt really is, but from what Sherm dug up, we know she's well over a hundred."

Eddie looked at the pictures of Aileen. "She's a kitty, isn't she?"

Ari stared at the little girl. "Yes, she is. How did you know that?"

Eddie shrugged. "Are we going on the plane again?"

"Yes. We're going to Texas! It's very hot there," Ari said.

"Can I bring my bathing suit?" Eddie asked.

"That would be a good idea," Ari said.

Eddie clapped with joy, slid off the sofa and dashed out of the room.

"She's so much fun," Kevin said as he watched Eddie leave the room.

ML

The next day, the jet landed at Hobby Airport in Texas. They deplaned, and a rental car person met them and led them to two SUVs.

"It's hot!" Eddie said, as she looked around.

"It sure is," Ari said. "Texas is a hot state, honey."

Sherm signed the paperwork, and they piled into the vehicles, one of which contained a child's seat.

Lonnie drove the lead vehicle with Kevin and Jason as his passengers, and Sherm drove the other with Roman, Gage, Ari and Eddie. They wove through the Hobby Airport Loop to Airport Blvd. Then they merged onto State Highway 288 S, took the McHard Road/Shadow Creek Parkway exit and turned onto Countryside Estates Boulevard.

The lead SUV pulled up to the guard shack. Lonnie provided the guard with information, indicating that both vehicles were together. The gate opened, and they drove through. Five-hundred feet down the road, they pulled into the immense parking lot on the left side of the road and parked in front of the community building.

Everyone piled out of the SUVs.

"Let me do the talking," Ari said. "We don't want to intimidate anyone."

That raised some eyebrows, but the men kept their lips buttoned. They followed Ari through the front doors of the community building.

A reception area blocked incoming visitors; it forced them to sign in. Ari approached the desk. "Hi, we're here to see my aunt, Aileen. Is she here today?"

"Aileen McCarthy?" the woman asked.

"Yes," Ari said.

"Your name?"

"Ari Davis."

"Why don't you and your party sit over there, and I'll contact Aileen," the woman said. She pointed to an area that consisted of several chairs and sofas and card game tables.

"Thank you," Ari said. She led the group to the appointed area, and they sat.

"They seem a little over the top in their security here," Kevin said. "It's an over fifty-five place, for Christ's sake. Do they have a lot of threats, or something?"

"I suspect the front desk is more of a nosy information-gathering spot than a security concern," Sherm said, as he snorted a laugh.

"That makes more sense," Jason said. "Still, it's irritating."

Roman observed heads popping out of doorways, looking in their direction. "I feel like a specimen."

A few minutes later, a vivacious woman with short, spiky white hair with teal coloring around her face walked up to them. She eyed Ari with a glint of warmth and confidence. "I figured you would make an appearance after the attorney contacted you. I'm your aunt Aileen, Ari."

Ari stood. She moved in for a hug. Aileen pulled her into an embrace, and they rocked in their hug. Ari cried.

"I wish I had had the opportunity to meet Uncle Charles. When we found out where you lived, I didn't want to waste any time," Ari said. She wiped her eyes. "These are my sons, Jason and Kevin." The boys shook their great-aunt's hand.

"And these are my life partners, Roman Davenport and Gage Stryker. This is Sherman Foo, the head of Panther Industries Security Division, and his second in command, Lonnie."

Ari grabbed up Eddie. "And this is our adopted daughter, Eddie."

"It's so nice to meet all of you. Why don't we go to my house so we can visit in private?" Aileen said.

"Good idea," Gage said. "I feel as if everyone here will have my suit size by the time we leave."

"You noticed that, huh?" Aileen chuckled. "That's the thing about an over fifty-five community. Everyone knows everybody's business, and gossip spreads faster than a brushfire." She linked arms with Ari and walked the group to the front door. "I'll have to hitch a ride with you because I walked."

They climbed into the SUVs. Aileen guided Lonnie down the street, directed him to turn left at the second street, and they pulled into the third driveway on the left. The house was a single-story, tan brick home with white accents and an iron-fenced backyard.

Aileen unlocked the front door and bid them enter. The house had a beautiful open-concept that flowed from the dining area, kitchen, living room and bar area. An enclosed back patio had screened panels where two cats snoozed in the sun. The wall of sliding glass doors showed a beautifully landscaped backyard.

"Please make yourselves comfortable. Itsy and Bitsy are regular house-cats, not shifters," she said. "Would you like some iced tea?"

"Oh, that would be wonderful," Ari said. "Let me help you."

They walked to the kitchen while the men chose their seating arrangements. Gage and Sherm walked into the sunroom, then returned to the living room and sat.

Ari noted the correct number of glasses on the kitchen island, including a child-sized glass. She raised an eyebrow.

Aileen noticed. "Our family has unique listening skills unless you block us out."

"Oh! I thought for sure you were psychic, or something," Ari said.

"I guess we fall into the *or something'* category," Aileen said, with a huge grin.

She pulled a pitcher of tea out of the refrigerator, then a plate of cucumber sandwiches cut on the diagonal. She lifted a dome from a plate on the counter to reveal bite-sized brownies and petit fours.

Ari poured the tea.

Aileen placed two trays on the island. One for the tea and one for the food. They carried the feast into the living room. Aileen returned to the kitchen for small plates.

"Dig in," she said as she returned to the living room. "I don't stand on formalities."

"I hope you don't mind my asking, but how long will you live here in this community?" Sherm asked. "When I searched for you, I tracked your movements."

"Now that we've connected, I'd like to stay close to my niece and her family," Aileen said. "If you plan to move to Charles' San Marcos estate, I'll sell this place and move there, or I'll move to wherever you live."

"Do we still have family in Ireland?" Ari asked.

"Yes, most of them are human, but there are a few that carry the gene," she said.

"You knew my mother, didn't you?" Ari asked. "I don't remember meeting you, unless I was a small child, but I remember my mother mentioning you by name more than once."

Aileen took a bite of a sandwich while she thought about Ari's question. "Your mother and Charles had a huge row decades ago. You most likely don't know this, but your mother was the youngest child. She came more than a hundred years after the rest of us, and as she grew up, she couldn't cope with the idea of having *mutants* for siblings."

"Do I have more aunts and uncles then?" Ari asked hopefully.

"Two uncles and an aunt, over in Ireland, and a horde of cousins," Aileen said.

"Did Alanna emigrate to the United States to get away from family?" Roman asked.

"Yes, but Charles and I decided we should emigrate as well, shortly after Alanna. We wanted to make sure she was safe. She left Ireland abruptly and was not in a good state of mind," Aileen said. "We worried people would take advantage of her. When we settled in the US, we found her living in Houston. Do you remember your father, Ari?"

Ari shook her head. "I don't even remember seeing a picture of him. Mom didn't even have any pictures of her family and refused to talk about my father. I figured he was either a one-night stand, or he abused her and she was hiding from him. I remember moving a lot when I was young."

Aileen closed her eyes longer than a blink. When she opened them, it looked as if she wanted to apologize for something. "Ari, your father is a shifter."

"IS?" Ari choked out. "Like, as in he is still alive?"

"No way!" Jason said. He and his brother shared a shocked expression.

"Our grandfather is alive? Where is he?" Kevin asked. Roman, Gage, and Sherm sat out the discussion, absorbing the details.

"He lives in the mountains in New Mexico," Aileen said. She turned her focus back to Ari. "Your father is a mountain lion. Your mother left him when she discovered he was a shifter. She most likely didn't even tell him about you—she was four months pregnant when she walked out and disappeared again. I can't imagine what she went through—leaving everything behind in Ireland only to discover the man she fell in love with was that very thing she ran from."

Ari reeled with emotion. How could her mother cut her off from not only her family in Ireland but her own father?

"Don't worry, Ari. We'll find him," Sherm said. "Travis can find anyone or anything."

"What's his name?" Ari asked.

"Kenneth Porter." Aileen appeared to want to say something, but decided against it.

Roman noticed her reticence. "What? Don't hold back now, Aileen. Ari deserves to know everything."

"I don't think they ever divorced. Alanna would have had to disclose her whereabouts to get a divorce, and there was no way she would have done that," Aileen said. "I don't even think your father knew of her background—that she came from a wealthy family. He certainly never reached out to any of our people."

Ari pinched the bridge of her nose. "I don't know what to make of this. All these years I thought I was alone. I mean, I realized you were out there somewhere, Aunt Aileen, but I didn't even have your last name."

"Mom's family is wealthy?" Jason asked. He thought of all the years they had struggled.

"Why couldn't your mother have been like Marilyn on the TV show *The Munsters?* Remember her? She was the normal niece," Kevin said. "Your mother could have been the Marilyn among all the shifters in her family."

Aileen patted Kevin's hand. "Don't fret about it. Things have all worked out, and now everyone can move forward." She turned her attention to Ari. "Soon, you'll meet your father, then you can meet your Irish family. But first things first—Charles' estate in San Marcos."

CHAPTER TEN

Sherm made all the ground transportation arrangements. They returned to Hobby Airport where Lonnie filed their flight plan to the San Marcos Regional Airport.

"Who would have thought San Marcos would have their own airport," Roman said, as he settled in his seat in their private jet.

"It's a very popular vacation destination," Aileen said. "It's smack-dab between Austin and San Antonio. You're lucky Ari has inherited the property because land and housing prices are skyrocketing."

"Do you know whether Charles had any aircraft?" Sherm asked.

"As far as I know, he still has a jet in a private T-hanger at the airport," Aileen said.

In less than an hour Lonnie landed the jet, and they drove off in two SUVs that awaited their arrival. Aileen guided them as they headed to Bradon Gorge Road, on the North side of the Spring Woods Preserve, where her uncle's estate was located.

They turned onto the road where a huge Private Property sign stood out, as it was reflective with large lettering. The cars meandered down a paved, forested road that could not be mistaken for a driveway. It ended at a massive stone dwelling. Off to the side stood a six-car garage. Beyond that, barely seen through the trees, was another massive building.

"Oh, my god, this is beautiful," Ari marveled, as her eyes darted from side to side taking it all in.

As they pulled up and parked in front of the garage, they noticed two people standing in the shade on the front porch. A middle-aged woman and a weathered man.

"Is that Mrs. Peña and Mr. Fuentes?" Ari asked as she turned to Aileen. "Are they shifters? How did they know we were coming?"

Aileen held up her cellphone. "They're not shifters, but they know all about us. I sent Mrs. Peña a text so they would be prepared to welcome you."

They piled out of the vehicles. Aileen led Ari and the others to the porch. "Mrs. Peña, Mr. Fuentes, this is Ari Davis, Charles' niece. I'll let her introduce her family."

Mr. Fuentes removed his hat and held it in a hand.

Mrs. Peña grasped Ari's hand in both of hers. "I'm so sorry for your loss, Ms. Davis. Your uncle loved you very much."

"This must be a great loss for you and Mr. Fuentes, as well," Ari said. She shook Mr. Fuentes' hand.

"Call me Pablo," the weathered man said.

"And call me Rosa. We are very down to earth here," Rosa said. "You should bring your luggage inside. It's much too hot outside to leave it in the car, especially if you have electronics. I'll give you the grand tour of the house, and Pablo can show you the property."

"Good idea," Sherm said. "It is a little toasty out here."

He, Lonnie, Kevin, Jason and Pablo returned to the cars and pulled out the bags.

They entered the house, and the boys crashed into their mother and Roman. A huge medallion of a cat in the wood flooring of the foyer stopped them in their tracks.

Strange words surrounded the image: Bí cúramach. Tá an teach agus an réadmhaoin seo faoi chosaint ag cait na hÉireann.

Roman squatted. He ran his hand over the beautiful wood that showed the cat in repose. "This is magnificent!"

Gage squeezed around the crowd, Eddie in his arms.

"Kitty!" Eddie squealed. She wiggled to get down and plopped herself on the floor by Roman. She touched the image of the cat that was created from pieces of wood.

"What does this say?" Ari asked.

"Be careful. This house and property are protected by Irish cats," Aileen said with a grin.

"Is that Gaelic?" Gage asked.

"No. The Irish language is Gaeilge, pronounced Gwal-gah," Aileen said.

Ari silently rolled the word in her head to get the feel for it.

They continued into the house.

"Why don't you leave the bags here in the reading room, and we'll get you settled into your rooms later," Rosa said.

Pablo settled his hat on his head. "Text me when everyone is ready to explore the property." He slipped out the door.

"He's a little shy sometimes," Rosa said.

Across the foyer from the reading room was an immense dining room.

Rosa led them to the kitchen, which was a chef's wet dream. The high-end Viking appliances were gleaming stainless steel. An enormous kitchen island with eight barstools sat in the middle of the huge room. There was a coffee and tea bar with two open shelves of labeled containers of both beverages to choose from.

"Oh! I love this coffee and tea bar," Ari purred, as she ran her hand over the smooth surface.

Besides all the cabinets, there was a butler's pantry, where they discovered a second dishwasher, and the laundry facility with a clothes-folding counter.

The living room was immense, with multiple sofas and chairs, and a huge wood-burning fireplace with a gas starter. The room also doubled as a library, with a library ladder. A wall of French doors led outside to a huge covered lounging and eating area. The summer kitchen, pizza oven, and sitting area were cooled with ceiling fans and misters to keep people comfortable during the scorching hot months.

A lagoon-style pool, a waterfall, and a zero-edge spa spread out before them. They stared at the setting, taking everything in.

They returned to the house and discovered a media room with ten recliners, beanbag-type chairs, a popcorn machine, a glass-door refrigerator filled with drinks, and a water stand. A wall of open shelves contained both DVDs and old VHS tapes.

They saw a game room, a fully geared-up gym with a sauna tucked away in a corner, and ten guest bedrooms, most of which held queen beds. Two of the rooms had two double beds. All the bedrooms contained a TV, a desk, two comfortable chairs, end tables, and lamps. There were five shared bathrooms in this section of the house.

"Can I move in here with you?" Sherm asked. Roman elbowed him.

"Me too," Kevin and Lonnie said at the same time.

Rosa then led them to the master bedroom. Evidently, Roman was not the only one with a custom bed. Charles' bed may have even outflanked Roman's by a couple of feet. Ari raised her eyebrows, but didn't even want to go there. She didn't know her uncle and surely knew nothing about his love life.

"Will you look at the size of this bed!" Kevin said. "This is bigger than yours, isn't it, Roman?"

Roman mentally took measurements. "Yeah, I think this has to be larger than our bed."

Gage sent a private mind message to Ari and Roman: *I have X-rated thoughts about you in this bed, Ari.*

Focus, Gage! We'll play later, Ari sent back.

Roman tried hard to keep a straight face.

A room-sized walk-in closet still contained Charles' clothing and accessories. The master bathroom had two farmers sinks, a vanity area, a large claw-footed tub, and an enormous walk-through shower with six shower heads.

They left the master suite, and Rosa brought them to Charles' office. Ari teared up as she saw walls of photos of her, her sons growing up, along with pictures of Roman and Gage.

Roman and Gage pulled her into an embrace when Ari started sobbing.

"It's just not fair," she wailed. "He should have approached me when I became an adult."

"Our family is a strange lot when it comes to privacy," Aileen said. "But I agree, he should have at least contacted you when your mother passed away."

"All his paperwork is in the filing system," Rosa said as she pointed to the lateral files. "He was big on order, so I'm sure you will find everything you need regarding the property and his life. Why don't we go to the kitchen? You could probably use a nice glass of iced tea and something to nibble on before you see the rest of the property."

They filed back to the kitchen and settled at the island and table. Gage stepped up to Rosa.

"What could I do to help?"

She pointed him to the ice machine. "Why don't you fill the glasses with ice?" She directed him to the cabinets that stored several sets of glasses.

Rosa retrieved the pitcher of tea from the refrigerator. Ari noticed another pitcher on the refrigerator shelf. She liked that the woman was prepared for their large party. The house-keeper pulled a platter of chicken salad and tuna salad finger sandwiches out of the refrigerator and placed them on the island. Then she grabbed a large stainless-steel bowl, went to the pantry and pulled out a large bag of chips.

Everyone dove in and prepared their plates. When they finished eating, Rosa texted Pablo.

"Why don't you leave Eddie here with me?" Aileen said. "We can watch a movie."

Ari looked at Eddie. "Do you want to stay and watch a movie with Auntie Aileen, or go outside where it's hot?"

"Can I stay with Auntie?" Eddie said.

"Of course, you can," Roman said. He ruffled her hair.

Pablo met them at the front door and started the tour. "There are rooms over the garage." He led them to the exterior stair-way, and he unlocked the door. He reached inside for the light switch, and the darkened area lit up. They marched inside and looked the place over. There were five bedrooms, a small kitchen, and a living room, all tastefully decorated.

"All these extra accommodations are wonderful for our large family and extended members," Gage said.

They left the garages and walked behind them to a large, multi-floored, rustic office building with a parking lot to the side that contained a couple dozen cars.

"This is where the offices are," Pablo said. "There's also some apartments and a gym in here." He ushered them into the building.

"I wonder why they don't have any signage?" Ari mused.

"Probably because it's private property," Roman said.

A receptionist stood and greeted them. "Welcome to O'Briain's, Ms. Davis! My name is Marcha, and I'm the receptionist-slash-administrative assistant."

Ari startled. She had no idea they were expected and had no clue that her uncle had an office building on his property. She extended her hand. "Hello, Marcha. It's nice to meet you." Ari introduced everyone.

"Why don't I take you to the conference room where you can meet the top tier of the company," Marcha said.

"I'll see you later," Pablo said. He nodded to Marcha. "Let me know when the meeting is over."

Ari glanced at Roman and Gage, then back at Marcha again. "Sure."

They walked down a hallway and entered a large conference room where four men and two women stood to greet them. Marcha made the introductions: Chewy, Viggo, Roger, Booker, who looked like a linebacker, Melly, and Judy.

Chewy took the helm. "It's so nice to meet you, your partners, and your sons, Ms. Davis. We find it tragic that we're meeting you after the end of Charles' life. Nearly all of O'Briain employees are shifters, but not all cats. Your uncle was adamant to employ as many of our kind as possible, because normally, shifters don't do well in the world."

"When I'm settled, I'd like to discuss how he went about this," Ari said. "Our people back in Reading seem to have a difficult time getting anywhere in life."

"We would be more than happy to help you with your people," Chewy said. He turned his focus to Roman and the others. "We are very pleased to meet you, Mr. Davenport, Mr. Stryker, and your security heads. We have used your services in the past for extractions on the African continent."

That got Sherm's attention. He pursed his lips, thinking through scenarios. "I don't recall doing business with O'Briain's."

"There are dozens of companies under the O'Briain umbrella," Roger said. "This would have been for Tenston Energy."

Sherm and Lonnie nodded, recalling the op.

"Oh, yeah," Lonnie said. "A team of eight to extract your senior VP after she was kidnapped from the hotel."

"Correct," Roger said. "It was a sensitive situation with the kidnappers. They tortured and raped her. We're grateful that your people got her out of there alive."

"And eliminated those fuckers," Melly said. She met her coworkers' shocked eyes. "What? I seriously doubt whether my language upsets anyone in this room." She rolled her eyes.

Lonnie winked at her.

They discussed business for the next hour. Ari discovered that O'Briain's was a large conglomerate of oil, gas, and energy holdings that included renewable energy. They owned real estate the world over, and Charles had philanthropic pledges worldwide.

Pablo met them at Marcha's desk when their meeting ended, and they resumed their tour. "Your uncle liked to be self-sufficient." They walked past the parking lot to an equipment building. "We'd better ride for the rest of the tour."

He led them through a door, and they climbed into a ten-seat, canopied, electric golf buggy. A worker pressed the overhead door button, and they smoothly rolled out of the building into the blinding sun.

Pablo drove down a path to a large orchard that contained pecan, peach, fig, avocado, and apple trees. There were berry bushes and a half-acre of strawberries. Then he drove them to the raised organic vegetable beds. There were also several vegetable arbors where veggies, melons, and squashes climbed up and over the wire. They saw workers tending to the trees, bushes, and arbors.

"Oh, I love these wire trellises!" Ari exclaimed as she walked through the center of one. Green beans, cucumbers, tomatoes, zucchini, and summer squash hung down.

"The employees take turns working in the garden," Pablo said. "Marcha keeps the schedule. Oh, and it's not just the employees in the building. All employees who live in the area and work in the gardens benefit. There's more than enough to go around."

"This is a great system," Roman said. He turned to Gage. "There's a lot we can do for our people back home. This has given me some good ideas."

"We raise our own chickens, beef, pork and lamb offsite," Pablo said. "Charles recognized the threat of commercial farming with all those antibiotics. None of that for our food sources. He heavily monitored the farms we purchased organic wheat.

Charles made sure they were not infested with GMO from cross-pollination or any type of what he called *drift*. He was a huge advocate of natural, chemical-free everything."

"I'm so happy to hear this," Ari said. "I spend a fortune feeding my family to keep the food as pure as possible. People don't even bother to read labels these days, then they wonder why they are so sick."

Pablo swung the golf buggy around and took them in another direction through a wide path in the trees. They came upon a house. "This is where my wife and I live, and there's another house over there." He drove to the next house that was at least ten acres away, maybe more.

Then they headed back to the house where Pablo dropped them off.

CHAPTER ELEVEN

They walked into the house and found Eddie at the kitchen island, coloring. Several stick figures were present on her drawing paper, along with what might have been cats and other animals, and a huge bright yellow sun overhead.

"Did you have fun?" Ari asked her as she studied the drawing. "This is a very nice drawing, Eddie."

"Yes! We watched the Minions! I love Bob!" Eddie said.

"Do you love Bob more than you do Tina?" Jason asked as he poked her in the side.

Eddie giggled. She turned to Ari with wide eyes. "I need a pretty dress for Lonnie's wedding next year!"

Lonnie howled with laughter. "Who am I marrying, Eddie? I don't even have a girlfriend."

"Melly!" she squealed.

All eyes focused on Eddie, who hadn't even met Melly.

"You know..." Gage rubbed his chin as he looked up and to the left for a memory search. "She did know Gowon was a king. She seems to know things." He cast his eyes on Lonnie. "Looks like you're getting married next year, Lon."

"Well, damn. I don't think I'm ready to settle down," Lonnie said.

"Settle down? All you do is work. You don't even have a social life," Kevin said.

All eyes were on Lonnie.

He huffed in exasperation. "I'm not a shifter."

"So?" Roman said. "Dr. Tanner isn't a shifter. His wife is. There's plenty of integrated couples. The fact that you work with so many shifters gives you an edge."

"Your little girl is prescient?" Aileen asked.

"I'm not sure if that's the correct term," Ari said. "Gowan, the Nigerian who came to America to help us with the gauntlet, was a king hundreds of years ago. Eddie picked up on it—that surprised everyone, especially Gowan."

"She's probably a little psychic," Jason said. "She's convinced she and Sherm are getting married, even though Sherm will be fifty or sixty by the time she's old enough to marry."

"And I'm not a shifter," Sherm said, amused.

"Perhaps things just float into her mind," Roman said.

"Whatever it is, I sure don't know how I'm supposed to get married next year. All I know is this woman's name," Lonnie said, with a hint of defensiveness.

"Everyone breathe," Aileen said. "Why don't we get you set up in your rooms?"

"Good idea," Sherm said. "Let's go grab the bags." "Can I go swimming?" Eddie asked from her stool.

"That's a great suggestion," Gage said. He looked around. "Did everyone bring a bathing suit?"

"Not to worry," Rosa piped in. "We have an assortment of suits for guests."

They headed to the reading room, grabbed their bags, and followed Rosa.

ML

Ari and Gage soaked in the spa. Eddie screeched atop Roman's shoulders as he, Kevin, Sherm, and Lonnie splashed each other. Jason was on a lounge chair texting with Janina.

Melly, Judy, Booker and Viggo joined them. Roger headed to the cabana and pulled out the pool volleyball net, while Chewy grabbed the ball. Marcha trotted over to the pool and joined everyone.

"Team up!" Roger yelled.

Gage smooched Ari. "I'm playing. Want to?"

Ari shook her head. "I'm very comfortable, thank you. Bring Eddie over here. Volleyball is way too active for her."

They split up the groups with Roman, Sherm, Judy, Viggo, Booker and Marcha on one team, and Lonnie, Roger, Chewy, Melly, Kevin and Gage on the second team.

Roger served the open. It turned out everyone was highly competitive. They made a ruckus with splashing, yelling insults at each other and cheering.

Chewy hit a wicked fastball right at Melly. She wasn't ready, and the ball bashed her off her feet. Lonnie reached out and grabbed her by the waist and pulled her head out of the water as she sputtered and coughed.

He lightly pounded her on the back until she recovered.

"Thanks. He caught me off guard," Melly said, her voice rough from coughing out chlorinated water.

Lonnie beamed at the raven-haired beauty. "Maiden rescuer at your service, mademoiselle."

She giggled and flirted back. "Have you ever been to this area of Texas before?"

"Nope. My first time," Lonnie said.

Her face lit up. "Why don't I show you around later?"

He stared at her, captivated. "Yeah, let's explore. We can grab dinner out."

The game petered out, and people got out of the pool. Some headed to the chairs to chat, drink, and relax, while others wandered toward the office building and their cars.

"I'll pick you up in half an hour," Melly said.

Lonnie stared after her, stunned.

Ari and Eddie got out of the pool. They walked toward the house behind Lonnie. "Looks like you have a date, mister."

He stopped and turned to Ari. "She's beautiful. I don't know what she could possibly see in me."

Ari balked. "Are you serious? You're a hunk of a handsome man with brains and skills as a double bonus. Don't sell yourself short, Lonnie."

He screwed his face up. "Really, you think women see me as a hunk?"

Ari rolled her eyes. "Honestly, when you get back to your room, clean your mirror and take inventory. You'd better hurry. She sounds like an on-time sort of gal."

Lonnie turned and trotted off to the house and disappeared inside.

Ari poked Eddie. "You're a little matchmaker. Lonnie and Melly are going out tonight and they'll have a lot of fun."

"I told you so," Eddie said. Her face held an expression of someone much older than the child she was.

Ari smirked.

Roman stepped into an active fire ant mound. The ants swarmed all over his bare foot, biting and stinging him by the dozens. He stomped around in a dance of pain and panic, trying to get them off his foot and leg. He, Gage and Sherm cursed up a storm.

Sherm spotted a garden hose, ran to it, turned the water on and blasted the ants off Roman.

Finally, ant-free, they entered the house by the sunroom.

Rosa met them.

She took one look at Roman's red, blistered foot and leg. "Go get dressed. I'll take you to someone who can fix you up and stop the pain."

Roman and Gage rushed to the master bedroom, and Sherm walked to the guest suites.

"What happened to your foot?" Ari asked as they entered the room.

"Fire ants! We'll need to warn everyone," Gage said.

"God almighty! They bite and sting like you wouldn't believe!" Roman said.

"Rosa is taking us to someone who can help him," Gage said.

They got dressed and left the bedroom. Sherm and Rosa waited for them in the kitchen.

"Aileen is watching Eddie," Sherm said.

Rosa entered the pantry, pressed a garage door opener, then retrieved keys from a key cabinet. "Let's go."

They hurried to the garage and piled into a Ford Explorer Limited Edition that seated seven. Rosa drove through the backwoods for several miles, while Roman cursed under his breath, trying to keep his hands off his foot and leg.

"The woman we're going to see may seem strange to you, but don't worry. She knows what she's doing," Rosa said.

"Strange how?" Sherm asked.

"The locals call her Witchy Woman, but her name is Cama,

and she's an herbalist. Everything she does is with natural medicines—all plant-based."

"Oh. Back home we have Mr. Tran," Ari said.

"Is she a shifter?" Roman asked.

"No, but you'd think she was. I swear she can read minds. It's most likely from treating so many of Charles' shifters over the years," Rosa said.

They pulled into a pitted dirt driveway. Rosa stopped the vehicle in front of a well-constructed cabin with add-on rooms. They piled out and followed Rosa to the door. She didn't even knock, just opened the door and walked inside.

"Cama?" Rosa called out. "Got a patient for you."

"Who goes there?" a woman's voice called back.

"It's Rosa."

They all piled into the room. Large bunches of herbs in various stages of drying hung from the ceiling along one wall. There were shelves crammed with jars, bottles, boxes, tins, and every other type of natural or metal container in all shapes and sizes. No plastic containers were in sight.

A woman of indeterminable age hobbled out of a back room. Her wiry, shoulder-length, dark brown hair stood out in every direction; there was so much of it. Amber eyes looked the group over.

"You're limping. What happened?" Rosa asked.

"Domino was spooked before I was settled in the saddle, and he threw me," Cama said. "Doc Benson's going to give me an adjustment this afternoon."

Rosa looked at the group. "Doc Benson is a chiropractor." She made the introductions.

Cama motioned for Roman to come to her, then she motioned for him to sit in what looked like a barber's chair. "Looks like you pissed off the entire mound."

"I had no idea there were such things as fire ants," Roman said. "This is agony! Can you help take the pain away?"

"Who knew panthers were such big babies?" Cama said. She pulled a small brown bottle off the shelf behind her and grabbed a cotton ball out of a jar. She shook several drops onto the cotton ball and dabbed the ball across Roman's affected foot and leg.

Roman sucked in a breath between his teeth, making a hissing sound as Cama applied the oil. After a moment, his face relaxed as the stinging eased up.

"What is that? The stinging has almost stopped," Roman said.

"Peppermint essential oil," Cama said. She grabbed three more bottles and shook oil into a small, shallow metal cup. She swirled the oil around, then dipped the cotton ball in the mixture and applied it to Roman's bites. "This here's camphor, menthol, and clove oil. I'll give you some. Apply it whenever you need it."

She grabbed a small brown bottle and handed it to Roman. "Give it a shake before you use it so the oils blend."

Cama looked Gage over. "You bumped your head?"

Gage, Sherm, Ari, and Roman stared at the woman in open surprise.

"He was in a car accident and had amnesia for a while," Ari said. "He's more or less back to normal."

Cama shook her head. "There's a piece that's not right."

"What do you mean?" Gage asked. He thought he was out of the woods with the wonky aggression and bizarre memory floods he experienced previously.

"There's a bruise in your brain. Needs healing," Cama said, scowling. She wandered around her shelves looking for what was required and grabbed four tins and set them on her working counter where her mortar and pestle stood.

She opened the tins and grabbed a handful of dried leaves from each and crumbled them into the mortar. She used her pestle to break the leaves down, snatched a small paper bag off a stack on the shelf and poured the leaves into the bag.

Cama looked over to Rosa. "You got a tea ball or something to put this in?"

"Yes, I do," Rosa said.

Cama closed up the bag, took a wooden clothespin out of a box and applied it to the bag. She shoved it at Gage. "Shake it up before you open it. Put one tablespoon of these herbs into the tea ball. Use boiling water, then steep it for no less than ten minutes. Drink two cups a day for the next three days, say morning and at night. You might feel a little weird after the second cup, but that's normal. Should heal that bruise."

Gage blinked at the strange woman. "Thanks. It was difficult getting through that amnesia."

"You've got good people," Cama said, as she appraised everyone. She zeroed in on Sherm. "Boy, you've got a surprise coming your way."

Sherm raised his eyebrows. "What do you mean?"

Cama shook her head. "Not for me to tell."

Sherm glanced over to Ari, Gage and Roman, a worried look on his face.

Cama laughed. "Don't worry, you're not going to die!"

Sherm let loose a breath he didn't realize he was holding in.

"What do we owe you?" Roman asked.

"A chicken and a pig," Cama said with a straight face. Then she burst out in a belly laugh at the looks on their faces. "You can pay me whatever you want. I call it a love offering."

Rosa smirked and shook her head. "That's our Cama, all right. Forever the jokester."

"I'd love to introduce you to our Mr. Tran," Ari said. "He's our herbalist back in Pennsylvania."

"Bring him with you next time," Cama said. "Is he cute?"

Ari winked. "He's a very nice-looking man."

Roman pulled his wallet out of his pants and laid a hundred-dollar bill on the counter. "Thank you so much, Cama. I can barely feel the ant bites."

"Watch where you're walking," she quipped. "God gave ya eyes for a reason, you know."

They piled out of the house and into the vehicle and headed back to Charles' estate.

"I like her," Ari said.

Rosa chuckled. "Cama is a live wire. And she knows her remedies."

They arrived back at the house. Rosa garaged the Ford, and they went inside to see what Eddie and Aileen were up to.

Roman slipped off his sandals to keep his feet free so the bites wouldn't get irritated.

Eddie bounced up to him. She bent over and examined his bites. "Boo-boos! What happened?"

Roman grabbed her and plopped her onto his lap. "There are fire ants in the grass and dirt here. Be very careful when you go outside. I stepped on one of their nests and they swarmed all over my foot and leg, biting me."

"What's a fire ant? Do they make fire?" Eddie asked.

"No, they're reddish-colored ants that bite so hard you think you're on fire," Roman said.

"Did you cry?" Eddie asked. Her little forehead creased with worry.

"I wanted to," Roman said. "They stung, but Rosa brought me to a lady who helped take the pain away."

"That's good!" Eddie said. "Maybe you should take a nap. When I don't feel good, Mommy Ari makes me take a nap, then I'm all better!"

Roman kissed her on the head. She squirmed out of his lap and crawled up onto Jason's chair.

"Hey, squirt," Jason said.

Ari and Rosa carried the bag of tea and the bottle of oil to the kitchen. Rosa entered the pantry, hung up the car keys, and retrieved a tea ball. She opened a cabinet and grabbed a cup, found a tablespoon and slid them over to Ari.

Sherm and Gage wandered in and sat at the island.

"You surely don't keep up the house by yourself, do you?" Ari asked. "The house has to be over ten-thousand square feet." She shook the bag, then filled the tea ball.

Rosa put the kettle on. "Heavens no. Lili is my head cleaner. She's a raccoon, and everyone knows how clean they are. She's meticulous, and drives her cleaning team batty at times, but she doesn't hold to laziness. I let her fire and hire people at will."

The kettle whistled, and Rosa poured the water into the cup. She set the timer on the stove for twelve minutes.

"Do you live here on the estate?" Sherm asked.

"Upstairs on this end of the house there's two apartments for staff," Rosa said. "The back stairs are through that doorway." She pointed to what they thought was a closet.

CHAPTER TWELVE

After a scrumptious home-cooked Tex-Mex dinner, everyone retired to the media room and examined the movies. Halfway through *Rocketman*, the movie about Elton John, Lonnie wandered in. Roman paused the movie, cued up the lights, and everyone zeroed in on the clearly love-struck man.

"Oh, man, you've got it bad," Sherm chided.

"Only took one date?" Gage asked.

"Where did you go? What did you do?" Ari asked.

"We went all over the place," Lonnie said. "Downtown's great. It has everything. Then she showed me Texas State University —the San Marcos River runs right through the middle of it! There's so many fun things to do here, not like Reading!"

"Did you eat?" Roman asked.

"We had the best food." "Melly brought me to a Tex-Mex restaurant. Man, that hot sauce takes a little getting used to,"

Lonnie said. "We talked forever." He paused for a long moment. "Are we going to move here?"

"We haven't discussed it yet," Roman said.

"Uh oh," Sherm said. "You'd better not quit on me!"

Ari piped up. She looked over at Roman and Gage. "This would be a much better environment to raise a child. As it is, we have to drive to a park, or drive over two hours to the house in the woods for Eddie to play outside. We'll need to give it a lot of thought."

They all settled back into their recliners, and Roman started the movie again.

Ari, Roman, and Gage entered the master bedroom. They eyed the bed.

They eyed each other.

Clothes dropped to the floor, then they were in the bed. It was as if they had never had sex before. They were on their knees. Ari kissed Roman. She licked and nipped his lips as she grasped his hair. Gage was behind her, licking her neck, teasing the rim of her ear while he tweaked her nipples.

Roman lifted Ari by the hips and positioned her over his cock. She slid down his shaft while she clutched his shoulders.

Gage waited patiently. He slid off the bed and entered the bathroom, retrieved a hand towel, and returned to the bed. He positioned himself behind Ari and pressed his rock-hard cock against her. She leaned back into him and groaned while still keeping up her rocking motion on Roman's cock. Gage reached around and rubbed her clit. She moved frantically, waiting for release.

Ari made the little mewling sounds that always preceded an orgasm.

"Come on, baby. Come for me," Roman said, as he pumped into her.

Within a little longer than a breath, Ari slammed down on Roman's cock as she exploded all over him. Her walls clenched his cock, milking every last drop of cum out of him. Then she collapsed against him, still breathing hard.

"That looked like a good one," Gage said. He grabbed the hand towel and reached around her, and was ready when Ari lifted off Roman. "Now, let me show you how it's done."

The three of them chuckled.

ML

After a week of basking in the Texas sun, meeting with the O'Briain team, and getting more familiar with the property, they packed up and returned to Reading.

The day after they returned home to the penthouse, Eddie made her wishes known, loud and clear.

"I want to play outside," Eddie said, her little face serious.

"Honey, there's nowhere to play outside the building, and we can't go to the house in the woods right now," Ari said.

"I want to go outdoors!" Eddie screamed and wailed.

"Eddie, we just got back home. Mommy, Daddy, Gage and I are trying to catch up from being gone for a week," Roman said, trying to reason with her. He picked her up, thinking he could appease her with cuddles and kisses.

She stiffened in his arms, screaming and crying. He was so far out of his short parental experience zone; he didn't know what to do. He implored Ari with wide eyes.

"Put her down on the floor," Ari suggested. "Tantrums can take a while to sort themselves out."

Eddie almost crashed to the floor, head-first in her throes, but Roman managed to ease the fall from his arms. He was breathing hard when he stepped back and stared down at his adopted daughter with panicked eyes.

"What brought this on?" he asked, trying to calm down.

Gage finally closed his mouth. He hadn't realized it was open as he gawked at Eddie, now sobbing more quietly on the floor.

Ari walked to the kitchen table and sat down . It had been decades since she had dealt with young children, and she forgot how nerve-wracking a tantrum could be.

"How can we make this work?" she asked. "It's pretty clear she wants the outdoors. She met some shifter children there, and it was her first experience of actually running wild outdoors."

"There's shifter children here," Gage said, his face showing total disbelief.

"It's not the same environment or freedom," Ari said. "She got her first taste of living among nature with few restrictions."

Roman and Gage joined Ari at the table. Eddie had curled up on her side, thumb in her mouth, and hiccuped herself to sleep.

"We'd better plan for thirteen or fourteen years," Roman said. "I don't know if the schools in San Marcos have Pre-K, but kindergarten is standard these days. There's already an office building, plenty of room in the house, extra rooms over the garage and apartments in the building."

"It won't be necessary to move the whole operation," Gage said. "It would be no different from meeting with Donatello, or having online meetings worldwide. Plus, I think there're opportunities for work for some of our people here who might want to move to San Marcos."

Ari nodded. "What about Sherm and his team? Would they stay here, or come with us?"

Roman didn't even think twice about it. "They'd come with us. They both loved the place, plus Lonnie now has a love interest. O'Briain's could use the help. Chewy told me they've had to farm out some IT issues in the past. I think it would be better to keep that in-house to protect those businesses."

"Okay, when do we want to do this?" Ari asked. "People here will need time to decide. Plus, Rosa will need a heads-up, as well as the O'Briain people. We need to think about exactly who we should approach to move."

Roman grabbed the grocery list pad and a pen. They began a list of names.

"Why don't we organize a Reading shifters meeting?" Gage suggested.

"Not until we approach our list of people," Roman said. "Once these specific people agree or not, then we can go ahead with the meeting."

"Are we going to call the people on the list, or invite them to a private group meeting?" Ari asked.

Roman thumped his thumb on the table. "Why don't we set up a group meeting? We can put together slides showing pictures of the property and the town so they know what to expect."

Gage jumped in. "We need to be very clear about how hot it is there. Reading is slightly larger than San Marcos, but San Marcos has a much cleaner feel and presence. After the meeting, we can email them the slides."

"We should provide links to the school district and attractions," Ari said. "So, when should we have this first meeting?"

"Let's all pool our pictures," Roman said. "We can choose the best ones to include in the slides."

"We should look up real estate taxes," Gage said. Then he thought of something else. "Maybe I can find a realtor who would consider taking a smaller commission if there were multiple house buyers in our group. We can ask Rosa and the O'Briain people for recommendations, then I'd talk to the realtor and come up with an agreement."

"That's an excellent idea," Roman said. He jotted that down on his list.

"I'll ask Lonnie if he took pictures when he and Melly were out and about," Ari said. "Don't worry, I won't say anything. I'll just tell him we're putting together a photo album."

"Upload everything to our Cloud account," Roman said. "I'll create a folder named SanMarcosTX."

"I'll see if I can find a playdate for Eddie. She definitely needs to be with other children," Ari said.

Two days later, Ari sent out a meeting notice to their short list. They met in a ground-floor meeting room that comfortably sat twenty. Roman took the helm.

"As most of you know, Ari's uncle Charles passed away, and she inherited his estate. We spent a week in San Marcos, Texas, and we've come to the conclusion that it would be the best place to raise a child. So, we are proposing a move to Texas," he said.

Sherm and Lonnie high-fived, excited. Fun and sun were in their future.

Kevin and Jason bumped fists.

"Before we meet with the Reading shifter community, we wanted to approach everyone in this room to find out if you would consider moving," Ari said.

Gage worked the laptop and pulled up the slideshow. "I'll email this slideshow to everyone once we leave this meeting. Please do not discuss the move or share the slideshow with anyone not in this room. The rest of the community will be in a separate meeting."

"It's paradise," Sherm said.

"A very hot paradise," Kevin said.

"There's so much to do there, and San Marcos is between San Antonio and Austin," Lonnie said.

They all watched the slideshow.

"Gage connected with a realtor in San Marcos. She's agreed to lower her commission to four percent for anyone in our group who wants to buy a house," Roman said. "She could easily have several sales in a short period of time."

Big Bear Muchisky and his wife appeared to be in the middle of a silent conversation.

"We're interested," Big Bear said. "We want to compare the school district to the Reading schools first, though."

"Great. We'd love to have you close by," Gage said.

"My cobra would be a lot happier there," Leander said. He fidgeted slightly. "It all depends on Trisha. I'm not worried about my store; I can open another one in San Marcos, and my store here would still be open."

Bruce and his team were in a huddle. Roman saw nods and shakes among them. Bruce spoke up. "Three of us would like to go. I don't see this as a bad thing though. We need a team here in Reading, and I could pull in more people and set the structure for both locations."

"Don't anyone feel threatened that they have to move," Roman said. "That's not our intention. The Reading offices are not going away. Our penthouse is not going away."

Mr. Tran raised his hand. "Where would I live if I were to move there?"

"There are some nice apartments in the building, along with what I'd call bachelor pads," Ari said. "There are also some great apartment complexes in town, and you could always buy a house again."

He nodded, thoughts rushing through his head.

"We're planning a community meeting," Roman said. "There would be opportunities for those in our town to gain skills and better employment. We should have invited Tommy Littlefield to this meeting. I'd like to bring him with us—he's multi-talented and eager to learn new skills."

"He'd love one of those bachelor pads," Lonnie said, nodding knowingly.

"Call him when we get back upstairs," Ari suggested.

By that evening, they had their core team. The Muchisky's compared school districts, looked at houses online and were overall thrilled with the adventure of moving to a hot climate. They wanted the best for their six kids.

Sherm and Lonnie had meetings with their people. They pulled in people to fill the slots on Bruce's team for the Reading area.

Roman and Gage met with Panther Industries department heads. Ari had been adamant that the top tier should also have the same opportunity to move. Their human team was just as important as their shifter people.

Next up was the community meeting. They made it a mandatory meeting, and as usual, Ari was in charge of refreshments. The large room filled quickly. People filled their plates with the catered goodies, ate and chatted with friends and neighbors. There hadn't been a mandatory meeting in a while, so people were curious as to what was going on.

Roman took center stage, with Gage and Ari flanking him. Behind them were Jason, Kevin, Sherm, and Lonnie. The room's occupants settled into the comfortable chairs and paid attention.

Roman eloquently presented his announcement. The slide presentation began after his initial explanation.

Gage took over when Roman finished. "We will email this slideshow to everyone in the room. Make sure we have your current email address. There are links to the realtor, the attractions of the area, information about taxes, school district information, and everything else you might require to make a decision."

Ari stood. "We understand not everyone will be interested in making this type of move, especially if your interests and families are here. We don't intend to make Reading a shifter ghost town. Panther Industries will remain in Reading. We will be opening another office in San Marcos, similar to the Italian office. We'll continue online community and worldwide meetings from Texas."

Two days later, the bigger picture was taking place. Twenty-two people stepped forward to sign up for the move, including two families. The majority were single men ranging in age from twenty to fifty. The six women were in the thirty- and forty-year-old age bracket. They all had various skills.

The Shilds would not be moving. That meant Alan, the disabled translator who worked for An Da Tran, would stay in Reading, along with Abbot Benston. No one had a problem with that.

Sherm stuffed the last bite of a peanut butter and marshmallow cream sandwich into his mouth. No one understood how he stayed so fit with his terrible diet. He swigged a mouthful of almond chocolate milk from a half-gallon container when the office phone rang. He attempted to chew through the sticky mess in his mouth, but shoved it into his cheek like a squirrel stuffing nuts into its mouth.

"Panther Security. Sherm speaking," he said. He spewed food and chocolate milk across his desk as he listened, his face showing more concern with each passing moment. "Ma! Wait! Ma, now's not a good time. Ma..." He opened a drawer and grabbed napkins.

He hung up the phone, bewildered. He jumped to his feet, grabbed his cellphone and thumbed a frantic text to Roman: *9-1-1! Personal emergency. Coming up. Need help!*

Sherm launched out of his office and bashed the elevator button. He paced, frantic. The doors finally opened, and he swiped his cardkey to ride to the penthouse. When the doors opened at his destination, Ari, Roman, and Gage greeted him with concerned faces.

Ari took one look at Sherm's freaked-out expression, gently led him by the arm to the living room, and pushed him to sit. "What in the world is wrong with you?"

Roman and Gage followed.

Eddie jogged into the room. "Don't worry, it's going to be okay."

Sherm stared at the child. "You sure?"

Eddie nodded. She sat beside him and held his hand.

Roman squinted at Sherm. "So, what's the emergency?"

"My mother and grandmother are on a plane," Sherm said.

Ari, Roman and Gage waited.

"Where are they going?" Gage asked, when it was plain to see that Sherm was stuck in his head.

"They're on the way here! What do I do?" Sherm belted out.

"Why are you freaked out?" Roman asked. "I'd think you'd be happy to see them."

"My place is a bachelor pad!" Sherm said.

"I translate that to mean it's a pigsty," Ari said. "Right?"

Sherm nodded.

"Gage, take Eddie down to Kevin," Ari turned to Eddie. "Is that okay? We have an emergency cleanup project."

Eddie clapped her hands. "I love working with Kevin!"

Gage and Eddie took off while Ari headed to the butler's pantry. She grabbed her cleaning tote, stuffed products into it and returned to the living room.

"Do you own a vacuum?"

Sherm shook his head.

"Roman, go get the vacuum," Ari directed. "How about trash bags?"

Sherm thought a minute. "I don't remember."

"Grab some trash bags," she yelled out to Roman.

Roman returned with the vacuum in tow and a few large kitchen trash bags.

"Come on, let's go," Ari said.

They rode the elevator down to the twenty-fourth floor, where

Sherm lived. He opened the door, and they entered the disaster.

Ari bashed him in the arm. "Sherm! Pigs would be ashamed of this place. What's wrong with you?"

"Time just seems to fly by," Sherm said, with a lopsided smile.

Ari grabbed the trash bags from Roman. She shoved one at Sherm. "Put everything that can be recycled in this bag." She gave Roman another bag. "Empty the trash cans, if he even has any, then check out the refrigerator. I'll head to the bathroom."

A pile of clothes and towels on the bathroom floor greeted Ari. She shook her head in disgust. Toothpaste blobs were in the sink. The medicine cabinet was smeared with gooey finger-prints. She walked to the toilet and peered inside.

Ari breathed a sigh of relief to see that it had been flushed, but it was filthy. She squirted toilet cleaner inside, then looked at the shower stall. She sprayed cleaner on all surfaces of the shower stall and turned on the overhead fan to suck away the chemical odors.

Ari turned on the water at the sink, slipped on a pair of cleaning gloves and went about cleaning up the sink, counter and mirror. She heard the vacuum, which meant the floor was one-hundred percent visible once more.

Roman ducked his head into the room. "I've thrown out just about everything in the fridge. Want me to start on the kitchen?"

"I'll do the kitchen. Ask Sherm if he has a clothes basket. If so, grab these things and see if he has dirty clothes in his bedroom. Make him sit down and prepare a list of foods his mother and grandmother would want. I know they like to cook," Ari said. "Oh, grab the dust cloth and the wood oil. He can clean up his end tables and the coffee table, and anything else that's wood."

Roman set about his tasks.

Gage stuck his head into the room. "The spare bedroom is clean. Should I strip the bed and put clean sheets on it?"

"Yes, granted Sherm has another set of sheets. If not, run all the sheets upstairs and start a load," Ari said. "I don't even want to think about the last time those sheets on his bed were changed!"

Under Ari's direction, Sherm's apartment became spotless. She left Gage and Roman in charge of the washer and dryer in the penthouse. They had found several sets of sheets. Ari determined that Sherm probably decided somewhere along the way that it was quicker and easier to buy new sheets instead of washing the dirty ones.

Ari dragged Sherm along to the grocery store where they loaded up a cart with everything his family would require for their stay. Once back at his place, he had a basket of clean laundry on his bed, his refrigerator and pantry stocked, and sheets drying upstairs. They went up to the penthouse.

"What time are they getting in?" Roman asked. "Are you supposed to pick them up in Philly?"

"Six-twelve," Sherm said.

Gage looks at the kitchen clock. "You'd better leave now. Might take anywhere from one and a half to two hours, depending on the traffic."

"I'll cook dinner," Ari said. "Once you drop their bags off at your place, come up for dinner."

Sherm let out a breath. "I'm so grateful. I don't know what I'd do without you guys!"

CHAPTER THIRTEEN

Emelina Foo and her mother, Teresa Wangdu, stood before the wall of windows in the penthouse, looking across the city of Reading.

"What a beautiful view," Emelina said.

Sherm's mother was barely under fifty-five years old and looked like Teresa's sister, instead of her daughter.

"Are you sure we can't help?" Teresa asked Ari.

"You two relax," Ari said. "Flying across country is stressful, even if you are only sitting. Those commercial seats are so uncomfortable."

Ari put the finishing touches on a salad, and Gage filled glasses with berry water. Roman sliced the roast, but not before it rested, as Ari had taught her men.

Sherm came down the hall with Eddie in his arms. "Ma, Grandma, this is Eddie. Eddie, this is my mommy and my grandma."

Emelina reached out her hands. "Oh, you precious little girl. Come here and give me a hug!"

Eddie hugged Sherm's mom, then his grandma. "Sherm and I are going to get married when I grow up!"

"You are?" Teresa asked. She chuckled.

"I approve of you as my daughter-in-law," Emelina said, smiling widely.

"Dinner's ready," Ari said.

Emelina carried Eddie to the dining room table and settled her in her booster chair. They all took their places at the table and passed bowls and platters. Then everyone dug into the food.

"This is a wonderful roast. What cut is it, if you don't mind me asking?" Teresa asked.

"Tenderloin," Roman said. "I've yet to roast one and not be happy with it."

Emelina crunched salad. "What type of salad dressing is this? It's nice and tangy."

"It's my homemade balsamic vinaigrette," Ari said. "I think it's better than anything I've ever had out of a bottle."

"You made this yourself?" Emelina asked. "Please share the recipe. I can't get enough of it."

Eddie followed the conversation. She took a bite of salad, which she typically never ate unless her family coerced her into eating it. "I love my salad!"

Ari, Roman and Gage raised their eyebrows.

Eddie stared at Emelina and Teresa across the table from her. "Are you bears?"

Forks clattered to plates, or stopped in mid-stride on the way to mouths.

Suddenly, all eyes were on the two Asian women, including Sherm's eyes, which were as round as saucers.

"Ma?" Sherm asked the unspoken question in a panic.

Teresa placed her fork on her plate. "Sherman, your mother and I came here to have an intervention with you."

His mother nodded, a hint of sadness on her face. "Son, you are thirty-five years old and there's no sign of you shifting."

"We're shifters?" Sherm asked, his voice squeaking with shock. His eyes darted from his mother to his grandmother, then to Ari, Gage, and Roman. "How come I didn't know?"

Emelina shrugged. "You have the gene. We didn't want to rush you."

"What are we?" Sherm asked.

His mother and grandmother showed their animal faces. "We're wolverines," Teresa said.

"Ari and her two sons recently found their animals," Roman said. "Sherm's probably a late bloomer like them."

"I'm a tiger!" Eddie said. She showed her kitty face.

"You're a beautiful tiger kitten," Teresa said.

Ari showed her liger face, while Roman showed his panther and Gage showed his eagle.

"Your eagle is very large," Emelina said.

"They're Tothars," Sherm said.

"We are aware of that. This was one of the reasons why we wanted to come here. We've attended the online meetings, and we are thrilled that you work for our kings and queen," Teresa said.

"Did Sherm mention that we're moving to Texas?" Gage asked.

"No! That's good. He will be closer! When are you moving?" Emelina asked.

"Within the next thirty days," Roman said. "There's a lot of preparation. The manufacturing business will stay here, as well as a lot of the corporate functions. Half of our security company will move to Texas, and half will be here to keep the balance."

Sherm was dumbfounded. "I can't get my head around this. I'm a shifter. Who would have thought?"

"Are you going to shift?" Eddie asked.

Sherm shrugged. "Not like I can schedule my first shift."

"What's a wolverine?" Eddie asked.

"It's in the weasel family. They're very ferocious. They can run really fast, and they don't back down when cornered," Roman said. "That explains a lot about you and your chosen profession, Sherm."

"How's that?" he asked.

"When you're on a mission, you don't back down," Roman said.

Gage nodded. "That's right. You're in command. And always in control. You never lose your cool."

164

Eddie threw her arms in the air. "See? I told you we would get married!"

Everyone laughed.

Sherm grinned widely at Roman.

"Don't you even think about calling me dad," Roman warned.

After dinner, Sherm and his family retreated downstairs to his apartment. His mother and grandmother sat on his now-clean sofa. It was clear to Sherm that they were nowhere near ready to retire for the night.

"Son, sit," Emelina said.

Sherm sat opposite them.

"From now on, make sure you carry a change of clothes with you. I'm sure, working with our kings and queen, you're experienced with shifters shredding their clothes," Emelina said.

"You must keep your head about you. Wolverines tend to be aggressive, and you don't know when you'll shift for the first time," Teresa said. "When you're in your animal form for the first couple of times, you may find that you lose much of your humanity. You can't afford to go wild unless it is absolutely called for."

Sherm worried as he listened to their advice. "I'm going to look up wolverines. I've got to know what I'm dealing with here. How come I didn't have a clue about this? Why'd you keep it a secret?"

"We left China long ago because the area where we are from, in the Altai Mountains, is a remote place where Russia, China, Mongolia, and Kazakhstan share borders. We wanted more than simple living, so we left," Teresa said.

"It was a difficult decision," his mother said. "Wolverines worldwide are dwindling in numbers. In some places they are nearly extinct. We had hoped that our move would bring us to new and interesting places where we could find our own kind. There are only a few wolverines in Canada, Alaska, and throughout the States."

"There just never seemed to be the right time to tell you, and we waited for indications you even knew of your animal," Teresa said, with a sad shake of her head.

"I hope to God I don't shift in public!" Sherm worried outright.

"Emmy, maybe we should shift. That might trigger Sherman to shift," Teresa said.

"Okay. Let's go change," Emelina said. "I like this outfit and don't want to ruin it."

They went to the spare room. Once they shed their clothes, Teresa opened the door more than a crack so they could leave the room once they shifted. She nodded to her daughter. They shifted effortlessly and shook out their fur.

Teresa nudged the door open with her snout. They trotted into the living room where Sherm sat on the sofa, lost in thought. His head jerked up as his mother and grandmother approached him from each side of the chair.

Sherm jumped to his feet. "Holy shit! You weren't kidding!"

Suddenly, his world tilted. His clothes shredded as he dropped to his hands and knees as brown, black, and a lighter reddish-colored fur sprouted all over his body. His face creaked and bones crunched as his nose altered into a snout. Then his teeth reformed into a mouth full of pointed teeth. Hands and fingers, feet and toes distorted into five-toed paws with crampon-like claws formed.

His body completely transformed from human to his beast.

What the fuck just happened? Did I shift?

Teresa growled at him. *Where did you learn such language?*

Son! You are so big and strong! Emelina sent with pride.

Sherm trotted into his bedroom and stood before the mirrored closet door. He stared at the reflection in the mirror. *Damn. Wolverines are ugly beasts.*

His mother and grandmother entered his room.

Shift back, his grandmother sent.

I'm not getting naked in front of you two!

For heaven's sake. We changed your diapers, Emelina sent.

Sherm snorted. *I'll give it a try when you go back to your room.*

Teresa and Emelina left his room and returned to the spare bedroom. They shifted and dressed, returned to the living room, and waited.

Sherm visualized his human form. Nothing happened.

He walked in front of the mirror, stopped, looked at his reflection and huffed in exasperation. Suddenly, it felt like his head tilted, then in the next moment, he found himself on his hands and knees in his human form.

Sherm stood, bones creaking loudly. He stretched out to pops and snaps. He grabbed some clothes and dressed, not bothering with shoes or socks. The new shifter entered his bathroom and turned on the light. He leaned in and stared at his face in the mirror.

"How could this face turn into that ugly beast?" He shook his head, then walked to the living room.

His mother and grandmother sipped freshly brewed tea. A third cup waited on the coffee table.

"Drink some chamomile tea. It will calm you down so you can sleep," Teresa said.

🦍**ML**🦍

The next morning, Sherm woke to a headful of conversations. *What the fuck is all this racket?*

There was a moment of silence, then a barrage of questions flooded his head.

Sherm, is that you? Ari sent.

You shifted? Roman sent.

Did you have any problems shifting back? Gage sent.

Language, son! His mother sent.

Yes, he shifted! Teresa sent.

I want to see your animal, Eddie sent.

Sherm's a shifter? Kevin sent.

Damn! Another voice in my head, Jason sent.

Sherm got out of bed and headed for the shower. He felt as if people were watching him get cleaned up. *You perve's stay out of my head while I shower!*

Thank God we only hear each other, Jason sent.

No one wants to see you naked, Roman sent.

For Christ's sake, everyone shut up, Sherm sent. He snorted when a thought passed through his brain. *I'm The Wolverine!*

You're A wolverine—you're NOT The Wolverine—Hugh Jackman, Sherm, Roman sent.

Sherm snorted, then stepped into the shower.

ML

He finished his shower, dressed and followed his nose to the fresh coffee. Moments after he swallowed his first sip, the doorbell rang. He went to the living room and opened the door. Roman and Gage stood there, huge grins on their faces.

"Welcome to your shifter family!" Roman said. He grabbed Sherm in an embrace and gave him a noogie to the top of his head.

"Damn. Cut it out," Sherm said. He batted Roman's hand off his head.

They came into the apartment. Sherm's mother and grandmother were busy in the kitchen.

"Good morning," Gage called out to them.

"Would you like coffee? Breakfast?" Teresa asked.

"No thanks, we just ate," Gage said.

"So, no problems?" Roman asked.

"No, my mother and grandmother shifted to show me exactly what we looked like, then I shifted. Man, what an odd experience that was!" Sherm said. "I swear I felt every single bone shift. For a minute, I thought they were breaking."

"Glad you didn't have any problems shifting back, like Ari did when we got back from Italy," Roman said.

"Yeah, she freaked out. We had to call Atsa to calm her down," Gage said.

"What's the plan for today?" Sherm asked.

"Groundwork," Roman said. "We need a meeting with Ari and the O'Briain team about the chain of command. I don't want anyone there to think we're muscling in on them and taking over. Also need to work out where our offices will be located in the building. I want to make a list of what equipment we should order, what we're going to take with us. We'll need to determine if anything has to be replaced here in Reading."

"Don't forget we need to work out living arrangements, and where people will bunk if they want to live on the property," Gage said. "Rosa needs to be kept in the loop for meals and housekeeping."

"O'Briain's should have plenty of room for our offices," Sherm said. "I don't know how many floors they occupy in that building, but that's something we need to discuss."

"If we have to, we'll build another office building, or add on to what's there," Roman said.

"Enough business. Come eat your breakfast, Sherm," Emelina called out. "We would like you to come for supper tonight. Authentic Chinese food!"

"That sounds good," Gage said.

"You'll love my mother and grandmother's cooking," Sherm said.

They stood. Roman slapped Sherm on the back. "Let me know when you're free. We should probably start off meeting with Ari, then pull in the O'Briain's."

⚔ML⚔

After the joking about Sherm's new animal, they got down to business. Ari, Roman, Sherm, Lonnie, and Gage sat in a conference room.

"Ari, I don't want you or your uncle's company to think we're taking over their business. We are only interested in the security end of the business," Roman said. "But we have to establish a chain of command."

Ari nodded. "I want to get into the books and see how things are set up, where the money comes from, and where it goes out to. One of the first things I want to do when we get settled is to go through my uncle's file cabinets in the house. I don't know if he has an office in the building, but I'll go through everything."

She turned to Lonnie. "Lonnie, I'd like you to pull profiles on the O'Briain employees in Texas. I think it would be a good idea to have Travis tunnel into their system. Let's make sure they haven't tried to hide something from us, now that they know I'm the one who will sign their paychecks."

"We should also check to see who handles their legal issues," Gage said. "Do they have a legal department? I don't recall."

"Why don't we send Lonnie, Kevin, Travis, and Tommy Littlefield to Texas to start things rolling with the Panther office area?" Ari suggested.

Everyone nodded.

"Ari, why don't you and Eddie go with them?" Roman asked. "You'll be able to establish the chain of command by being there, and you can go through the files."

"Plus, Eddie will be a lot happier. She's already made friends there," Gage said.

"Okay, we have our work cut out for us," Ari said. "I figure we should be able to leave in three or four days, tops. Ask Travis to do his thing before we inform them that I'm on the way."

Lonnie worked his phone. "He's on it."

"I've got Kevin pulling profiles," Sherm said.

"What about the house in the woods? What do we need to do to close it up and protect it?" Ari asked.

"Empty the fridge and freezer—we could have a huge going away party," Roman said.

"We could hire one of the bears to maintain the place," Gage said. "We have to make sure it's winterized so none of the pipes burst."

"Don't forget, we installed surveillance cameras. Bruce's Reading team can monitor them," Sherm said.

CHAPTER FOURTEEN

The house in the woods was hopping. Music played, food was devoured, and lively conversations competed. The grill cooked the chicken and the burgers. Roman carved a roast that Ari had cooked in the oven. They had frozen meats and refrigerated items bagged for people to take with them when they left. Eddie was the center of attention and soaked it up.

Gage showed Hurly Burly, one of the bears, around the house. They walked room by room while Gage pointed out where all the light switches were in the house. They discussed the security system and everything else he would need to know to maintain the place.

They talked about the weapons they were leaving behind at the house in the gun safe. Hurly would fire them on occasion, clean them, and make sure they were all accounted for. He and Gage made sure his set and the spare keys worked.

Mr. Tran brought one of his sons to the party. Douglas was forty, single, and maintained cellphone towers for a living. His father worried about those heights and the danger of the job. He approached Roman at the grill.

"Mr. Tran! I'm so glad you could make it," Roman said, as he shook the man's hand.

"Roman, this is my youngest son, Douglas," Mr. Tran said. "He's going to move to Texas with me."

The three of them talked for a long while. Roman mentally called out for Sherm to join them.

"Sherm, this is Douglas, Mr. Tran's son. He's a cellphone tower climber. Think you can find a place for him in Texas? He's going to move with his dad."

Sherm and Douglas moved off to the side and started a lively conversation.

"Thank you," Mr. Tran told Roman. "He's been at his current company for over four years, but I worry about him climbing those towers."

"I don't blame you. One mistake is all it takes—not securing a harness properly, something dropping on you—any number of things could go wrong, then you're done for," Roman said.

Sherm and Douglas walked back to the grill where Roman and Mr. Tran were.

"Your son's giving his two-week notice on Monday, then he'll start at Panther," Sherm said. "He'll be able to get his feet partially anchored in the week before you move, so he's not adrift when the entire operation moves. Lonnie will put him to work as soon as you're both settled."

"Excellent!" Mr. Tran said. "I wish he didn't have to give two weeks, but that's the least an employee should do to keep in good standing."

"Sandy will set up a time to go over the paperwork. Do you think you can sneak away while still working for your current employer?" Roman asked.

"No problem, I spend hours on the road going from tower to tower," Douglas said. "I'll make myself available!"

Gage and Hurly Burly walked up to their small group at the grill.

"Everything all set?" Roman asked.

"Yup. Keys work, everything's in order," Gage said.

"Big Bear said you'll be the local head of the clan," Roman said. "Make sure Greg McMahonas takes his meds!"

Hurly laughed. "We've got him on a short leash and under control... for now."

🏯 **ML** 🏔

The party wound down, and the place was quiet once again.

"I'll miss this place," Ari said.

"It's not like we're never coming back," Gage said. "I suspect we'll make periodic trips throughout the years."

"We'll have a wonderful life in Texas," Roman said. "It's the best thing for Eddie." His eyes roamed over to the sofa where Eddie was sprawled out, sound asleep.

"She's excited to go on the plane tomorrow," Ari said. "Rosa talked to the children she met, and they're happy to have their new friend move there permanently."

Ari grabbed her purse, Gage gently gathered up Eddie, and they headed out the door. Roman locked up the house.

Eddie played with Tommy Littlefield and Kevin on the jet, while Ari plowed through the O'Briain profiles. She had found nothing to alert her that there was anything fishy going on. They all seemed like upright people with excellent backgrounds.

Travis and Lonnie plunked down in the seats opposite Ari.

"The company seems spotless," Lonnie said.

Ari frowned. "That's what I'm worried about. Am I being ridiculous? Panther is spotless. Could O'Briain's be spotless as well?"

"Your uncle Charles seemed to be the type that didn't put up with anything. Reminds me of Roman—very straightforward," Lonnie said.

"Guess we'll see how this pans out when we get settled," Ari said.

"There was something I needed to check out further," Travis said. "Looked suspiciously like a back door. Could have been from someone helping on an IT matter, but I don't like it."

"Show me," Lonnie said.

Travis pulled up a bunch of code and showed Lonnie. "I blocked this, but left it here so we can trace back to the originator."

"We may have our work cut out for us," Lonnie said.

"I can't wait to see my aunt again," Ari said. "I hope she finds a buyer for her house so she can move to the estate."

🏠**ML**🏯

The jet set down at San Marcos Regional Airport. Everyone piled out, helped retrieve the luggage, and hauled it over to the two waiting vehicles. They stretched before settling into the vehicles and took off to the property.

When they arrived at the huge stone house, Aileen dashed from the house to greet them. She rushed up to Ari.

"Guess what? I have a contract on the house! Full price!" Aileen said, excited.

Ari grabbed her in a hug. "That's amazing! Congratulations! Do you want to move into the house, the building, or somewhere on the estate?"

"Guess I'd better work that out, huh? I need to know what to pack to bring with me, or sell—I don't want to put anything in storage. What's the point?" Aileen said.

Eddie looked down at the ground. "Is that one of those bad ants?"

Aileen checked it out. "No, that's a regular old ant. Let's look for a fire ant mound so you stay away from them." She took Eddie's hand and led her over to the lawn. "We'll be in soon. Rosa has lunch ready for y'all."

Ari turned to the guys. "Let's go see Rosa and get something to eat before we get started."

They all headed into the house, luggage in tow so it didn't roast in the hot sun. Rosa met them halfway to the kitchen, arms up wide.

"Welcome home!" Rosa announced.

Ari hugged her. "It's so good to be back. We love it here."

"Eddie's boxes arrived, and I have everything set up in her bedroom," Rosa said. "I put the office boxes in Charles' office, and your boxes in the master bedroom. I didn't unpack them because I didn't know how you wanted to set up the closets."

"Oh, thank you. I think I have things figured out how I want to arrange our bedroom. Back home, we each had a separate bedroom we could escape to when we needed our space, along with a sitting room where we kept our home offices," Ari said. "I'll be using Uncle Charles' office, but Roman and Gage have to determine where to set up their personal offices here."

After lunch, Ari brought Eddie to her new bedroom. "This is your new bedroom. What do you think?" Ari asked.

"I love it!" Eddie was delighted to see all her clothes in the closet and her toys present and accounted for. She rearranged the toy placement for a couple of her favorites.

Ari patted the bed. "Eddie, come sit with me for a minute. I want to talk about something very, very important."

Eddie's eyes widened. She climbed onto the bed and sat facing Ari.

"Now that we live in a house, I want you to think about being safe," Ari said. "Never, ever go anywhere with a stranger. We would never tell a stranger to come get you, do you understand? There are a lot of people here who we trust, like Sherm, Lonnie, Travis, Tommy, Rosa and Pablo. They are the only ones who would ever come to get you in an emergency."

Ari noticed Eddie was confused. "If a stranger drove up in a car, or even walked out of the woods and told you one of us was hurt, run for the house or the office building. Scream as loud as you can to alert people. Also, you can scream in your mind so we hear you immediately."

"My other mommy told me not to go with strangers," Eddie said.

"I'm glad your birth mother taught you that," Ari said. "Being safe is very important. If someone tried to grab your hand and drag you, what would you do?"

Eddie's face transformed into an angry expression. "I'll scream very loud, then I'd let my kitty claws come out and hurt him!"

"You have to be careful, Eddie. If the stranger is human, you can't shift all the way," Ari said. "But you could use your claws to make him let go of you."

ML

The doorbell rang. Rosa answered the door to two little girls who appeared with older siblings. "Come in! Let me tell Eddie you're here."

The girls and their siblings came into the house. Rosa showed them to the reading room, then she went to Eddie's bedroom.

"You have company, Miss Eddie!"

"I do?" Eddie's face lit up. She raced out of her room to the reading room near the front door. She was beside herself with happiness to have friends.

Ari went into her office. Even though she still considered it her uncle's office, she worked to adjust her perspective. She ignored her office boxes beside the desk and went directly to the wall of lateral file cabinets. She wondered where she should start. Would her uncle have worked right to left, or left to right? Ari pulled the rolling desk chair over to the cabinet on the left side of the wall, sat and opened the cabinet.

Charles had labeled the hanging folders, as well as the manila folders in each hanging folder. She closed that drawer and opened the bottom drawer. These hanging folders were a different color. She perused the labels, closed the drawer, and rolled her way across the room. The last lateral file on the right side of the room was empty. She determined that was where she would store her files from Reading. Ari was sure her uncle cleared that cabinet for her. She teared up at the thought.

Now that she understood his filing system, she could decide what to go through first.

Lonnie, Travis, and Kevin walked through the main distribution frame (MDF) on the second floor of the office building in a large room, while Tommy looked on. There were rows of cabinets housing patch panels and network switches.

They trekked up to each floor, looking over intermediate distri-bution frames (IDF)—small telecom closets—a single point where all end-user network cabling drops came into. This included the wide area network (WAN) and local area network (LAN) environments that connected cabling to each user. The IDF also contained backup systems, switches, hubs, routers, and connections.

"Whoever wired this shit didn't know what they were doing," Kevin said. "What a mess."

"We'll tackle that later," Lonnie said.

Next, they went to the floor allocated to Sherm's group. Lonnie sat at a desk and logged into the computer with the temporary password Viggo provided. He made his way to the system files, and he, Travis, and Kevin studied the coding. They found the back door that Travis had identified.

Lonnie studied the office phone list someone had left on his desk. He picked up the receiver of the desk phone and called Chewy. He switched to the speakerphone.

"Do you know someone who goes by the name Leonardo?" Lonnie asked.

"No," Chewy said. "Why?"

"Travis found something suspicious that looks like a back door to your system. We traced the code to someone who uses the signature, Leonardo," Lonnie said.

"We'll be right up," Chewy said, and disconnected the call.

A few minutes later the elevator dinged and Chewy, Viggo, Roger, Booker, Melly and Judy filed into the office.

Lonnie switched his view from the twenty-four-inch monitor on the desk to the large monitor on the wall.

"Who could that be?" Roger asked as he stared at the screen.

"Leonardo is most likely someone's code name," Kevin said.

They all stared at what Lonnie had highlighted.

Chewy hit the phone and called the front desk, on speaker. "Marcha, drop what you're doing and pull all the invoices for anyone who has worked on our computer systems in any capacity." He looked at Lonnie and the team. "How far back do you think this may have occurred?"

Travis stood in front of the large screen. "Maybe until January 2018." He pointed to several lines.

"Marcha, focus on all of 2018 and forward to the present day," Chewy said. He cut off the call and turned to everyone else in the room. "Fuck! Someone may have stolen secret company information."

Travis sat down and went to work backtracking the potential saboteur. "Not happening on my watch."

Lonnie shared the story of the Wall Street project Travis and Sherm worked on last year.

Marcha buzzed the office phone. Chewy answered on speaker. "I have those files, Chewy."

Lonnie turned to Tommy. "Can you get those files? We need to get on top of this right now."

"Sure!" Tommy left the office.

"Tommy's on the way down," Chewy said.

Several minutes later the elevator dinged Tommy back on the third floor. He entered the office with several file folders.

Lonnie turned to the O'Briain crew. "We'll tackle this. Why don't you go back to what you were doing? I'll let you know as soon as we have something solid."

Chewy, Viggo, Roger, Booker, Melly, and Judy filed out of the room, spewing curse words.

"I want to learn what you're doing," Tommy said.

"You'll be learning by fire," Lonnie said. "Sit with Kevin and watch what he does, and ask questions."

Lonnie divvied up the file folders. "Look through these invoices and whatever paperwork is in the file. Tag any name, whether an O'Briain employee who signed off on the job, or vendor employee names. There may be several technician names, depending on the size of the job. Once we have those, we'll do discovery to find out their usernames within their company, their own private accounts, or anything tracked back to them."

Lonnie called Chewy. "Have you fired anyone, or has anyone left on their own within the past eighteen months?" He listened. "Okay. I want to see his file." He turned to the group. "One disgruntled employee quit last year over a bonus check."

Melly came upstairs, a file folder in hand. She passed it to Lonnie. "Charley Richmond. Human. Worked in the solar division. He thought his year-end bonus check should have been higher. Some of the deals were still pending, so the sales data wouldn't have shown up until the following year, if they were signed off and funded. From what I remember, it sounded as if he had a lot of debts and was counting on more money to get his head above water."

"Tommy, I want you to nose around the solar division and ask questions about this Charley Richmond," Lonnie said.

"Hit up Denise Squalter. She's the biggest gossip, but she only passes along good stuff—after she's researched it to death," Melly said.

"Huh. I guess there's run-of-the-mill gossip and there're factual gossips," Travis said, as he snorted and shook his head. "Who knew?"

"Don't let on you work for Panther," Lonnie said. "Someone might clam up."

"Why don't you say you're a liaison in training for the solar group—learning the ropes about all things solar and alternative energy," Melly said. "I'll introduce you around so everyone knows you're legit."

"All right," Tommy said.

Lonnie lowered his voice and directed it at Melly. "Want to grab a bite to eat later?"

"You're on!" She winked at him. She turned to Tommy. "Come on, I'll show you where this group works." They headed for the stairs. "It's down one floor."

Melly led the way into a hive of cubicles. She walked up to a cubicle where a forty-something, not a natural redhead with a widow's peak, sat having an animated conversation on her phone via a headset.

"Gotta go," the redhead said as she pressed a button on the headset. She turned to Melly and Tommy. "What's up?"

"Hi, Denise. This is Tommy Littlefield," Melly said. "He's the liaison in training for your group. Can you introduce him around, then let him see what you do over here?"

Denise looked as if she were about to devour Tommy. "Sure, be happy to." She waited until Melly was out the door, then turned her full attention to Tommy. "So, Tommy, where are you from?"

Tommy did a quick assessment of the woman. "Little Rock, Arkansas."

"What brought you to San Marcos?" Denise asked, curious as she snooped for more information.

"My uncle died, and my aunt really needed help. She's moving from a small town outside of Houston to San Marcos to be closer to more of our relatives," Tommy lied.

"Oh, that's so sad. Is she elderly?"

Tommy nodded. "Yeah, but she tries to be independent." He looked around the huge office maze where at least twenty cubicles were situated. "So, do you sell solar and alternative energy here, or what exactly do you do?"

"Some of us sell existing solar from solar farms, some of us sell solar panels, and some of us broker between the farms and utility companies," she explained.

"How long have you worked here?" Tommy asked.

"Eight years," Denise said. "O'Briain's is an excellent company to work for. They have significant benefits, and the company is stable. Mr. O'Briain recently passed away, and his niece is taking over the company." She made a scary face.

"What? You don't like her? Is she bossy?" Tommy asked.

"We're all worried she'll make changes we don't like," Denise said. "She's the queen of our kind, after all."

"I met her and the kings in Little Rock," Tommy said. "They had all these commandos with them when they were passing through."

"Commandos?" Denise asked, her eyebrows raised almost to her hairline.

"Yeah, weapons and everything. I sure wouldn't want to mess with them," Tommy said. "So, does everyone in your group like working here? I need a stable job where there's not a high turnover."

Denise waved his comment off. "Not to worry. People love it here. Well, there was one idiot who quit last year over a bonus. If he had kept up with his sales, he would have realized his pending sales would have applied to this year."

She whispered conspiratorially, "He has gambling debts and the wrong kind of people want to be paid."

Tommy's eyes widened. He whispered back to her. "You mean a loan shark, or the mob?"

"Yes," Denise said, as she nodded his way. "They came looking for him once. Thought he was going to pee in his pants!" She stood. "Let me introduce you around."

🏯ML🗾

Kevin, there's this oily-looking character named Leo down here, as in Leonardo, Tommy sent.

Oily? Kevin asked.

Literally. Shiny face. Has the personality of a snail; I can't imagine him as a salesperson.

Ask the gossip woman about him when you're out of his sight, Kevin sent. *I'll tell Lonnie.*

Denise finished with the introductions, and they returned to her cubicle.

"Who was that guy with the oily face?" Tommy asked.

"That was Leo. Poor guy. His face just oozes oil. Don't get too close to him; he doesn't have good dental hygiene," Denise said. "He's not good on the computer, either. He always requires someone to fix his mistakes in our database."

Denise checked her cell phone for the time. She stood. "I've got to head out for an appointment."

"Thanks for taking me under your wing," Tommy said. "I'll see you tomorrow."

She gathered up a pink briefcase, lifted the long strap of her purse over her head and across her body, pushed in her chair, then left the cubicle.

Tommy waited until she was through the elevator doors before he slipped out of the room and headed to the stairwell. He took the stairs two at a time and entered the Panther floor.

"Lonnie, forget that Leo guy," Tommy said as he settled into a chair. "Denise said he doesn't have very good computer skills and they have to fix his mistakes in their database."

Lonnie stopped what he was doing and swung his gaze over to Tommy. "That could be a cover-up. Did you find out anything about Charley Richmond?"

Tommy shared what Denise had said about his debts and the visitors.

"Travis, check on local loan sharks," Lonnie said. "Maybe we can connect the dots."

CHAPTER FIFTEEN

Ari left her new office and walked over to the O'Briain building.

Marcha greeted her. "Hi, Ms. Davis. What can I help you with?"

"Hi... Marcha, right?"

"Oh, you remembered!"

"Where are the Panther offices?" Ari asked.

"On the third and fourth floors," Marcha said.

Ari thanked her and walked to the elevator. She stopped at the third floor and exited. "Hi everyone!"

"Hi, mom!" Kevin called out.

"Hi, Ari," Lonnie said. "Getting settled?"

Ari pulled up a rolling desk chair to sit in front of Lonnie's desk. "There's no security in the building. No badges, nothing.

Anyone can walk in here anytime." She looked around the room. "And this open cubicle farm—I doubt Sherm's going to like this setup. Do you have any idea where the executive suite is for Roman and Gage's offices?"

"Yeah, we need to make a lot of changes, especially with the security," Lonnie said. He brought her up to date on the back-door issue.

"Oh, no! I don't like the idea of starting out with problems, especially when they could be internal," Ari said.

"Let's go see the offices they've allocated to the execs. For this floor, we need to get this built out differently. Sherm will want glass between us and the elevators for sure, and probably signage," Lonnie said.

He and Ari took the elevator up one floor. They looked around.

"Are you kidding me? Two desks out in the open, and that's it?" Ari cursed under her breath, but Lonnie heard her. "I'll start looking for a company that can build out our floors. I'm pretty sure I have the final headcount. Jason and Mr. Tran should be up on this floor."

"Let's go back down to my domain and call Roman, Gage, and Sherm. I want to talk to them about the security system I'd like to install, including the same badging system we use in Reading. It's no wonder they have this backdoor issue," Lonnie said.

They walked down one flight of stairs, and Lonnie set up the online call. Roman and Gage were in Sherm's office.

"Hi, honey," Roman and Gage said at the same time. "Can I say *hi, honey,* also?" Sherm quirked.

Ari and Lonnie explained their plans, and Lonnie talked about the issue they discovered.

"Are you going to be okay with having offices in the building instead of having an office in the house?" Ari asked. "There are plenty of bedrooms in the house and we could convert two of them into offices for you two."

"I'd still like a home office," Roman said, as he caught Gage's eye.

"Same here," Gage said. "Like you said, there's plenty of room in the house."

"They can network us to the office building and to Reading. I don't like the idea of us having to walk to the building in the middle of the night when we get a hankering to work on something," Roman said.

"Do you think I should schedule a meeting with the O'Briain workers and let them know about the changes I'm proposing? Or, should I wait until everyone is here, onsite?" Ari asked.

"You're not nervous about taking the helm, are you?" Roman asked.

Ari bit her bottom lip. "It's a lot of responsibility, and I don't want anyone to be upset."

"Honey, it's not a popularity contest," Gage said. "You're the CEO of O'Briain's, whether anyone likes it or not. Don't get all apologetic with them. They will expect changes. That happens anytime a company restructures."

"Start with a memo," Roman said. "Tell them about the new badging system that we will install for their security."

"We need to take a really good look at that lobby structure and the whole first-floor layout," Sherm said. "Let's find out how many visitors come through the front doors, what their conference rooms contain—they looked bare bones from what I can remember. I'd like security at the front desk as a deterrent."

Ari nodded. "Okay. Lonnie and I will walk the floors and see what needs to be done. I'll write up a memo and Marcha can distribute it."

"That's our gal," Gage said.

"You're still feeling okay?" Ari asked Gage.

"Yeah, that tea from the witchy woman worked," he said. "No issues whatsoever."

They cut the call, and Ari grabbed a lined tablet of paper off Kevin's desk. She wrote out a draft of the memo she wanted Marcha to distribute. She had Lonnie, Kevin, Travis, and Tommy read it.

"How should I sign it?" Ari asked.

"Create your electronic signature to say Arianna Davis, CEO, O'Briain's," Lonnie said. "You could always change it later."

"Okay. Can you get away now, or do you want to wait until tomorrow to do our walk-through?" Ari asked.

"Let's do the walkthrough tomorrow," Lonnie said. "I'd like to get to the bottom of this Leonardo issue."

"I'll bring this to Marcha and ask her to type it up and distribute it," Ari said.

The next morning, Ari and Lonnie stopped outside the glass

front doors to the building. They looked through the doors into the reception area.

"I don't like it," Lonnie said. "Sherm will hate it once he gets here and takes it all in again. There's nothing barring anyone from entering the building and walking to the offices or taking the stairs to wherever. What happens when Marcha takes a break? Or has to make copies or something? We definitely need security at the front desk."

When Ari and Lonnie walked through the front doors of the building, two people who were talking with Marcha at the front desk scurried away.

Ari didn't give Marcha any sign as to why she was there. "If you need me for anything, page me," Ari said. She and Lonnie walked behind the desk and studied the layout.

Lonnie sketched on a large iPad with a stylus. Ari watched as he drew a wall that blocked off the hallways.

"There needs to be secured entrances to these corridors," he said. "And a guest bathroom out here prior to entering the badged area."

He sketched a larger reception area to include a security guard.

"Let's look at the conference rooms," Ari suggested.

They walked down a corridor. The conference rooms were scattered throughout the floor, and all contained the basics. Old conference tables, chairs, side tables for refreshments, overhead projectors, wall monitors, conferencing call equipment, and laptop setups.

"I'd like to pull these conference rooms to the front of the floor, like the layout in Reading. There's nothing worse than having clients, or complete strangers wandering around the cube farms," Lonnie said.

"I agree," Ari said. "Things seem pretty lax here. I'm so used to the Panther security setup back home that this place looks vulnerable on several fronts."

They found a copy and office supply room and looked it over. The copier was networked.

Lonnie took out his phone. "Travis, there's a copy center on the first floor. I want you and Tommy to check every floor and get a printout summary of incoming and outgoing faxes, along with a summary of copy and print jobs. Maybe our suspect copied, sent, or received something."

He turned to Ari. "Most people don't realize there's a function where you can see what they printed, copied or faxed, which is good for our end."

The summary alone from the first-floor copier was one-hundred twenty-five double-sided pages. It showed the user ID, date, the number of pages, and the first couple of lines of what they sent to the printer from a networked computer.

Travis discovered he could email the summaries to a user account, so he sent them to his Panther email account.

Faxes were easy to identify with the date, to and from fax numbers, and the sender and recipient of the correspondence.

The trickier summary was the copy and print jobs anyone could walk up and perform.

Lonnie scowled. "These machines will require a login and pass-word for all functions. I'll require the employee badges be programmed for the new compliance."

"I'll add that to the list. These are most likely leased machines," Ari said.

Roman, Gage and Sherm flew in for a week of work setup. They met with Lonnie and Ari about the build-outs of each floor, looked at Lonnie's suggestions with sketches, and discussed the badging and security systems.

"People live on the fifth and sixth floors," Sherm said. "I want security here twenty-four-seven, same as Reading. I'd prefer shifters, so their senses can pick up on anything unusual."

The five of them walked the floors to go over Lonnie's suggestions, while looking at the sketches. They made a few changes.

"I wonder what the apartments are like upstairs?" Ari asked. "Let's ask Marcha if we can access one of the vacant ones."

They walked to the front desk, and Ari asked the receptionist.

Marcha opened a drawer in her desk and fumbled through a mess of keys with ID tags. She pulled a spreadsheet, folded in half, out from under the keys, and checked tags against apartment details.

Sherm buttoned his lips, but Roman, Gage and Lonnie knew what their head of security was thinking. Anyone could access those keys.

"Here you go, room 505 is vacant," Marcha said as she handed the key over to Ari.

"Thanks. If you need us, please page us over the intercom," Ari said.

Once they were in the elevator and the doors shut, Sherm lit up and let go. "Those keys should be secured in a lockbox," he said.

"I'm cringing thinking about the liability," Gage said.

"We've got our work cut out for us," Roman said.

The elevator door opened, and they exited on the fifth floor and walked up to a door sporting 505 in brass letters. Ari unlocked the door, and they ventured inside. To say the place was drab and unwelcoming was an understatement. The small kitchen contained old avocado green appliances.

The rooms were like boxes. The most recent update was the Berber carpeting.

"I'll bet my salary they yanked out shag carpeting when they installed the Berber stuff," Lonnie said. "This place is hideous! Those apartments over the garages were nice. What the hell happened here?"

"Not what happened, what didn't happen," Ari said. "I'll get bids on this work. The contractors can start on all the vacant apartments, then we can move the residents to updated accommodations while we tackle those older places."

"Let's try to find shifter contractors for all the work," Roman said. "We should schedule a community meeting that would include this entire area of the hill country."

"We don't have a conference room large enough to do that," Gage said.

"Let me look at my spreadsheet," Ari said. "I'll sort it by zip codes and see how many shifters are in this area. There may not be that many."

"I think it's time to arrange an O'Briain leadership meeting so we can inform them about all the changes that will take place," Roman said. "They can let their staff know."

"That sounds like a good idea," Ari said. "I'll ask Marcha to set up a meeting before lunch."

ML

Booker, Judy, Viggo, Chewy, Roger, and Melly entered the conference room and sat opposite Ari and the Panther execs, Sherm and Lonnie.

"Hi everyone," Ari said. She made her voice light and friendly so as not to make the O'Briain team think they were coming into an axing meeting. "You've most likely seen Lonnie and me walking the floors and making assessments prior to Roman, Gage, and Sherm arriving. We've made additional assessments since they arrived, and I wanted to let you know about the upcoming changes."

She noticed the body language change across the table. Fear wafted off the six employees.

"The first thing you need to understand is that these are structural changes for security purposes. I have not assessed employees, but that will happen sometime in the future. Those assessments will entail one-on-one meetings, much like your annual reviews. For today, I'm going to turn the meeting over to Sherm."

Sherm started with the overall lack of security. "Lonnie and I were alarmed at the complete absence of security measures in this building. We're not surprised that we found an attempt at embezzlement."

Lonnie manned a laptop and brought up a slideshow of the Reading facility ground floor. Sherm eyed the first slide and continued with his talk.

"As you can see right from opening the door from the street at the Panther Industries building in Reading, security is present. There's a guard there twenty-four-seven, which is what we will implement here."

Lonnie progressed to the next slide.

"This badging system requires authentication for visitors to enter the conference rooms, which are separate from any of the office suites. Visitors receive a badge at the front desk, along with a code that they manually key into the keypad," Sherm explained. "If a counterfeit cardkey is inserted, or they enter the wrong code more than three times, it will not release the card. A silent alarm alerts security."

"The only badge-free access anyone will have on the ground floor is to the restrooms," Lonnie interjected.

"All employees will have a badge with their specific security clearance," Sherm said. "Elevators and copy machines will require a badge. This building will be the most secure building in the area, I guarantee it."

Sherm, Roman, and Gage explained the structural changes of moving the conference rooms and other changes.

"Are there any questions?" Ari asked. She studied the people across the table from her. The O'Briain team sat stunned.

"Wow," Chewy said. "To say you're hitting the ground running is an understatement."

"I'm glad you're here," Booker said. "I've never really given thought to our security before, but now that you've brought it to my attention, we literally don't have any security at all."

"Anyone can wander around in here. If Marcha leaves her desk to use the restroom or to make copies, the entire company is vulnerable," Sherm said. "Back in the fifties, that may not have been an issue, but nowadays? Security should be the first line of defense against any attempt to steal information or to harm employees."

"What will be the protocol when a client pays a visit?" Roger asked. "We're used to bringing people to our offices for meetings."

Roman swiveled his chair, then met Roger's eyes. "I'll bet you've never thought about the secrets that might be on your desk. You turn your back for an instant, open a drawer in a file cabinet, and someone snaps a picture with their cellphone of your desktop. You'd never suspect. You can't afford people wandering around unescorted. Security is our business. We'll make sure no one steals yours."

The team across the table had wide eyes.

"I'm almost embarrassed at what you probably think of as our Flintstone operation," Chewy said. "Charles probably thought his company would be protected since most people here are shifters. Hell, your people were here only a couple of hours when Travis found that Leonardo problem."

"How's that coming, by the way," Judy asked.

"We're almost there," Lonnie said. He asked if they were aware of Denise's revelation about Charley Richmond's visitors.

"A loan shark thug was here?" Melly and Viggo exchanged a shocked glance.

Melly ran a hand over her arm. The hairs stood on end when she digested the threat.

"Either a loan shark, or the mob. We'll know today," Sherm said.

They finished the meeting. The O'Briain's returned to their offices, and the Panther Industries team rode the elevator upstairs. Ari returned to her home office.

CHAPTER SIXTEEN

Ari began with the shifter spreadsheet. She sorted by state, then looked up zip codes for the Hill Country. She included Austin and San Antonio in her search, since San Marcos was in the middle of those larger cities. Then she sorted the database again by zip code. Next up, she copied all the data for those people into another tab in the spreadsheet titled TX Local.

There were over four hundred shifters in the area. There was no way they could meet in any of the conference rooms. She called Roman via FaceTime on her iPhone. He put her on the large monitor.

When she told them the number of people, they were all surprised. "Should I zero in on San Marcos alone, for contractors?"

"We're proposing a lot of work," Gage said. "We will require companies experienced in these types of projects that have the resources to do the work. We don't want someone to juggle people from job to job."

"That makes sense," she said. "Let's throw a *Getting to Know You* meeting under an open-sided tent and serve food. There're plenty of open acreage. I can ask Marcha to find all the resources we'd need."

Heads nodded at her suggestion.

"It would be like the one we had in Reading, where people told us what they did for a living. It's better to share resources among our own people," Ari said. "I'll ask Rosa if she has any favorite caterers before I start looking at restaurants. Should this be a lunch event, or an after-work event?"

Gage said, "After work might be better. If it's going to be like Reading, we were there for longer than an hour. Plus, if people come in from Austin and San Antonio, the drive here would take up much of their lunch hour."

Ari made notes. "Okay. A lot of people start their weekend on Thursday night. Do you want this party on a Thursday or Friday? It will most likely take several days to make all the arrangements, so we're looking at next week to host the event."

"I'd say Thursday," Roman said. "That way, people who do this type of work can get started on Friday making lists or whatever they do before they make an appointment to meet with us."

"Should this be a Panther Industries event, or an O'Briain event?" Ari asked.

Roman and Gage shared a thoughtful, questioning expression.

"It's both when you think about it. We've brought Panther Industries and the Panther Security Division to the area. We're their kings and queen, and you, Ari, are the new CEO of O'Briain's," Roman said.

"Plus, we're setting up a shifter network here," Gage said.

Sherm tapped a pen on his desk. "The buildings need to be secured, so make sure there are porta-potties in abundance. There may not be enough time to install a badge entry at the front door of the office building."

"Okay. I'll set this up for six-o'clock next Thursday," Ari said. "I'll walk over and sit with Marcha after I speak with Rosa and Pablo."

They ended the call, and Sherm and Lonnie met about the badging system.

"Let's get a secure box for the apartment keys while we're at it," Sherm said.

ML

Ari texted Rosa to contact Pablo so that she could discuss the event with them. She headed to the kitchen as Pablo entered through the kitchen door.

"Next Thursday we're going to throw a party on the property, and I need your advice. This is a Panther Industries *getting to know you* meeting for all the shifters between San Antonio and Austin," Ari said. "Pablo, can you help with the best location on our land? There will probably be over four hundred people here, and we're going to have open-sided tents, porta-potties, and catered food."

"Rosa, I'm going to meet with Marcha to help pull this together, but I wanted to find out who your favorite caterers were so we can get menus. It will require several restaurants and companies to prepare enough food for that crowd. Now I'm wondering how we'll be able to provide running water for the outside kitchen and refrigeration!"

"We've never had a function this large, but once we get everything worked out, we'll have a plan in place for future events," Pablo said.

"Why don't you get with Roman and Gage once you find an area that is large enough? It has to be somewhere that will withstand being trampled by people. You can discuss the water and refrigeration resources, as well," Ari said.

She turned her focus on Rosa. They chatted about restaurants, and Ari made a list. Then she took her lined tablet and iPad and walked over to the office building.

ML

Marcha made a list of everything. She was excited to be involved in the first undertaking of its kind at O'Briain's. After Ari left, Marcha went online and searched for party rental services. She lucked out on the first link on Google and pored through tabs. She picked up the phone and called Ari on her mobile.

"Ari? I found a company that has open-sided tents, generators, upright refrigerators and freezers, plus ovens and everything for the caterers. I'll find out what the caterers require. The man I spoke with said he could come by tomorrow to speak with you."

"Excellent! That was quicker than I ever expected," Ari said.

"I'll call a porta-potty company, then the restaurants," Marcha said.

After speaking to a representative at a porta-potty company, they determined it would require six porta-potties. Marcha booked them.

Pablo, Roman, Gage, and Sherm rode in a golf cart to a tract of land away from the house, gardens, and buildings. Pablo pointed out an entrance off the road in the preserve that sported a large, reflective Private Property sign.

"This area might be good for parking," Pablo said. It was a flat, grassy area.

Gage had been working his phone. "I found a site that calculates parking spaces to acreage. We will require two to three acres alone for parking. It's hard to tell if four hundred people will drive themselves or share rides. We need to determine where all the catering and service companies will park. That should be off to the side close to where they will set up. It would be difficult to haul their food and equipment over grass and dirt. Their people may also come in separate cars."

"This area is four acres, so it should be large enough for guest parking," Pablo said. He drove the cart through the four acres to the next plot of land, which was fifteen acres with scattered trees. "Will this work for the tents and all the people?"

They got out of the cart and looked around.

"I think so," Roman said. "The trees shouldn't be a problem. They add shade. The event company can let us know how they could set things up."

"Should I contact Bem? He mows fields around the county," Pablo said.

"Wait until we know whether this place will work for the tents, then you can get him out here to mow," Roman said.

Pablo nodded. "I'll put him on alert." They climbed back into the cart and returned to the office building.

"We'll need signage so people can find the place, then signage from the carpark to the event tents," Gage said.

"We should get Jason involved. He can set up the purchase orders, invoicing, and payment process for the service providers," Roman said.

🏛**ML**🛡

The day of the event arrived. There were signs for the Panther/O'Briain party along the road. A steady stream of vehicles drove into the mowed area and parked. Ari's invitation specified six-o'clock sharp, so that they would get the most people on time. She included a bold note that stated *Don't park lopsided,* so there would be enough room for everyone.

A gigantic tent, which was actually three large tents put together, stood majestically in the middle of the event area, with long tables and decent seating. Off to the side, but close by, was a large, enclosed catering tent with all the equipment the service providers needed. Generators were lined up along the back of the tents. They provided all the electrical needs, including cooling misters for the event tents, and actual air conditioning for the caterers.

Panther Security was present at the tents, the house, and office building, to make sure no one strayed where they weren't supposed to go. Sherm and Lonnie determined that those people would be rotated often with security in buildings because of the heat. They made sure all security personnel had a cooler of ice and water bottles to avoid dehydration. Ari insisted they should be shaded, so each security detail location had a canopied area for the guard to stand under.

The venue included a bar area with three bartenders and two bar-back helpers to keep the place stocked. Two large ice machines worked hard at keeping the ice flowing.

Once the quarter hour arrived, the royal family lined up on the stage. Roman took to the microphone on the small stage and called for people to settle down at the tables. He introduced Ari as the new CEO of O'Briain's, then introduced himself, Gage, Kevin, Sherm, and Lonnie.

Ari took the microphone. "Thank you for coming to our first San Marcos event. I'm sure you've attended online events we hosted in Reading, Pennsylvania, but we thought it would be nice to bring everyone together for this local event."

"One of the first things we did in Reading was to create a data-base of local services provided by shifters, which we shared with the shifter community. We want to establish that here, because of several projects I'll let Roman and Gage tell you about in a minute. It's important to build this database so we know whom among us we can support through your businesses and services. You'll see on the tables a card where you can fill in your information, along with a box to drop the card into. If you'd rather email me the information, that makes it easy for me."

She told them her email address was on the card, and provided the email address verbally, then handed the microphone to Roman.

He outlined the work that Panther Security required for the O'Briain building, which included the conference rooms, the reception area, apartments and other reorganization of areas in the building. He and Gage specified companies and contractors to contact them as soon as possible.

"There will be an open meeting with all companies and contractors to go over the work line by line so people can bid on projects," Roman said.

Sherm summarized Panther Securities. Just as he was finishing, Big Bear Muchisky, his wife and their six kids filed into the tent.

"You're just in time, Big Bear!" Sherm said. "This is Big Bear Muchisky and his family, who have just moved from Reading, Pennsylvania. Big Bear is a grizzly bear you don't want to cross. In his bear form, he stands around nine feet tall."

Big Bear waved Sherm off and found seating for his family.

"I don't even come close to Larry," Big Bear called out.

"You're right. Larry is a Kodiak bear," Sherm said. "We tiptoe around him."

As Sherm was finishing up, Jason arrived.

Gage grabbed the microphone. "And here's Jason Davis, the man with the checkbook."

Jason waved. He walked onto the stage and joined his family.

Gage thrust the microphone at him.

"Just so you know, I handle all the financials for Panther Industries and Panther Securities Division. I scrutinize all purchase orders. I pay invoices within a short window of time because we realize that small businesses need cash flow," Jason said. "If you're slow in getting your purchase orders in order, or slow in invoicing us, don't expect me to drop everything to pay you."

Ari retrieved the microphone. "All right. I think everyone wants to eat and have a good time. Before they serve the food, are there any questions?"

Marcha walked to the side of the rows of tables holding a microphone.

A man raised his hand and staggered to his feet. Marcha walked over to him and handed him the mic.

"Who the hell are you to come in here and tell us how great you are and how little we are?" the man said. "I don't work for you and I don't want to!"

A man at the table grabbed the guy's arm. "Butch, sit the hell down and shut up!"

Butch shook him off, staggering into the table and jarring the utensils.

Roman grabbed the mic from Ari. His voice boomed out. "What are you doing here then? Do you plan to go rogue? If so, you can't stay in this territory. We are your kings and queen— your royal family. We will not put up with any bullshit whatsoever."

Two commandos made their way over to the man through the tables. They apprehended him.

"Come with us peacefully, or we will use force. You are not to disturb this event," a commando said.

Marcha grabbed the mic from the drunk, then backed out of the way.

Butch struggled for a bit, but they dragged him back from the table, jostling attendees on either side of him, and people at the table to the back of his chair. The commandos assisted him out of the tent.

Sherm left the stage, Lonnie on his heels. They exited the tent.

"Where are we going to put him? Can't let him wander around drunk," Lonnie said.

"Do you have Pablo's number?" Sherm asked.

Lonnie looked through his phone, shook his head. "No."

Sherm texted Ari. *Need Pablo's number. Do you have it?* Ari texted him Rosa's number. It was obvious they needed a contact list update.

Sherm texted Rosa. She must have texted Pablo because he called Sherm.

"Pablo, did Charles have a holding cell for troublemakers?"

"No, but there's an old storm cellar room," Pablo said.

"Is it empty?" Sherm asked.

"Yes. I'll come get you."

Pablo drove a mid-size golf cart and stopped where the group was. He saw the commandos with the belligerent Butch. They all piled into the golf cart. The commandos shoved Butch into a seat and secured him with heavy-duty zip cuff ties to the seat.

The golf cart jerked forward and Pablo drove around and through the trees for several minutes. He approached the back of the house where there was a set of Bilco storm doors. He stopped the cart, got out and approached the doors.

"It may smell down there. I don't think it's been aired out in decades," Pablo said.

Lonnie opened the doors. Dust billowed out, along with a dank, musty odor. He took the stairs down and looked for a light switch along the wall. A long string from a lone bulb in the ceiling was all he could find. He pulled the string, but the bulb was either burned out, or the power was no longer active in the cellar.

The only furnishings was an old dusty bench.

"This is going to have to do until we can find something better," he said, as he resurfaced.

Sherm nodded to the commandos. "Put him down there and secure the door." He turned to Pablo. "Would you be able to get him a bottle of water? I want to make sure he stays hydrated."

"It's cool down there, so he should be okay," Lonnie said. "Leave a guard here," Sherm said.

"I'll be right back," Pablo said. He trotted along the house to a door and entered. He returned moments later with several bottles of water and a lightbulb.

Lonnie followed Butch and his team members down the stairs. They pushed Butch onto the bench.

"Hold your hands out in front of you," Lonnie said.

Butch obliged without talking back.

Lonnie withdrew a knife from a pocket and cut through the zip cuff ties.

People were eating when Lonnie and Sherm returned to the

tent. They joined Roman and the family at the table in the two vacant places.

"Everything under control?" Roman asked Sherm.

"We put him in the old storm cellar—not ideal, but it's all we have for right now," Sherm said. He turned to Ari. "Need an updated contact list."

"Looks like we need to add a secure place to the contractor list," Gage said.

"Any problems after we left?" Sherm asked.

"No, everything went according to plan," Ari said.

CHAPTER SEVENTEEN

Butch smacked his lips, then snorted. He woke to a growling stomach in a dimly lit room he didn't recognize. He sprang upright on the filthy bench, which made his head clang. He looked around the small room and noticed a sliver of light at the top of the stairs.

He stumbled over to the stairs and climbed to the midpoint where two doors secured the room. He pushed on the door on the right. It wouldn't budge. He tried the door on the left. Then he pounded on the doors while hollering.

"Open up! Open the door! I'm trapped down here!"

Butch truly thought he had stumbled upon the place while drunk, and no one knew where he was. He freaked out a little. He turned and walked down the stairs. Butch noticed two plastic liter bottles of water on the floor in front of the bench. He grabbed one, uncapped it, and took a swig. Water dribbled down his chin. He scraped the back of his hand across his chin.

Butch sat down on the bench. He heard muted conversations outside. He was up off the bench and onto the stairs where he pounded on the door to his right. "Hey! Open the doors! I'm trapped down here."

He heard a noise overhead. The door opened, and a flashlight blinded him. He covered his eyes with his fingers. "I don't know how I got down here, but I'm sure glad you came to my rescue."

Butch climbed the stairs. Two men in what looked like military ops uniforms apprehended him. They jerked him over the threshold, while another man jogged down the stairs, turned off the light and returned to the surface. He closed the doors.

It was pitch black outdoors. The house was also dark.

Butch didn't know where he was.

The commandos led the sobering drunk around the house to the front door. Another man jogged ahead to the front door and rang the doorbell.

Roman, Gage, Sherm, and Lonnie came to the door in pajama pants with tousled hair and stepped outside.

Butch stared, wide-eyed, at the kings. His bloodshot eyes darted from one to the other, taking in Sherm and Lonnie as well. He bowed, half-assed, still a little wobbly. "Your highnesses. I'm sorry these guys disturbed you. I must have wandered into the cellar... I don't remember a thing."

"You disrupted our first meeting with your drunken, obnoxious behavior," Roman said, keeping his voice steady. He wanted to lash out at the idiot in front of him.

Butch stared, open-mouthed, at Roman's pronouncement. "I did? I'm sorry. Look... bear with me. I know this sounds crazy, but I have this medical condition which makes me seem drunk..."

Four pairs of eyes glared at him. He squirmed.

"You think that excuses your behavior?" Sherm asked.

Butch's stomach chose that moment to roar loudly. He slapped a hand on his gut and looked embarrassed. "Sorry, I must have missed the meal."

"What's this medical condition?" Gage asked.

"Auto-brewery syndrome," Butch said. "Makes me go off my rocker. I must have accidentally eaten something that triggered it. That makes me go bonkers."

Sherm was working his phone. "A doctor diagnosed you with this condition?"

"Yes. About five years ago," Butch said. "I'm on a special diet. I can't have anything that breaks down into sugar. No white bread or pasta—things like that."

"Come in. We'll get you something to eat," Roman said.

"I don't want to put you to any trouble," Butch said.

"No trouble at all," Roman said.

They all turned and walked into the house with Butch between the kings.

The next morning, Roman's email inbox contained six emails from companies who wanted to bid on the projects. He forwarded them to Gage so they could both read the summaries about the companies.

By noon, there were three more emails from companies who wanted to bid on projects.

Roman rolled his chair over to Gage's desk. "Want to set this up for Monday morning?"

"Yeah. That way, if more emails come in this afternoon, we can send them the meeting information," Gage said.

"Let me call Sherm and see how he wants to handle the security," Roman said. He rolled back to his desk and called via the office phone. He mentioned the meeting on Monday.

Sherm came upstairs. "The new security system won't be in place for another week or two while we wait for the equipment to arrive. We'll have to use the old hand-created method of printed name tags and sign-in sheets at the front desk."

Roman and Gage nodded.

"We'll have to specify in the email we need the names of attendees so Marcha can create the tags ahead of time," Gage said.

"I'll have security at the front desk to monitor things, because she's going to be busy," Sherm said. "I'm also going to post security at both ends of the hall to keep track of guests. We don't want them wandering around unescorted."

"Good idea," Roman said. "I'll send an email to these people to get the ball rolling."

"We may have to run to the office supply store for name tag

sheets, holders and lanyards," Gage said. "Let me go see what supplies Marcha has."

Sherm worked his phone. "I've got Big Bear at the front desk to attend to things while Marcha is tied up with this."

Kevin, Travis, and Tommy were in a huddle when Lonnie returned from the restroom.

"What's up?" Lonnie asked. He walked up behind them, bent down and looked at Travis' computer screen. "What's that you've got there?"

"Leo Dagistino, downstairs, IS Leonardo," Kevin said. "He's convinced everyone he doesn't know a lot about computers, but that's a lie. Everything traces back to him."

"We've gone through all the paperwork, all the murky user-names and activity on all these accounts, and it all leads back to Leo," Travis said.

"Does he live here in the building?" Lonnie asked.

"Yes," Tommy said. "I wonder if he sneaks downstairs in the middle of the night to do things?"

Lonnie's eyes went wide. He left the room without saying a word. They heard him running up the stairs.

Lonnie burst through the stairwell door and into the executive area where Roman, Gage, Jason, and Sherm were. Jason was in a corner, working diligently on his laptop.

They all looked up when Lonnie came into the room. "What's going on?" Sherm asked.

Lonnie pulled up a chair and sat down. "Our team has finished with discovery, and all roads lead to Leo Dagistino downstairs. Tommy said that he lived in the building. He also brought up a crucial point."

He mentioned what Tommy said about possible nighttime activities.

"We need to handle this immediately," Sherm said as he got to his feet. "Roman, can you call the O'Briain team together? We'll have to do a house arrest. Lonnie, have Travis disable all Leo's access to O'Briain's immediately. When we put him under house arrest, I want to remove all electronics from his apartment. We'll confiscate his phone as well."

Roman and Gage stood. "Let's go. We'll grab people downstairs, whether or not they're busy."

They all thundered down the stairs and through the stairwell door in the lobby.

Marcha looked up. Big Bear was ready to jump into security action, if required.

Roman changed his trajectory and headed for the reception desk. "Marcha, we're going to have an emergency team meeting. Hold all calls for the next hour."

"Do you need me to accompany you?" Big Bear asked.

"Stay here. Keep this front secure," Sherm called out.

Marcha wanted to ask questions, but they were down the corridor at a brisk pace.

They stopped at each of the team leaders' offices. They all piled into the conference room. Sherm shut the door. Tommy tapped on the door, then entered with file folders of paper. He set them on the table, then exited the room quickly.

🏛**ML**🗿

Leo sat at his desk, clacking away on his keyboard. He couldn't save his file to the server. He looked across the cubicle farm to see if anyone else was having problems. Everyone else seemed busy.

"Hey, I can't save my file to the server," he called out.

"Save it to your desktop," someone yelled back.

He saved his file to the desktop.

"Reboot your system," one of the guys suggested.

"Okay. I'll try that." Leo clicked on Restart. He sat back and waited. After a few minutes, his system came back online. When he tried to login, the system rejected his password. "Now I can't login."

One of the guys huffed out a frustrated curse word, got up and went to Leo's cubicle. He looked at the screen and noticed the Invalid Password box.

"Call Chewy," the guy said.

A few minutes later, Booker came into the room and walked up to Leo's desk. "Got a minute?"

"Sure. I can't seem to login now, and I don't know where Chewy is," Leo said.

"He's in the conference room. Come on," Booker said. He and Leo left the room, and they walked to the conference room. There were piles of paper across the table. The O'Briain team glared at Leo.

"Sit," Sherm commanded, as he pointed to a chair.

Booker stayed at the closed door. No one was getting past his enormous bulk. He was a former linebacker, and his animal was a gorilla.

Leo slunk into the proffered chair and stared at the men and women around the table, his eyes wide with trepidation.

"You're fired, Leo," Chewy said, barely civil.

"What? I've worked my ass off for this company!" Leo stated.

"And pending arrest for embezzlement, stealing company secrets, and insider trading," Roman said.

Leo's mouth turned into a grim line.

"Hand over your company cellphone," Sherm said, with his hand stretched out.

He thought about it for a moment, then Leo dug his phone out of his pants pocket and slid it across the table to Sherm.

"You will be under house arrest pending further notice," Sherm said. "Until which time we determine whether to involve the feds."

Leo slumped lower in his chair.

Sherm stood. He and Booker escorted Leo to the elevator. They rode up to the apartments, exited and walked down the hall.

Leo noticed the security guy outside his door. Then he noticed the bolting mechanism on his apartment door.

Sherm nodded to the guard. He opened the door, placed his hand on Leo's back and pushed him inside. "You will notice we have confiscated all your electronics. If you need anything, you'll have to resort to the old-fashioned way and ask the guard."

"You took my TV?" Leo asked wildly. His eyes scanned his apartment. He rushed from room to room, then returned to the door. "You took my laptop and my iPad?"

"Evidence," Booker said.

"What am I supposed to do?" Leo asked.

"What every criminal does when they're in a jail cell," Sherm said. With that, he closed the door and slid the bolt into the locked position.

"Never did like that fucker," Booker said. He and Sherm returned to the conference room.

Everyone looked up when the two men entered the room. "We've decided to get Ari involved," Gage said. "This is her area of expertise."

"Good idea," Sherm said. "Did you tell them her code name?"

Melly smiled. "The Sifter. I like it."

"I wonder if anyone else has stolen from us?" Judy asked. The O'Briain team scowled.

"Don't worry, Ari is a forensic accountant. She'll go through his bank accounts to discover what he's gained from his activity.

She'll also go through all the O'Briain accounts for several years to see if there's any other suspicious activity."

"Charles must be turning over in his grave," Viggo said. He shook his head. "I can't believe we were so unaware of this theft."

"It won't happen again," Roman said. "That's a promise and a guarantee."

The meeting broke up, and everyone went back to their offices. Roman discovered two more emails from contractors and sent them the meeting information, along with a request for the names of attendees so Marcha could make badges.

"Monday morning can't get here fast enough," he said.

Monday morning, Marcha and Big Bear badged visitors at the front desk. They were asked to wait in the lobby until everyone had been accounted for. When the last person on the list showed up and received a badge, Big Bear escorted them to the conference room. They all filed in and took a seat around the table where Roman, Gage, Sherm, and Lonnie sat.

"Good morning, gentlemen... and lady," Gage said. His eyebrows rose as he noticed Butch among the group.

They made introductions around the table, and people provided short descriptions of what their company brought to the table in terms of its services. Everyone brought a packet of information about their company. Gage gathered those in a pile.

"Thank you for this information," Gage said, as he patted the stack of packets in front of him. "We'll go through them so we can learn more about you and your services."

Sherm explained why some changes were required regarding security.

Roman and Gage provided explanations why other changes were needed. They handed out sheets of information with current room sizes and what the new requirements would entail. Then, along with Sherm and Lonnie, they escorted the people on a visual tour of the building.

When they concluded the tour and the prospective contractors had all the information they required, Roman addressed them again in the lobby before they all left.

"You might consider pooling your resources among yourselves to bid on your specialty project to get this work done. We require not only craftsmanship but also expediency. In no way should you bid on a project if you do not have the resources to complete the project within the timeframe required."

"If you don't know each other, you might want to exchange business cards before you leave," Gage suggested.

"Good idea," Butch said. He pulled his cardholder out of his suit pocket and handed out his cards to his competitors.

CHAPTER EIGHTEEN

Eddie, Cassie (short for Cassiopeia), and Kylie splashed in the pool while wearing their puddle jumper life jackets, as Ari watched over them. When someone wandered too far from the shallow end of the pool, Ari blew a whistle.

They finished their pool play and ran over to the monkey bars that had been installed a week earlier, along with tree swings. Pablo had attached thick ropes to smooth boards for the seats on the swings. He had the ropes tied to the enormous oak tree branch way above, and Kevin, Lonnie, and Roman tested the swings to make sure they were safe.

"Why don't we all go inside so you can change, and we can have some lunch?" Ari asked.

"Can we have ice cream?" Eddie asked.

"After you eat your lunch," Ari said. "But we should see what Rosa has prepared. She may have something yummy for dessert."

The girls giggled, ran screeching toward the back door and disappeared inside the house.

Ari carried her laptop and phone into the house and dropped them off in her office. She wandered into the kitchen, where Rosa was finishing up lunch prep.

"Can I help you with anything?" she asked.

"No, I've got everything under control, thanks," Rosa said. "Your men should be here soon." She had taken to calling the assorted men *your men* when addressing Roman, Gage, Kevin, Jason, Tommy, Sherm, and Lonnie.

Rosa had set up a small table, like the one in Eddie's room, for Eddie and her friends in the corner of the kitchen. The grown-up kitchen table sat eight without the additional leaves.

Ari delivered the children's plates to their table. Their lunch consisted of bologna sandwiches with lettuce and tomato, cut in fours, a quarter of a little cucumber, and some chips.

The men were having thick roast beef sandwiches, dill pickles and a side of chips.

Just as Rosa placed everything on the table, the girls rushed into the kitchen, chattering up a storm, and settled into their chairs.

"It's so nice that you have your own table!" Cassie said.

"My mom thinks of everything," Eddie said.

"What's this?" Kylie asked as she held up her cucumber wedge.

"It's a baby cucumber," Eddie said. "They're great—I love them."

"Cucumber? Eewww," Kylie said.

"You should try it," Eddie said. "You might like it."

Ari and Rosa held back laughs listening to Eddie try to talk her friend into trying the new food.

Kylie took a tiny bite. She nodded as she chewed. "This is good! I like it better than the cucumbers my mom buys."

Rosa and Ari shared a thumbs-up sign.

"Tell your mom and she'll talk to my mom!" Eddie said.

The front door opened, and the men filed inside.

Ari received cheek kisses from her partners and her sons. "Everyone settle in. I'm hungry!"

A guard knocked on the door. Rosa grabbed a covered plate and headed for the door. She handed the plate over to the guard. "Food for the prisoner."

Even though they had tried to convince Rosa to eat at the table with them, she stuck to her old-fashioned habit. She ate her lunch upstairs in her suite, where she watched one of her TV shows.

"I came across an account I can't access," Ari said, as she looked across to Sherm.

"Email it to me. One of us will be able to get through," Sherm said.

"What have you found so far?" Gage asked.

"I've discovered six accounts he's skimmed off," Ari said. "I'm not finished yet, so there's most likely more. He was brilliant, to the tune of almost two-hundred-fifty-thousand dollars. But, like I said, I'm nowhere near finished yet. The way he skimmed would have gone unnoticed for a long time, until someone performed an audit."

"Yeah, the way he fooled everyone with his klutziness and lack of computer skills, made it easy for him to get away with what he did," Gage said.

"That woman Denise told Tommy they always had to clean up his database messes," Roman said.

"He was making sure they didn't look at him too closely for anything else that could have gone wrong," Lonnie said. He chewed on his sandwich, his expression thoughtful. "I wonder if he had anyone else working with him?"

"Maybe someone on the outside, perhaps?" Sherm asked. "Did you guys finish looking through all the documentation?" Roman asked.

"We're still sifting through things," Lonnie said.

"What about cross-checks with names at all those companies to find out if there were any links to his name?" Roman asked.

The peanut gallery at the little table finished their lunch. "What's for dessert?" Eddie asked.

Ari stood and went to the refrigerator. "Wait until you see what Rosa prepared!" She pulled out three dessert dishes that contained a small brownie topped with whipped cream.

The girls squealed in delight.

"Do I get some?" Sherm asked.

Ari looked down at his plate. "When you finish your sandwich. You know the rules." She winked at Eddie.

The girls finished their dessert.

"Can we go outside and play?" Eddie asked.

"Yes. Remember to be on the lookout for fire ants," Ari said.

The girls stood and ran to the front door, giggling all the way.

Roman watched them all the way to the door. "It's amazing how Eddie has transformed in the short time since we moved here."

"This was the best decision ever," Gage said. "I feel like we have our own little paradise."

Sherm nodded. "I thought we had everything in Reading. Now, though, I can't imagine living there after experiencing this place."

"Let's not get all mushy about things," Ari said. "We are so lucky to be this privileged. Most people don't even have a tenth of what we experience every single day."

Gage stood. "Come on. We've got a lot to do."

They pushed their chairs back and stood. Roman and Gage kissed Ari on the cheek, then they all headed out the front door.

ML

The girls played hopscotch over on the side of the parking area where Kevin had drawn the layout with colored chalk. He had made the squares smaller for their size, with each square a different color. Overhanging trees partially shaded the area from the hot Texas heat.

Jason had found small, flat rocks the size of a quarter that they used for their markers. He painted the first letter of their names on the rocks so they knew which was theirs.

Eddie watched from the side as Cassie hopped and jumped the squares.

"Don't step on the lines!" Kylie yelled as she encouraged her playmate.

Next up was Kylie's turn. Cassie joined Eddie on the side as their friend tossed her rock, ran and jumped. The spectators squealed giggles.

Just as Kylie finished up, a pair of hands reached out from behind a tree and grabbed Eddie.

She screamed loudly in fright. Eddie bit the man's hand with all her strength, then twisted out of the stranger's grasp. He grabbed one of her arms before she slipped away.

"You're hurting me!" Eddie screamed.

All the girls were screaming. The front door opened, and Ari and Rosa rushed out. Pablo came running from the rear of the house. He saw the man with Eddie. He ran up to the man and slugged him in the mouth.

The kidnapper pulled a gun out of the back of his jeans and slammed it into Pablo's head. The older man collapsed on the ground, out cold.

"Pablo!" Rosa screamed.

Ari slammed her arm in front of Rosa. "Stay here with the girls!" She ran straight for the man and her little girl. The kidnapper pointed the gun at her.

"Stay where you are, or I'll shoot."

Ari stopped in her tracks. She held her hands out in front of her in surrender. "Don't hurt her. Let her go."

228

The office building door opened and Roman, Gage, Jason, Kevin, Sherm, and Lonnie piled out, followed by a score of shifter workers who heard Eddie and the girls screaming.

He's human. Don't shift! Roman sent to everyone.

Sherm was out in front of the runners. By that time, the kidnapper had Eddie through the trees, and the girls were screaming hysterically and crying.

Stay with the girls! Roman commanded Ari.

It conflicted Ari. She wanted to shift into her liger and go after the kidnapper, but she allowed the men to take charge. She and Rosa comforted Kylie and Cassie as they all watched the drama unfold.

Halfway to the scene, Sherm started yanking off his clothes. He shifted into his wolverine and charged across the parking area and crashed through the trees.

Sherm! Do not kill the human! Roman demanded.

The men plowed through the trees after Sherm's wolverine. They heard ferocious animal sounds.

Moments later, Eddie ran into Gage's legs, screaming hysterically. He picked her up and held her tight. They all heard the wolverine attacking the man. Then there was silence.

Gage stayed behind as everyone else rushed to the scene. "It's okay, honey. You're safe now. Sherm has everything under control." He rubbed Eddie's back as she sobbed into his chest.

This may remind Eddie about her birth mother's attack by the wolves, Gage sent to Ari, Roman, Kevin, Jason, and Sherm. He blocked everyone else, especially Eddie.

"Someone get Pablo into the house," Gage directed to the crowd from the building.

Sherm, as his wolverine, had the man down on the ground, still alive, with one paw on the human's back. The animal growled viciously, its snout with bared teeth drooling over the man's ear.

The man whimpered, scared out of his mind.

Kevin and Lonnie hauled the man to his feet. His exposed skin had bite marks and deep claw gouges everywhere that they could see, and more through his torn clothing. Blood dripped down his face and arms.

Roman played it cool. He patted Sherm's animal on the back. "Good boy. Go back to base." He eyed Sherm.

The wolverine looked from Roman to the kidnapper. His lip curled up, and he let out a low growl, then he trotted off toward the building. When he reached his clothes, he shifted back and dressed quickly. He was glad he hadn't shifted without remembering this part. After he had dressed, he returned to the scene he had left.

Roman, Gage, holding Eddie and Jason walked behind Kevin and Lonnie, who had the kidnapper in their grip.

We'd better call the police since he's human, Sherm sent, as he walked up to the group.

"Take him to the building. The girls are traumatized, so we need to secure him away from the house," Sherm said.

They walked out of the woods to a large group of shifter employees. Everyone was tense.

Sherm took charge. "Chewy, call the police. Tell them there was an attempted kidnapping of a child. Booker, need you to be on guard duty for this scumbag. We'll put him in a conference room while we wait for the cops to get here. I want to question him before they arrive."

Chewy had his phone out and placed the call.

Gage walked over to Ari and transferred Eddie to her waiting arms. "Maybe you should call Cama, that herbalist, for help with Pablo and the girls," Gage suggested. He kissed Eddie on the head, then headed toward the office building.

"That's a good idea. We'll call the girls' parents," Ari said to Rosa. "Do you have their phone numbers?"

Everyone sent pulses of love and warmth to Eddie, the other two little girls, and Pablo.

They hauled the man into a conference room. Lonnie had him in cuff ties within moments, then shoved him into a chair.

"Go find that gun," Sherm told Roger. "Don't pick it up; just find it."

Roger headed to the conference room door.

Roman pulled a chair out from the table, turned it around, and sat facing the man. "Who are you? Did you plan this kidnapping by yourself, or did you have help?"

He turned to Lonnie. "Someone needs to find the getaway vehicle."

Lonnie and two of the Panther guards hurried from the room.

The kidnapper refused to talk.

Roman nudged the kidnapper's foot with his shoe. "We can do this the easy way, or the less comfortable way. Your choice."

The kidnapper squirmed in his chair. He looked at all the large, muscled men. "Dagistino said it would be easy as pie. Grab the girl, hold her for bargaining power until you released him from house arrest, then he'd pay me fifty-thousand dollars."

"Leo? Leo Dagistino?" Roman asked.

"Yeah," the man said.

"How'd he contact you?" Sherm asked.

"Called me on my mobile," the man said.

"That fucker!" Chewy spat. He was out the door and running to the elevator.

"Kevin, you and Travis get upstairs and tear that apartment apart. He must have another cellphone stashed away," Sherm said. "Booker, go with them. Secure the prisoner while they search."

Kevin, Travis and Booker beat it out of the room. They made it to the elevator just in time to ride up with an enraged Chewy.

I want to shift and tear him a new one, Melly sent.

Do you think there was anyone else working with him? Viggo asked.

No telling, Gage sent.

We found the gun, Roger sent.

Don't touch it, Roman sent.

They heard sirens approaching fast. Multiple cars skidded to a halt in the driveway and parking area.

"Let's go," Roman said. He motioned for Gage to join him. They headed out the door to greet the emergency responders.

Two other cars screeched up the drive into the parking area. Frantic parents rushed to the house.

Found a pickup truck, Lonnie sent.

CHAPTER NINETEEN

Kevin, Travis, Chewy, and Booker rushed out of the elevator. The guard in front of Leo's apartment reached for his gun, but relaxed when he saw who was coming.

"What's up?" he asked.

"He's got another phone in there somewhere. Tried to kidnap Eddie," Kevin said.

The guard unbolted the door, and the men went inside. Leo jarred awake from where he sprawled on the sofa.

His feet hit the ground as he felt the rage wafting off the men.

Booker grabbed Leo and hauled him to his feet. Chewy patted him down and found a cellphone in his pants pocket. He held it up for everyone to see.

"Need to search the place thoroughly for electronics—anything that can communicate," Kevin said.

Kevin, Travis, Chewy and the guard started a methodical search, while Booker sat Leo down in a kitchen chair and zip-tied him to the slat on the chair back. Then he did a thorough search of the kitchen.

Roman and Gage met the law enforcement people as they piled out of their vehicles. There were both police and sheriff department vehicles, besides an ambulance.

Two big, burly policemen and the sheriff approached them.

"You called in an attempted kidnapping?" one of the cops asked.

Roman and Gage introduced themselves, then provided the information, while Sherm joined them.

They mentioned the little girls, Pablo being unconscious, and the kidnapper who had been mauled by their dog. That segued into Leo's embezzlement that led to the kidnapping.

Roman prayed they wouldn't want to see Sherm in his wolverine form, or, heaven forbid, confine him for a rabies check.

Guess that wasn't the best idea I've had, Sherm sent. *What if they want to take me in?*

Let's not worry about that right now, Gage sent.

The police took statements from everyone. Roger showed them where he had found the gun in the woods. Lonnie led them to the pickup truck.

They took the kidnapper into custody and placed him in the back of a police car. They also took Leo into custody. They placed his phone, the kidnapper's phone, and the gun in separate evidence bags, then a police tow truck hauled away the pickup truck.

"We'd like everyone to come down to the station as soon as possible to give their statements and get further details about the kidnapping and embezzlement," one of the policemen said. He indicated the larger group, which included Roman, Gage, Ari, Chewy, Sherm, Pablo, Rosa, and Lonnie.

Cassie and Kylie and their parents stood to the side. As soon as the last emergency vehicle drove down the road, they all converged into a more controlled question-and-answer session.

Ari herded everyone toward the house as Cama drove up and parked. Her VW Thing was paint-wrapped with flowers, peace signs, rainbows, and all things hippyish from the late sixties and seventies. She got out of her Thing, clutching a bag of herbs.

"Everyone okay?" Cama asked. She spotted Pablo. "Looks like you took a beating." She looked the girls over.

They all went inside.

ML

The next day they all drove into town to the police station to give their formal statements. A police child psychologist worked with Eddie and her friends to extract the details of what happened.

They questioned Ari about the embezzlement. Evidently, the San Marcos police were smart enough to look her up online and discovered her credentials.

Gage, Roman, Sherm, Lonnie, Chewy, and the rest of the lot confirmed the sequence of events. Every detail that led up to

Pablo being slugged with the gun, the dog attack, and securing the kidnapper until law enforcement showed up to take over.

Roman got Dr. Tanner on the phone and begged him to create a file for Sherm's wolverine, that they named Spike. He brought the paperwork to the police station that showed Spike to be a five-year-old Caucasian Shepherd dog, which was similar in coloring to the wolverine. Luckily, no one wanted to see the dog.

Gage and Roman chose the bedrooms that would house their home offices. Sherm's team wired the place. They discussed whether to have a contractor add soundproofing to the walls that butted against guest bedrooms and decided it would be worth the expense for the privacy.

Pablo took charge of having the bedroom furniture moved to the storage facility that looked like a furniture store. Ari went along for the ride so she could "shop" for desks and required accessories and furniture among the items. She still could not believe her eyes when she walked through the door after the guys who hauled in the bedroom sets. It was like walking into a high-end furniture showroom.

"Why didn't my uncle sell these things when he made changes?" she asked Pablo.

"Who knows? But, on the bright side, you don't have to buy new desks or anything else—it's all here," Pablo said with a chuckle.

ML

Gage, Roman, and Sherm perused the proposals they received from the contractors. They chose four companies for their specific expertise. A small company took over the reception area. Their prior work looked promising.

Two companies combined forces for the interior office projects, which included the two Panther floors. Another team of two companies pooled their resources to work on the apartments. They would report to Ari.

A mid-sized company took on the conference room project. They had seen the slides of the conference room conversion in Reading and planned for similar configurations.

Everyone was happy with the prospect of working together on the projects, and getting in good standing with Panther Industries and O'Briain's.

Roman, Gage and Sherm met with the O'Briain leadership team and employees.

"The work will start in two days' time," Roman said. "It will be noisy, and you may have to move your office more than once."

People openly groaned.

"We're expecting at least four to six weeks of construction—maybe more, depending on the manpower," Gage said. "If your work is the type that you could work from home, you might want to consider that."

Sherm held up a hand in a stop motion. "As long as you have a secure network that's password-protected, so no one can piggyback on your user account. And, remember, if you do work from home, or meet a client somewhere, securing your laptop, devices and paper files is of the utmost importance."

A woman slowly raised her hand, her face a giant question mark.

"Yes?" Roman asked. "What's your name? What is your function here? And how may I help you?"

She wobbled to her feet, nervous. "I'm Mary Margaret in the accounts receivable department." She stopped, looked around the room, then plunged into her question. "What's going to happen to us because of Leo?"

Roman stared, thoughtful at the tense woman. "What exactly do you mean, Mary Margaret?"

"Leo stole from the company, and now he's in jail," she said. "Are you going to fire us for not catching his scam—I mean the accounts payable and accounts receivable departments?"

"Not unless you were an accomplice to Leo in his scam," Gage stated. "No one has to worry about that, if you had nothing to do with it."

"We are pretty sure that was a one-off situation," Sherm said. "You have absolutely nothing to worry about."

Mary Margaret heaved a swoosh of breath from her lungs. "That's good. I just bought a new car. It worried me that that piece of excrement jeopardized my job." She plunked her butt down into her chair.

"I do need to inform everyone that Ari is performing a complete forensic audit on all the O'Briain accounts," Roman said. He established her qualifications for regular employees. The leadership team already knew about Ari's background.

Suppertime included Sherm as a regular, as he was living in the house, and Jason. Lonnie had moved into a room over the garage, along with Kevin and Tommy, while they waited for the completion of the apartment renovations on the fifth and sixth floors. Lonnie and Melly were supposedly out and about, but most likely in her bedroom.

As everyone settled at the table, Ari made an announcement. "Company's coming!"

Eyebrows rose in curiosity. "Your aunt?" Gage asked.

"No, she's packing the house in Pearland and moving. She'll be here this weekend, though, but she's not the company I mentioned," Ari said. "Atsa's coming for a visit!"

"Oh, that's wonderful," Roman said. "He's joked about now that we're closer, we'll never see each other."

"When will he be here?" Sherm asked. "Tomorrow," Ari said.

"Is Yiska coming with him?" Kevin asked.

"Don't know," Ari said. "We'll find out when he shows up."

"We have to pick him up at the airport?" Gage asked.

"He didn't mention whether he was flying or driving," Ari said. "He can be quite mysterious."

"Who's Atsa?" Eddie asked.

"You don't remember Atsa?" Roman asked.

Eddie shook her head.

"I'm not sure she met him during that difficult time," Ari said.

Pablo was sweeping up the parking area in front of the garages when a pickup truck pulled up. He rested the large broom against the debris cart attached to the smaller of the golf carts.

Atsa and Yiska got out of the truck. "Buenos días," Atsa said.

Pablo tipped his hat. "Morning. Just in time for breakfast. Come!" He led them to the kitchen door, wiped his feet on the mat and opened the door, calling out. "Dine' are here."

Ari pushed her chair back, hurried over to the Navajos and hugged Atsa, then Yiska. "I'm so glad you're here. Come sit down; we were just starting breakfast. Coffee?"

"Hello, beautiful," Atsa said. Then he walked to the table and grasped Roman's extended hand. "Hello, my friend."

Introductions were made around the table, chairs pulled up, coffee offered, all the while Eddie stared wide-eyed at the newcomers.

"Eddie, this is Atsa and Yiska," Gage said from the chair beside her.

She acted shy, lowering her head and toying with her fork.

"What a pretty little princess," Atsa said.

Eddie grinned and peeked up at him, then at Yiska.

Atsa stared at Sherm. "Wolverine? Really?"

Sherm grinned.

"He's been insufferable with the Hugh Jackman thing," Gage said.

"You really had no idea?" Yiska asked.

Sherm shook his head. "No clue. My mom and grandmother about freaked me out."

"I can attest to that," Ari said. "Sherm was a hot mess of freaking out when they sprung his heritage on him."

Atsa laughed. "Man, I wish I could have been here for that!"

Sherm scowled across the table at Atsa. "How would you like it, say, if your mom told you that you weren't a Dine', but Polish or something?"

Everyone laughed at Sherm's expense.

Yiska gave Atsa the once-over. "Yeah, I can see how you'd pass for Polish."

"God, none of you will ever let me live that down, will you?" Sherm asked.

"I expect we can have fun with this for years to come," Roman said.

"So, is everybody here and settled in?" Atsa asked.

"Almost," Ari said.

They talked about who was moving, who was staying back in Reading, all the renovations to the building, and the most recent event with Leo and the kidnapping attempt.

"Oh, and Roman got into fire ants," Sherm said.

"You didn't know about fire ants?" Atsa asked.

"We don't have them on the East Coast," Gage said. "They're on our radar now, though."

"Rosa's friend fixed him up," Ari said.

Roman sighed. "That was a painful half hour or so. Those damn ants are relentless. I still get a twinge of an itch every once in a while." He shook his head. "How long did it take you to drive here?"

Atsa and Yiska shared a calculating look. "About fifteen hours," Atsa said.

"Just under a thousand miles," Yiska said.

"That's a long drive," Gage said. "Should have flown."

Ari met Atsa's eyes. "My father lives near you."

Atsa squinted at her. "Your father?"

"Not only did I discover my uncle passed away and left everything to me, but my Aunt Aileen informed me that my father was alive and well. He lives in the mountains in New Mexico," Ari said.

"And he's a mountain lion," Kevin said.

"Oh, and my grandmother was using a false name, so Mom didn't even know her real name," Jason said.

"Sounds like years of therapy to me," Yiska said. "You going to look him up?" Atsa asked.

Ari nodded. "Yes. I want to meet him and all the relatives I have over in Ireland. I just don't know how he'll take to having a daughter he never knew existed."

"Family dynamics," Gage said. "You can never tell how things will turn out."

They finished breakfast, and Jason and Kevin left to go to work.

"We want the grand tour," Atsa said.

CHAPTER TWENTY

Atsa, Yiska, Roman, Gage, Ari, and Sherm settled in the living room.

"This is quite a spread you have here," Atsa said.

Ari shook her head. "It's funny. When we found out about my uncle, his estate, and all the rest of it, someone mentioned moving to Texas, and I practically bit their head off. I couldn't imagine wanting to leave Reading."

"Then we flew in," Roman said. "When we drove up the drive and saw the house, it was as if we had entered another world entirely."

"Even after the kidnapping attempt, Eddie still loves it here," Gage said.

"I think we should hire a nanny to help out with Eddie," Ari said. "If just for the next few months until things quiet down. Rosa is the housekeeper, not a nanny, and even when my aunt moves here, it's not her job to babysit all the time."

Roman nodded in thought. "That's not a bad idea. We need to make sure whoever we choose is a shifter. They need to be mature and conscious of their surroundings at all times, and will know what to do in an emergency."

A car horn tooted outside. Roman got up and walked to the front door, and stepped outside. Mr. Tran powered down the driver's window and waved at him.

"You made it! Park over there and come inside," Roman said. "Leave your windows cracked a little, and if you have electronics, bring them inside so they don't cook."

He watched as Mr. Tran parked in front of the garage, popped the trunk, got out of the car and grabbed his rolling suitcase and a briefcase. He and Roman shook hands.

"Come in!" Roman said. They joined the others in the living room.

"Mr. Tran!" Ari said. She was off the sofa and pulled the Asian man into a hug. "I'm so glad you made it. Your son isn't with you?"

"No, he's a couple of days behind me. The truck we reserved had problems, and he had to wait for another one to become available," he said.

"Better to know that ahead of time, instead of getting on the road and breaking down," Gage said. He turned to Atsa and Yiska and introduced the men to each other.

Mr. Tran did a little bow to the Dine'. "I've heard many good things about you."

"And we know all about your herbal remedies," Yiska said.

Mr. Tran turned to Roman. "Just before I left, Leander and Trisha were combining households and getting ready to pack up."

"Good to know," Roman said. "In another month or two, we'll have everyone here and everything in place."

"Oh! Mr. Tran! There's a woman I want you to meet," Ari said. She told him about Cama. His eyebrows raised.

"I will have to see what she mixed together for those ant bites," he said.

"It was a bunch of different essential oils," Ari said.

"I have a case of our books out in the car," Mr. Tran said. "Should I bring them into the house, or the office?"

"I've got to head over to the building," Sherm said. "I'll take them to your office, and someone can show you the way later, after you've rested up."

Sherm and Mr. Tran left the house, and Mr. Tran returned in a few minutes.

"Don't freak out when you see the offices," Gage said, as he shook his head. "These people don't really know how to set up offices, Mr. Tran. We've hired several companies to renovate the building. On top of that, they have no security whatsoever."

Mr. Tran, Atsa, Yiska, and Ari had a long discussion about herbal remedies and other natural things, including food and drink intake.

The next morning, Mr. Tran, Atsa and Yiska were rested from their long trips.

Mr. Tran brought a small notebook to the breakfast table. Over his last cup of coffee, he opened to a flagged page. "I have found something significant in the translation of the big books."

"About shifters in general?" Gage asked.

"No, I think this is specifically about Tothars," he said. Roman, Ari, and Gage stared at their translator.

"What did you find?" Roman asked.

Mr. Tran flipped the notebook open to the flagged page. "First, I should tell you, there are a few words I couldn't translate. I snapped a picture of a page and sent it to Alan to see if he could translate it. There's a picture I want to show you."

He pulled out his cellphone and sifted through his photos, then tapped on the picture of the page. He held his phone out to Roman. Ari and Gage leaned in, and the others around the table stood and looked over their shoulders.

The photo showed a sketch and Chinese words. There was a picture of a half-man, half-animal, which looked like a yak, down on the floor in what they could only construe as a submissive, prostrate position.

A regal-looking man with a very long, thin drooping mustache, stood over the creature, in what appeared to be a temple. The man standing had fangs and claws extended, but wore colorful, draping clothing of royal quality. A hint of a cat's tail emerged from the bottom of the clothing.

The room was so quiet they could hear a fly buzzing at a window.

"This is remarkable! What do the words say?" Ari asked.

Mr. Tran read from his notebook. "Blank (I don't know this word) before the blank king. Blank must choose whether to grant life or to bring death." He flipped his notebook shut. "I've thought about this, and it seems as if the yak-man was a subject of a Tothar, and perhaps he did something wrong and he was begging for his life."

They studied the picture again.

"That makes sense," Roman said. "I'll be interested to learn what Alan comes up with."

"Would I be able to send this to the elders back on the rez, along with what you translated?" Atsa asked.

"Of course. I'll type out the words and include the picture. What's your phone number or your email address?" Mr. Tran asked.

Atsa gave him both.

"Let's go over to the building so you can see where our offices will be," Gage said as he stood. "Currently, all we have are desks and chairs. There's no offices or even cubicles. The O'Briain people never built those two floors out for offices."

"I'll be in my office," Ari said. "I'll send out an email to the locals about a nanny."

The men left the house and walked over to the office building.

Tempers were stretched thin with all the construction, which seemed to be on every floor in the office building, and even in the house. Workers tore the sheetrock out of Roman and Gage's chosen bedrooms, which they were converting into offices. Contractors installed sheets of soundproofing material on the walls that butted up to guest rooms.

Ari was at her wits' end, trying to get anywhere on the O'Briain accounts audit. Then there was the issue with Eddie grumping at nap-time because there wasn't a quiet place to sleep.

After a thorough background check that would pass any government security check, they hired Phoebe June Blassingame as Eddie's nanny. The pit bull shifter was thirty, with dark brown hair and brown eyes with gold flecks. She was very active, had a trim figure, and came with glowing references. Her new residence was the bedroom beside Eddie's.

Phoebe grabbed Eddie's hand. "Come on. Let's grab a quilt and take a nap in the woods."

Eddie's face lit up. She hopped in a circle and clapped. She squealed as she ran to Ari with the news. "Mommy! Guess what? Phoebe and I are going to the woods to take a nap!"

Ari joined Phoebe in the foyer. The nanny had a metal thermos of ice water, one of Eddie's favorite books and a quilt, all thrown into a large bag.

"This sounds like an adventure!" Ari said. She knew her daughter would be safe. Phoebe had stopped an abduction at her former employer's when her pit bull took down two men.

"We just need to get away from the racket," Phoebe said. "It's stressing Eddie out."

"Believe me, I understand," Ari said. "They should finish the hammering tomorrow. After that, it's painting."

Eddie and Phoebe headed out the door.

Ari gave up and walked over to the office building to see what was going on.

They situated Marcha at a desk out of the way of the construction, with Big Bear at another smaller desk. A wooden wall, floor to ceiling, was being constructed that cut off the view of the elevators and most everything else behind it. The long reception counter that was being installed had three seating areas. One for security, one for the receptionist, and another that would be used by a second security person when they needed manpower for special events.

After everything was set up, they would install the electronics. That comprised the phone system, security monitoring system, badging equipment, the key box, and a host of other things.

Ari came through the front door to more hammering. She waved at Big Bear and Marcha and walked directly to the elevators. She rode upstairs, thankful for the relative quiet inside the car. But the doors opened to more racket when she stepped out into the corridor.

The bulletproof glass wall was being installed to make the open area into an office suite. Sherm, Roman, Ari, Lonnie, and Gage determined that extra security was required on the executive floor, the lobby, and conference rooms. Anywhere they were building out areas. All glass walls would be bulletproofed. The new front doors to the building were being swapped out after the construction and renovations concluded.

Ari ducked around two construction workers through the new doorway. Roman, Gage, Jason, Mr. Tran, and Sherm greeted her.

"Why don't you pack up and use the area over the garage until things settle down?" Ari suggested.

Roman was on his feet. "Good idea. Who's living there right now?"

"Lonnie, Tommy, Travis and Kevin," Sherm said. "Come on, Mr. Tran," Gage said. "Let's get out of here!"

Roman picked up the phone and called downstairs. "Travis, tell everyone to pack up their stuff and head over to the garage. We'll use that until we can think straight."

"It's going to be crowded," Sherm said.

"I'll take quiet and crowded anytime!" Roman said. "Gage and I will only be there for one or two more days, then we'll be able to work from our home offices."

"Phoebe and Eddie are napping in the woods," Ari said. "The O'Briain's are working from home for the next week or two," Gage said. "We may need to bring desks and chairs, but let's check it out."

"Make sure no one leaves any paperwork behind." Sherm shoved his laptop into his backpack. He grabbed the box of Mr. Tran's books and walked out the door, followed by everyone else.

They walked to the two elevators and waited for the cars to arrive.

"My head is pounding to the beat of hammers," Gage said.

Ari looked him over. "I hope that won't cause a problem with your head injury."

"That's long over, so I shouldn't have to worry about anything," Gage said.

Dual dings sounded. They piled into the elevator and headed down to the ground floor. They stopped on the third floor and called out for Lonnie and the guys to join them. Everyone skirted the workers at the front doors as more bullet-proof glass was being hauled from a truck.

Kevin, Tommy, Travis and Lonnie were on the way to the garage, ahead of them.

"Each floor needs signage," Roman said.

"Do you want the same as the Reading office building?" Jason asked.

"Should have O'Briain's first, then the Panther companies," Roman said.

"I'll get on it," Jason said.

"You should have signage on our two floors," Gage said.

"I'll draw something up for your approval before I issue a purchase order," Jason said.

They arrived at the garage and everyone climbed the stairs. Kevin unlocked the door, and they all piled inside.

"Mr. Tran, you take the kitchen table," Sherm said. "The rest of us should be okay on the sofas and chairs."

Tommy was the last one through the door. He closed the door behind him. They all stood for a moment when they realized how quiet it was.

"What a difference!" Ari said.

Mr. Tran set up his laptop on the kitchen table. His phone rang. He pulled it out of his pocket and noticed his youngest son was calling.

"Douglas, are you in San Marcos?" He listened. "The building is being renovated. We'll stay at a hotel until the renovations are finished. I'll get a storage unit. Drive here to the house while I make the arrangements. You have the address?"

When he disconnected the call, he noticed everyone standing, empty-handed, waiting for him.

"Do you want to store your things in the garage, or should they be in a climate-controlled environment?" Gage asked.

"The garages are air-conditioned," Sherm said.

"I've booked you two rooms in a hotel downtown," Jason said.

"That is so kind of you!" Mr. Tran said.

"We had no idea of the shape of things in the building when we made the announcement in Reading," Roman said. "Trust me, you would not want to live in one of the apartments in their current state."

"Remember shag carpet and gold or green appliances?" Lonnie asked.

"Shag carpet? I didn't think they still manufactured that," Mr. Tran said.

A car horn sounded outside, and they all piled out of the door.

"Lonnie, move the Navigator out of the garage," Sherm said.

Lonnie ran to the last garage stall, pressed the garage fob, and waited while the door slid up. He backed the huge SUV out of the slot and moved it over to the parking area, close to the trees.

"Douglas, we can store everything in the garage," Mr. Tran said.

His son pulled the moving truck over to the open garage door and got out of the truck and stretched.

Everyone shook hands, then the men began to unload the truck and move the furnishing and boxes into the cooled interior. Mr. Tran directed them on what to set aside for his immediate needs.

ML

Phoebe and Eddie were splashing in the pool when Ari came through the French doors.

"Have you seen Rosa?" Ari asked.

"Not since this morning when we moved into the woods for our nap," Phoebe said.

"Maybe she went to the store," Ari said, more to herself than to Phoebe. She returned to the house and ducked into her office. The house was quiet now that the contractors had left for the day. Ari sat at the desk and started going through paperwork, but looked up. Her forehead crinkled in thought.

She didn't smell anything cooking. That was odd. She got up and walked to the kitchen. Nothing was prepared. Ari opened the refrigerator and saw thawed meat on a shelf. She pulled her phone out of her pocket and perused her contacts.

"Pablo? Have you seen Rosa?"

"No, not since after breakfast," he said.

"Do you think she went grocery shopping?" Ari asked.

"No, all the cars are here," Pablo said.

"Maybe she's taking a nap," Ari said.

"Not this time of day," Pablo said.

Ari climbed the back stairs to the two apartments and knocked gently on Rosa's door. She knocked harder. "Rosa?"

After no one answered, Ari opened the door and stepped inside. The place was immaculate. "Rosa?"

She checked the kitchen, bathroom, and headed to the closed bedroom door. She tapped on the door. "Rosa?" Ari opened the door. She found Rosa on the bed, propped against the pillows, eyes closed, the TV remote beside her hand.

Ari stood stock-still for a moment. Then she snapped out of it and hurried over to the bed and touched Rosa's hand. It was cold. She checked for a pulse and didn't find one.

"Oh, Rosa," Ari said with a little sob. Ari left the room, closed the door, and left the apartment. She stood in the hall, back against the door. She covered her face with her hands.

Roman! Rosa's dead, she sent. *She must have had a heart attack.*

Where is she? he asked.

In her bed. I looked everywhere, even asked Pablo if he'd seen her. She must have been going to watch one of her shows at lunchtime, but died before she turned on the TV.

A few minutes later, the front door open and feet rushed up the back stairs, Sherm in the lead.

Roman stopped to take Ari into a hug. He turned to Kevin and Jason. "Why don't you take your mother downstairs and make her a cup of tea?"

CHAPTER TWENTY-ONE

Pablo clutched his hat in his hands in the kitchen, his eyes downcast. "Poor Rosa."

"Was she divorced? Did she have children?" Ari asked.

"She was a widow," Pablo said. "She has four grown children. I can call them."

"Thank you, Pablo," Gage said. "I'm afraid we didn't know her that well and haven't had a chance to have more personal conversations."

Sherm called the police to report the death. The coroner removed the body and took it to the mortuary.

Ari, Roman, and Gage prepared dinner.

"Did we make a mistake in moving here?" Ari asked.

Roman and Gage stopped their preparations to stare at her.

"Why would you think that?" Roman asked.

"Look what's happened so far," Ari said with heat. "Embezzlement, attempted kidnapping, the fire ants, now this."

"Hon, the kidnapping was a plan gone wrong because we discovered the embezzlement," Gage said. "Rosa's death was most likely due to a heart condition."

"And we didn't know about fire ants," Sherm said. "We've had a lot on our plates over the past few months.

Things will calm down," Roman said. "I'm sure you'll feel different after a good night's sleep."

🏯ML🏯

They met Rosa's family at the viewing. Almost all the O'Briain people attended the funeral. Afterwards, Ari approached Rosa's oldest son.

"Carlos, you and your sisters and brother can come to the house whenever you have time to go through your mother's things," Ari said.

He nodded, solemn. "She loved working for Charles and was so happy to meet you and your family."

Ari dabbed a tear. "I didn't even have a chance to get to know her. It's sad. I never got the chance to meet my uncle, and now Rosa is gone."

Carlos patted her hand. "It's okay. I'll get in touch with my family and we'll figure out when to get over there. She didn't have much. After our dad passed away, she threw her whole life into Charles' house and property."

They said their goodbyes, and Ari allowed Roman and Gage to

steer her toward the car. They drove home and entered the house.

Giggles greeted them as they walked through the door. Eddie, Kylie and Cassie clomped around in Ari's shoes, each with a purse draped over their arm, and a dress hem dragging the floor. Their cheeks were dusted with blusher, and lipstick smeared more than their lips.

"Goodness, are you girls famous movie stars?" Ari asked.

Phoebe looked guilty. "They tricked me. I was okay with them playing dress-up because you allowed that, but I didn't give them permission to get into your makeup. I've cleaned up the mess, but your lipstick didn't survive."

Gage and Roman snapped photos of the girls.

"Don't feel too bad," Ari said. She scrutinized the girls. "At least they didn't get lipstick on the clothes."

"Would you have a minute to talk?" Phoebe asked.

"Sure," Ari said. "Would you like some tea?"

"No, thank you," Phoebe said.

"You want hot tea?" Gage asked Ari.

"Yes. Come on, Phoebe, let's go to the kitchen. I'll get the girls something so we can keep an eye on them and see what they're doing," Ari said.

After they settled the girls at the little table with veggies and dip, the adults settled at the big table. Ari sipped her tea.

"I wanted to discuss Eddie's education," Phoebe said. "You mentioned when you hired me that she hadn't attended Pre-K yet. Kids typically get into Pre-K at four years old in Texas, and they have to be five years old by September 1st to enroll in kindergarten. But during my interactions with Eddie, I've noticed her keen intelligence and insights. I'd like to order some books and start working with her."

"She's been through a lot in her young life," Roman said. "She witnessed her birth mother's murder. We didn't want to push anything on her through all of that."

Ari and Gage nodded, digesting what Phoebe said.

"That's a good idea," Ari said. "I believe she'll excel at learning. When I read to her, she either has learned the story and can recite it by heart along with me, or she knows how to read."

"I noticed that as well," Gage said. "Maybe we should have her tested."

"I'll have Jason set up an account for her educational materials," Ari said. "He'll most likely get you a credit card for that account."

"While they're occupied, let me do something real quick," Phoebe said. "It will tell me if she can read, and at what level."

She was up and out of her chair in a jiffy and heading down the hallway toward Eddie's room. Phoebe returned in a few minutes, a big smile on her face.

"Now we wait," she said. "They're just about finished."

As if they had heard, the girls moved away from the table and shuffled their big shoes toward Eddie's room. A few minutes later, Eddie stomped over to the table, minus her shoes, with a note on a piece of copy paper and an irritated expression on her face.

"There's nothing wrong with my TV!" Eddie looked from one to another at the table, then settled on Phoebe.

"What does that say?" Phoebe asked.

"You can't watch TV. Your TV is broken." Eddie huffed after she finished reading the note.

Ari, Gage, and Roman controlled their shocked expressions.

"I'm sorry. I tried to turn the TV on to check the weather and I couldn't get it to power up," Phoebe said.

Eddie placed her hands on her hips. "Next time, ask me and I'll show you how it works." She stomped out of the room.

"That's a far cry from See Spot Run," Ari said.

"I guess that answers that," Gage said. "Looks like we have a little genius on our hands."

"We'd better alert Sherm and the guys. Eddie might see something inappropriate when she's with them," Roman said.

"Eddie will test out as gifted," Phoebe said. "There's a great possibility she may skip a few grades."

"She'll be turning four in two weeks," Ari said. "Instead of mostly toys and clothes, I'll find educational toys for an older child."

"The San Marcos Independent School District offices are open," Phoebe said. "You should call them and talk to someone in the gifted and talented program and ask about testing and grade placement."

Eddie stomped into the room in Ari's shoes. She leaned on Phoebe's legs. "I checked the weather for you. It's currently ninety-nine and will be seventy-seven overnight. The barometric pressure is thirty, and tomorrow is going to be one-hundred degrees."

"What's barometric pressure?" Phoebe asked. She made a questioning expression as she looked at Eddie.

"That's when you can tell if it's going to rain," Eddie said. "If the barometer has a high number, it will be sunny. If it's low, we'll get rain."

"Oh! Thank you! I never understood that before," Phoebe said.

"Just ask me, and I'll try to explain things," Eddie said.

She waddled off to play.

"Now she probably thinks I'm an idiot!" Phoebe said, as she pushed her chair back and stood. "I'd better go tend to the flapper girls before they get into trouble."

"You should start her with writing so those skills can catch up with her reading ability," Gage said.

"Why don't we get her started on the language learning programs we have subscriptions to?" Roman asked.

"All good ideas," Phoebe said. "She will let us know when or if she gets overwhelmed."

🏛️ML🏚️

Ari returned to her office and looked up the phone number for the school district. She learned that kindergarten registration would begin the week after Eddie's birthday, but in Texas, she would have to be five years old to enroll.

She decided to call and speak with someone, anyway. After a long conversation with someone in the Gifted and Talented department, they told Ari she would have to seek private testing. The school district would not test Eddie unless she was enrolled in school.

Ari harrumphed. She walked over to the office building and approached Marcha.

"By any chance do you know anyone I could call about having Eddie tested for academic placement?" Ari asked. "The school district won't test her until she starts school."

Marcha tapped her chin. "I would assume you could call a child psychologist for that information." Then her face lit up. "Guess who might be a good resource? That guy Butch."

Ari remembered the man who disrupted the meeting. Marcha gave her his contact information. Ari thanked her and left the building, heading over to the garage. She wanted to pass this by Roman and Gage before she contacted Butch.

She climbed the stairs to the living quarters over the garage. The men took up every chair and sofa. Lonnie and Kevin worked in their bedrooms. Tommy sat in a chair in Kevin's room with his stocking feet on the bed, while clacking on his laptop keyboard.

Roman and Gage stood and hugged Ari one at a time.

Sherm joined them.

She passed on what she had learned from the school, then Marcha's suggestion about asking Butch about a referral.

"I'll bet Butch went through not only medical testing but also psychological testing," Ari said. "His psychologist should be able to steer me in the right direction, don't you think?"

"I don't see the harm in you talking to him," Gage said.

"We may end up having Eddie homeschooled with private tutors," Roman said. "Phoebe has a master's in early childhood education from Stephen F. Austin University. She could get her started, then be a liaison for the rest of Eddie's education."

"That may be the route we have to take. For now, though, I believe having her tested will help Phoebe get centered on where to start and how to proceed," Ari said.

"We already know she's smart," Gage said. "We have to make sure she doesn't get bored."

"I'd better sit in on those lessons," Sherm joked. "If Eddie and I are going to get married, she's not going to want an idiot."

"Honestly, Sherm. Don't knock yourself down; there's nothing idiotic about you," Roman said. "Well, for the most part." He faked a punch to Sherm's bicep.

"Okay, I'll call Butch," Ari said.

"Ari, I have three strong candidates for Rosa's position," Sherm said. "Two women and one man."

"A butler? Set up interviews, Sherm." She kissed Roman and Gage goodbye, patted Sherm on the cheek, and headed back to the house.

As she reached the front door, Pablo pulled up in the golf cart.

"Ari, with Rosa's passing, I forgot all about the mail," Pablo said.

"The mail?" Ari asked.

"Rosa used to ride the buggy to the mailbox and get the mail for the house," Pablo explained. He got out of the cart and pulled a mail bin out of the back. "I'll carry it inside for you."

Ari gawked at the bin that was half-filled. "Oh, no! I hope none of the accounts will be overdue because we forgot to get the mail! Where is the mailbox?"

"Hop in and I'll show you," Pablo said. "When you find a replacement for Rosa, I'll show her the mailbox and explain everything to her."

"Or him," Ari said. "We're interviewing two women and a man."

They rode down the long driveway to the main road. A large mailbox, with a flag, was on a metal pole. Beside it was an elevated, closed metal container.

Pablo pulled the wooden handle and showed her how the bin fit inside so the mail was protected from the weather. "We installed the wooden handle because the metal one was hot enough to burn. The mailman leaves packages if they aren't too large for the container. Sometimes he'll drive up to the house, but I hate to say it, he's pretty lazy."

"Okay. This is good to know. Is the mail for just the house, or do we get the office building mail as well?"

"House and offices," Pablo said.

They got back into the cart and drove back to the house.

Pablo carried the bin into Ari's office.

CHAPTER TWENTY-TWO

Butch turned out to be a great resource. Through unraveling his affliction, he had been through the gauntlet of healthcare professionals. He referred Ari to Dr. Gregory Sarantopoulos. The doctor was on vacation in Greece for the next six weeks, so Ari set the appointment for October.

In the meantime, Ari, Roman, Gage and Phoebe worked out a plan for Eddie's immediate educational classwork. Learning to write was first on the list. Languages were next, along with math, science, grammar, spelling, and the whole lot that made up English taught in school.

Sherm arranged interviews for the three people vying for Rosa's replacement. Finding a quiet place on the property was a challenge during business hours because of all the renovations. They made arrangements to meet people at Mr. Ortega's office, Charles' attorney in San Marcos.

Louellen Pringle was the first candidate. She sat across the conference table from Roman, Ari and Gage. A prim woman with iron-gray hair, she sat ramrod straight in the chair. They discussed the duties, the size of the house, the apartment and determined from her facial and body postures she wasn't a good fit.

There is no way in hell she'll work out, Gage sent.

I get the impression she's going to whack my hand with a ruler, Roman sent.

She'll probably whack you alongside the head, Ari sent, while trying to suppress a giggle.

The gentleman was next. Joshua Butler looked just under fifty, had trained with the exclusive British Butler Institute in London, and had moved to the US with his employer, who had recently passed away. His goal was to secure another position so he could stay in the United States. The interview went smoothly.

I think he'll work out, Roman sent.

I agree, Ari sent.

Seems very down to earth, Gage sent.

The last applicant was Leona Davis. They kept their facial expressions pleasant when the obese woman waddled into the room.

"Hello," Leona said as she approached the table. She sounded a little winded.

"Hello, Leona," Roman said. "Thank you for coming to meet with us. Did the agency give you the scope of the position we're hiring for?"

"They told me this was a housekeeper position," Leona said. She smiled at her prospective three employers across the table.

Ari held pages in her hand. "It says here that you spent the past fifteen years working for Martin Wortham as his housekeeper. Why did you leave?"

"Mr. Wortham remarried, and his new wife and I didn't get along," Leona said. "She didn't like the way I ran the house or doted on her husband."

"Their loss," Gage said. "What size was the house, and what did you do?"

"The house was around four thousand square feet. I cooked the meals, took care of the laundry, cleaned the house—just basic housekeeper duties."

"The position we are trying to fill belonged to a woman who spent the past twenty years taking care of my uncle's house and estate," Ari said. "It's a fast-paced household that includes a house that's over ten-thousand square feet, with anywhere from a minimum of six people to as many as fifteen or twenty on any given day for meals and laundry. There's an apartment upstairs for the housekeeper."

Leona's eyes widened. "Oh, my goodness. If the agency had provided me with these details, I would not have wasted your time. Your household would be a little too much for me to take care of." She stood.

"I'm so sorry," Ari said. "I know what it's like to get your hopes up about something. Let me walk you out."

Ari and Leona left the room together.

After Ari returned, they thanked Mr. Ortega for the use of his conference room, then they headed back to the house.

By the time they arrived home, the house was quiet.

Sherm, come to the house, Roman sent.

Within a few minutes, Sherm entered the front door and headed to the kitchen.

"What were you thinking?" Gage asked.

"What do you mean?" Sherm asked. He didn't know what was wrong.

Roman shared a mind picture of the two women with Sherm.

"Seriously?" Sherm said. "Those two looked nothing like the women in the pictures the agency sent me." He shared pictures of two completely different women. "What about the guy?"

"We like Mr. Butler," Ari said.

"Lonnie will do a thorough background check on him. I don't trust anything the agency provided," Sherm said. He worked his phone and texted Lonnie. "He looks good on paper, but we'll see if there's anything hidden. We should have everything, including his shoe size, within the hour."

"You need to consider taking action against that agency," Ari said. "At the very least, get the owner on the phone and ream him out."

"I guess it's time for me to get to know the police chief and the sheriff," Sherm said.

Before Sherm left, Lonnie sent a complete background analysis on Joshua Butler. He was single, fifty-two years old, a British citizen, had no traffic tickets, no criminal record, not even any infractions as a teenager. He had glowing recommendations from past employers.

"Mr. Butler looks clean," Sherm said. "He'll need a new work permit, Roman. He no longer has legal status to stay in the US, so if you want him, you need to make an offer before he's deported."

"Let's get him out to the house for a more detailed interview," Roman said.

"I'll reach out to him," Gage said.

"Ask him to bring his paperwork," Roman said. "I can take a look at it."

🏯 **ML** 🏞️

At ten-thirty the next morning the doorbell rang. Roman answered the door and invited Joshua Butler into the house. The British man was immaculately groomed, in a three-piece charcoal gray suit, with his brown hair styled as you would expect of a professional butler, and shiny black shoes.

"Any problem finding the place?" Roman asked. He guided the man to the kitchen, where Ari, Gage, and Sherm sat around the table. They all stood.

All the men, including their guest, were approximately the same height with similar builds.

"No, your directions were precise," Joshua said.

Gage stuck his hand out.

"It's good to see you again, Mr. Stryker," Joshua said.

"Gage," Gage said. "Thanks for coming, Joshua."

"Please, call me Mr. Butler," he said. "I realize that may sound formal to you Americans, but that's what all my employers called me, and I was a butler in London."

Roman introduced Sherm.

"What do you prefer, tea or coffee?" Ari asked.

"I've grown quite attached to coffee, thank you," Mr. Butler said.

Ari guided him over to the coffee and tea bar. "There's just about every flavor, thanks to Rosa."

"This is quite an assortment of coffee and tea," Mr. Butler said. A dimple in his right cheek appeared when he smiled. "How does this machine work?"

Ari showed him how to fill the reusable K-cup.

"Your kitchen is a dream," Mr. Butler said, as he looked the room over.

"I thought our kitchen back in Pennsylvania was fabulous until we came here," Ari said. "This kitchen is hard to beat."

"This is like a shiny new toy," Mr. Butler said, as he studied the coffee machine with wonder. He made his coffee, and they all sat at the table.

"My uncle passed away and left me his estate," Ari began. "We haven't been here that long, and I didn't know Rosa's routine. So, this position will be somewhat of a challenge as we discover things Rosa took care of that I'm unaware of, such as the mail." She explained about the mailbox and bin.

Sherm sat up straight. "We need to get the business mailing address changed to a post office box. Anyone coming down the street has access to that mailbox, which means anyone can steal checks and business correspondence."

Ari startled. "I'll have Marcha set up a post office box. She can email the new mailing address to all the O'Briain's business accounts."

She sent Marcha a note from her iPad. Then she turned her attention back to Mr. Butler.

"Sorry. You see how it is. The job includes preparing three meals a day, laundry—but I prefer to do my own, and I'm set in my ways. So, the laundry will entail the sheets and towels from all the beds and baths, Roman and Gage's laundry, as well as Eddie's and Sherm's," Ari said. "Our bed is a large, custom-sized bed, and the bedding is enormous. It will take two people to fold sheets, believe me!"

"There's a woman that comes in two or three times a week. Her team cleans the house, the apartments over the garage, and the apartments in the office building," Gage said. He looked to Ari. "Is her name Lilly?"

"No, it's Lee-Lee, but spelled L-i-L-i," Ari said. She turned to Mr. Butler. "I know Rosa coordinated different things with Pablo, our property manager, and Marcha, who keeps the worker schedule for the garden worker shifts. I don't know what else, but whatever else has fallen through the cracks since Rosa's passing, we'll figure it out as we go along. You would be in charge of the kitchen, groceries, and making sure the house runs smoothly. Do you have any questions?"

"Not at this time, but I may jot things down for clarification later," Mr. Butler said.

"I noticed on your CV, your education included a graduate degree in European Languages, Culture and Society," Roman said.

"Yes. The focus was quite broad. I studied literature, linguistic traditions, history, sociology, philosophy, art, film, and other cultures associated with the languages taught at University College London. I decided I needed the degree for my chosen work," Mr. Butler explained. "My former employers entertained dignitaries and people from across Europe. I also took several culinary courses, so my cooking skills are restaurant-worthy."

"Do you have any friends or family here in the States?" Gage asked.

"No, unfortunately. And I do not plan to find someone to marry to stay here, either," Mr. Butler said, with a quirked smile.

"Why don't we show you the house and grounds," Roman said. "I'll introduce you to Pablo. He manages the grounds and the groundskeepers."

Ari showed Mr. Butler the enormous butler's pantry. They walked through the rest of the common areas of the house: living room, media room, library, gym, game room, then the bedrooms and her office. They climbed the kitchen stairs to the apartments upstairs.

"This is where Rosa lived," Ari said. "We've removed the furniture that was here before with what you see now. We didn't want whoever we hired to feel uncomfortable about sleeping on a bed where someone died."

Mr. Butler took in the living room: a leather sofa, comfortable side chairs, a coffee table, end tables, and a good-sized TV. The kitchen was a much smaller version of the kitchen for the household, and contained high-grade stainless-steel appliances.

Ari showed him the bedroom which held a queen-sized bed and all the accessories, then the bathroom which included a claw-footed tub and a separate walk-in shower.

"This is quite nice," Mr. Butler said.

"We can swap out any of the furniture. My uncle kept everything, and I swear I thought it was a furniture showroom when I first saw it," Ari said. "You would have full access to the pool, gym, media room, game room, and the sauna. If you are not too uncomfortable, we would like you to join us for meals at our table. We could never convince Rosa to sit down with us."

They returned to the kitchen. Roman, Gage and Sherm toured Mr. Butler outside.

After he had seen the entire property, they returned to the kitchen.

"We'd like to offer you the position, Mr. Butler, but there's one critical thing we need to bring to your attention," Roman said.

🛕**ML**🏯

After Mr. Butler recovered from witnessing their true identities, he was even more enthusiastic about moving on to a new life.

"What is your current situation?" Gage asked. "Did you give your notice yet?"

Mr. Butler winced. "Mrs. Cheswick, my late employer's wife, decided to return to London as soon as possible. She had no desire to retain my services, as her husband was much older and she felt stifled by my presence."

"Let's get your employment contract set up," Roman said. He called Marcha. "Can you print out an employment contract for Joshua Butler?"

Roman led the way to the front door. He, Mr. Butler, Gage and Sherm walked over to the office building. Roman retrieved the contract from Marcha, and they all walked to the offices over the garage, where he introduced Mr. Butler to everyone.

They sat at the kitchen table, which Mr. Tran had vacated, to settle into his hotel room with his son.

Roman discussed the contract with Mr. Butler. He pointed out the generous salary, the benefits that took effect upon signing the contract, and all the legal jargon. Mr. Butler signed the document.

"Jason, can you make a copy of this for Mr. Butler?" Roman asked. "We'll be over at the house."

"Sure," Jason said. "Welcome aboard, Mr. Butler." He took off down the stairs with the pages in hand.

They walked back over to the house.

"Everything all set? You're welcome to move in immediately," Ari said.

"Did you bring your I-766 employment authorization paperwork?" Roman asked. "I'll work on securing a new work permit for you. Now that you're gainfully employed, there shouldn't be any problem regarding your being able to stay in the country."

"I can't tell you how much I appreciate the expedience," Mr. Butler said.

"Do you need help moving your things?" Gage asked.

Mr. Butler looked embarrassed. "I'm staying in a hotel. Mrs. Cheswick asked me to leave before her husband's body was cold."

"That's shameful," Ari said.

"Is the car a rental?" Sherm asked.

"Yes," Mr. Butler said. "Mrs. Cheswick barely gave me enough time to pack and call a cab. I can't help how her husband treated her, but the way she treated me was uncalled for."

"Why don't we follow you back to your hotel? You can check out and return the rental car," Roman said. "You won't need a vehicle for a while. There are a half-dozen or more that will be at your disposal."

"I would be most grateful for the help," Mr. Butler said.

Roman, Sherm, and Gage helped Mr. Butler move his belongings from the hotel to the Navigator. Then they returned the rental car.

"You were forced out rather quickly, and there's no telling if you left anything behind," Roman said. "I believe we should pay a visit to Mrs. Cheswick so you can make a more thorough move-out. You most likely forgot things in the kitchen and other places that you were too unaware of at the time to take notice of them."

"Do you think that's a good idea?" Mr. Butler asked.

Roman, Gage and Sherm smiled.

Sherm plugged the address into the GPS, and within minutes he pulled up in front of a monstrosity of a house. "This the place?"

"Yes," Mr. Butler said.

"Horrible taste in housing," Sherm said.

They all got out of the Navigator and walked to the front door. Mr. Butler rang the doorbell.

A straight-faced woman in her mid-fifties answered the door. "Yes? What are you doing here, Mr. Butler?"

Roman stepped in front of Mr. Butler. "Mrs. Cheswick?"

The woman looked Roman over. "Yes. Who are you?"

"I'm Roman Davenport, the CEO of Panther Industries, and an attorney. This is my business partner, Gage Stryker, and Sherman Foo, the head of our security division," Roman said.

"What business do you have here?" Mrs. Cheswick asked.

"You dismissed Mr. Butler unfairly after your husband passed away," Roman said.

Mrs. Cheswick lifted her chin and sniffed, affronted. "I had no further use for his services."

"That may be so, but he had just lost his employer of several years. You did not give him ample opportunity to make a clean exit from your household with all his belongings," Roman said. "I'm representing Mr. Butler, and I would hate to disrupt your move back to the UK with an ugly lawsuit."

She looked at Mr. Butler with contempt. "You're suing me?"

Mr. Butler was about to answer when Sherm elbowed him in the side.

"My client is under advisement not to comment, or communicate with you until we have resolved this situation," Roman said. "We would like access to your home. In his haste to follow your wishes to vacate the premises, Mr. Butler may have left behind personal belongings. He will carefully check for anything he overlooked."

Anger smoldered beneath the surface of the spiteful woman. "You have one hour."

"My client will take as much time as necessary to go through each room he typically worked in," Roman said. He turned to Mr. Butler. "Did your employer ever require you to go to his office?"

"Yes, but I did not work there," Mr. Butler said. "He would ask me to deliver things he needed—changes of clothing and little gifts for his secretary."

Mrs. Cheswick gasped. "How dare you imply my husband behaved improperly with his secretary!"

"May we come in?" Roman said.

She reluctantly stood aside, and they entered the house.

Twenty minutes later, they marched out of the horrible house with three boxes of Mr. Butler's belongings, after Mrs. Cheswick approved the items. They carried his laundry, dry cleaning, kitchen tools, books, DVDs, shoes, and a pair of winter boots. He discovered his London rain gear and a shoebox of letters from family and friends that was in the back of his closet.

Sherm drove to the house. They made two trips from the Navigator to the house with their arms full, marched up the kitchen stairs and set the boxes and bags in the living room. A copy of the signed employment contract was on the kitchen counter in the apartment.

"Thank you so much for your help," Mr. Butler said. "I can't tell you how grateful I am to retrieve the rest of my belongings. I was overcome with the abruptness of my termination and didn't even realize I had left behind so many things."

"Settle in," Ari said, as she patted him on the back.

"You'll need a few days to learn our routines, the layout of the house, especially the kitchen, and how things function around here."

Mr. Butler hung his dry cleaning in the bedroom closet. "Let me assist you with the evening meal. That would help me become grounded."

"Come downstairs when you're ready, and I'll give you a more thorough tour of the kitchen and pantry," Ari said.

Ari opened all the kitchen cabinets so they could explore the contents. Even she was unaware of everything they contained.

"Feel free to change things around," Ari said. "Just don't change the coffee and tea bar unless we discuss the reason."

They explored the butler's pantry, and Ari opened the upright freezer. Mr. Butler noticed labels on all the shelves. There were bins that held chicken, beef, pork, seafood, wild game, vegetables, casseroles, and desserts. On the door were jars of soups and sauces.

"This is wonderfully organized," Mr. Butler said.

"There's also a root cellar. Did Pablo show you that?" Ari asked.

"No, I don't recall seeing a root cellar," Mr. Butler said.

"I love it. Pablo stores fresh carrots, potatoes, sweet potatoes, and a lot of other things, so we enjoy fresh vegetables and fruit through the winter. There's also shelves of canning jars," Ari said.

"This household is certainly self-sufficient," Mr. Butler said. "I'm impressed. In the UK, many country estates are self-supported with vegetables, poultry, beef, lamb and pork."

"We've gained a lot of ideas for the shifter community back in Reading," Ari said. She showed him Rosa's recipe binders on a shelf in the pantry. "We'll have you making Mexican food before long."

CHAPTER TWENTY-THREE

Dinner was a boisterous affair. Mr. Butler was a little shy to be eating with his employers, but after a while, he loosened up and joined in the conversation. A week later, he was thoroughly settled and knew his way around the kitchen, the pantry, the entire house, and the gardens. He followed LiLi and her crew to make sure he understood what they did and how they did it. He liked the raccoon's professionalism and her passion for cleaning.

The following Monday, Pablo wandered through the kitchen door. He didn't see Mr. Butler, so he entered the pantry where he found the man folding towels. He took his hat off.

"Have you ever canned food?" Pablo asked.

"No, I have never had the opportunity," Mr. Butler said as he stopped folding a towel.

"My wife will come help you," Pablo said. "We need to harvest tomatoes and other vegetables."

"When should I plan this for?" Mr. Butler asked.

"Tomorrow," Pablo said. "My wife will come and show you where all the supplies are and what to do."

Pablo plopped his hat on his head and left through the kitchen door.

Mr. Butler finished folding towels, stacked everything in a basket, and made a trip to each bathroom and replaced them in the linen closets. When he returned to the kitchen, he started lunch preparations. He made egg salad, tuna salad, turkey, and roast beef sandwiches. The butler made Ari's berry water, another pitcher of iced tea, and a vegetable and fruit platter. He also included small bowls of egg and tuna salad and a basket of mixed crackers.

Everything was on the table when the family filed in.

Eddie looked at the offerings. "I love egg salad! What's that?" She pointed to the tuna salad.

"That's tuna salad," Ari said. "You've had tuna salad before. You love it."

"Are you sure?" Eddie asked.

"Yes, I'm positive. Your kitty loves tuna."

Everyone settled around the table.

Phoebe nudged Eddie. "Eddie has a progress report."

All eyes were on the munchkin.

"I've finished my geometry workbook," she boasted.

Mouths dropped open. Eyes drifted to Phoebe.

She shrugged.

"She took to geometry as if she were born knowing it," Phoebe said.

"Why did you start her on geometry?" Roman asked.

"I planned to begin with basic English. She picked up the book, and that was that," Phoebe said.

The doorbell rang.

Mr. Butler placed his napkin on the table and rushed to the front door. Aileen greeted him.

"May I help you?" The woman stunned him. She was gorgeous.

"Hi. Where's Rosa?" Aileen asked.

"I'm sorry to inform you, but Mrs. Peña passed away. I'm Mr. Butler, her replacement. And you are?"

"Oh, no! I'm Ari's aunt, Aileen."

They shook hands and didn't release immediately. They seemed to realize their hand connection after more than a long blink and let go of each other.

"Come in, we just sat down to lunch. Won't you join us?" Mr. Butler asked, a little flustered.

They walked to the kitchen.

"Aunt Aileen!" Ari was on her feet and swooped her aunt into a hug.

Roman, Gage, Sherm and Jason were on their feet and gave Aileen a welcome hug.

"Aileen, it's good to see you again," Roman said.

They all made their greetings while Mr. Butler pulled together another place setting and sat Aileen across from him.

"Is that house near Pablo's place still vacant?" Aileen asked.

"Yes. Do you want to go see it after lunch?" Ari asked.

"Do you have time? I close on my house in Pearland next week," Aileen said.

"Oh, Aunt Aileen! It will be so wonderful to have you close by!" Ari said. "Oh, and this is Phoebe, Eddie's nanny-slash-tutor, and you met Mr. Butler."

"I'm so sorry to hear about Rosa. What happened?" Aileen asked.

"Heart attack. Ari found her," Gage said.

Aileen looked over to Ari. "Oh, no. I'm so sorry you had to experience that so soon after everything else." She looked over to Eddie. "So, missy, what are you learning these days?"

"Geometry!" Eddie squealed.

"Geometry?" Aileen asked. She looked at her niece and the men around the table. "Really?"

"She's looking more and more like a little prodigy every day," Roman said.

"Guess who's a shifter, Auntie!" Eddie said. "Sherm! Now we can get married when I grow up!"

"She's still stuck on that, hmmm?" Aileen asked.

"Even more so now that Sherm had his coming-out moment," Gage said.

Aileen eyeballed Sherm. "Well?"

"I never had a clue. My mother and grandmother came for a visit and let the wolverine out of the bag, so to speak," Sherm said.

"Wolverine?" Aileen asked. "Aren't they cold-weather animals?"

"Yup. So, Mr. Butler may find me sitting in the upright freezer one day," Sherm joked.

"You'd better plan to remove several shelves before you climb in," Mr. Butler joked. He turned to Ari. "Pablo stopped by earlier and said we needed to can tomatoes and other vegetables tomorrow. His wife is supposed to stop by in the morning to show me where the supplies are and what to do."

"Oh, that's interesting. I've never canned vegetables before," Ari said.

"I'll help," Aileen said. "It's not difficult, but it can be time-consuming, depending on the amount of produce to be put up."

After lunch, Ari retrieved the keys to the vacant house, and she, Aileen, Roman and Gage walked through the woods to where the house stood. It was a single-story house, similar to Pablo's, with a river rock front, along with sand-colored bricks.

Ari opened the door, and they went inside. It was an open floor plan with a nice kitchen and a living room with a fireplace. The house felt cool. Roman found the thermostat. The temperature was set at seventy-seven. The interior plantation shutter blinds were closed.

Aileen and Ari opened the blinds, and the house lit up. It was light and bright. They looked around, with Aileen mentally placing furniture.

"This looks ideal," she said. "I'm pretty sure it's the same size as my Pearland house, and everything will fit. I'm glad I won't have to sell or give away my furniture."

Ari slipped her arm through her aunt's arm. "That's good. I know how you feel about downsizing. It can be difficult if you've had things for a long time."

They finished and returned to the house. Ari returned to her office and pulled the labeled bag of keys out of a locked drawer. She dumped them out on the desk and pulled out the spare key to Aileen's new house. She found her aunt in the kitchen with Mr. Butler.

"Here's the key to the house," Ari said. "Do you have movers, or would you want us to get a truck?"

"Oh, no. It's much easier to use a moving company," Aileen said. "Now that I have an address, I'll be able to book the move."

ML

Pablo's wife, Minerva, showed up at eight o'clock the next morning. She was a plump, chatty, likable woman. Mr. Butler, Ari and Aileen followed her into the pantry to a closet hidden out of the way. There, they found a pressure cooker and a large, covered pot. The pot contained a wire rack, a heavy-duty jar lifter, a ladle, a canning funnel, a bubble freer, and a big wooden spoon. There were several cases of different size canning jars.

Minerva handed out supplies, and they marched back to the kitchen.

Pablo entered the kitchen with boxes of tomatoes, followed by zucchini and yellow summer squash, green beans, and carrots.

Minerva clasped her hands together in front of her chest. "I know it looks like a lot, but don't panic. We already put up berries and jam from those harvests."

"First, we need to get all these things washed; then we have to prepare the different jars," she said. She placed her hand on the big pot that contained all the supplies. "There's two different types of canning methods for different types of foods. We use this for the water bath method. The water bath is for fruits and fruit juices, jams and jellies, salsa, tomatoes, pickles and relishes, chutneys, sauces, pie fillings, condiments and vinegars."

Next, she patted the pressure cooker. "This guy is a pressure cooker. It's used to put up meats, poultry, vegetables, chili, and seafood. You can find a lot of cookbooks online with recipes for both methods."

By the end of the day, with a break for lunch, they filled the counters with a colorful variety of canning jars packed with their bounty. Minerva guided them to the root cellar, where they placed their jars in the proper place. She and Rosa had a method for the storage and use of vegetables and fruits. All the jars were labeled with the date. Most vegetables would last up to five years, while tomatoes and citrus fruit only had a shelf life of eighteen months. They filled their boxes with jars from the shelves to stock the pantry.

Once they were back in the kitchen, they cleaned up and stored the canning tools.

"We're going out to dinner," Ari announced. "Everyone go get cleaned up. I'll tell Roman and Gage. They can pull together whoever wants to join us. Mexican, Italian, Indian, pizza? What does everyone want?"

Mexican was the unanimous vote. Ari mind-messaged Roman and let him make all the arrangements.

They all piled into vehicles and headed to Mamacitas on Aquarena Springs Drive. Roman had called and talked to the manager, and had him reserve enough tables to seat twenty. He arranged a buffet of enchiladas, fajitas, rice, beans, quesadillas, tacos, and tamales. When they arrived, three large, round tables were waiting for them. After they were seated, Roman told the waiter to put everything on one ticket and to give him the bill.

They took drink orders and delivered chips and salsa to the tables. Lively chatter drowned out the rest of the restaurant, while people gawked at their group. The waitstaff set up the private buffet, and their hungry party emptied the metal food pans. Roman paid with his black American Express Centurion card. When they left the restaurant ninety-minutes later, Roman, Ari, and Gage seemed to be best friends with the wait-staff and the manager.

🏛ML🗿

Ari tucked Eddie into bed. Roman and Gage kissed their adopted daughter goodnight. They returned to the living room where Aileen, Kevin, and Mr. Butler were engaged in a lively discussion. Roman headed to the bar.

"Who wants what?" he asked.

"Whiskey," Gage said.

"Gin and Tonic," Ari said. "Use that lime gin and tonic."

Kevin got up and strode over to the bar. "I'll take a beer."

"Red wine," Aileen and Mr. Butler said at the same time.

When everyone had settled with their drinks, Ari started the conversation. "I want to have a meeting with our Reading shifter family about a community garden and preserving the food in a root cellar or pantry for our people."

"The more we learn here, the more we can pass along to them," Gage said. "We'll have to see if there're any gardeners among our people back there, because I have no idea what they can plant now. The cold weather is right around the corner. Someone will have to check with the city to get permission to start a community garden."

"Why don't you send out an email first to see if there are any gardeners?" Roman asked. "Once you find someone, then you can plan what they need before you get everyone's hopes up about a sustainable project like this."

CHAPTER TWENTY-FOUR

Jason flew to Italy to lead a meeting with Donatello, Marco, and clan leaders throughout Europe, the UK, Russia, and Asia. Roman, Gage and Ari discussed what to do about Greenland, Africa, Australia—including all the islands, and South America. Currently, the US (including Alaska and Hawaii), Canada, Mexico, and Central America had solid connections to the Tothars. The rest were still trying to establish unwavering connections to the kings and queen of their kind.

During Jason's three-week stay at the palazzo in Fiuggi, Donatello and Marco snapped pictures of Jason and Janina in various poses of lip-locks.

"She's going to have to move here," Ari said, glaring at her life partners. "I don't want Jason to move to Italy! We'd rarely see him."

"Ari, that's not our choice to make," Roman said. "Besides, they aren't even engaged."

"Honey, calm down," Gage implored. "To me, it looks like they're headed to the altar. They're the ones to decide where they live. We can't. You don't want to appear as the mother-in-law from Hell if they do get married."

Ari paced the kitchen as everyone else at the breakfast table ate in silence, eyeing her.

"Ari, Jason is almost fifty. Your apron strings not only need to be snipped, but that man is not the baby bird you envision in your head," Aileen said kindly.

Ari fretted, then returned to her seat. "What about the library project? If Janina moves here, who's going to be there to lead the people?"

"Someone else will fill that spot. It's not like they aren't capable," Gage said. "Mr. Tran, Alan, or Abbot Benston can take turns going abroad. They're all familiar with the library and the people doing the work. I'm sure Mr. Tran will choose someone to be their lead."

"Ari, I'm firm on this. You cannot pressure Jason into deciding to please you," Roman said. "I realize he's your son, not mine, but he's one of my best friends and I won't allow you to jeopardize his happiness."

"Who do you think you are?" Ari was on her feet, eyes blazing.

Roman shoved his chair back, not put off. "I'm your life partner and Jason's stepfather for all intents and purposes. I HAVE a say in this. You're being too overprotective."

Gage stood and faced them. "Everyone calm the fuck down, right now. Ari, either your hormones are whacked out, or something else is going on for this type of reaction. I agree with Roman."

In less than a long blink, Ari's clothes shredded, and she shifted into her liger and roared.

Aileen threw herself in front of Mr. Butler.

Eddie screamed and shifted into her tiger kitten. She jumped out of her booster chair and onto the kitchen table and hissed in all directions. Phoebe grabbed her and ran to the bedroom and slammed the door shut.

Roman, Gage and Kevin shifted.

The kitchen door opened and Sherm entered. He stopped in his tracks.

Ari's liger shoved the table across the floor as she advanced on Roman, snarling.

Aileen shoved Mr. Butler toward the stairs. "Go upstairs and stay there until I come for you."

He didn't hesitate, but took the stairs two at a time. His door slammed at the top of the stairs.

Aileen approached the liger. She grabbed fur on its cheek and forced Ari to look at her. "Stop this instance, Ari."

Ari snarled at her aunt.

Aileen swatted the liger's face. She shook the fur gripped in her fist. "STOP! Shift back right now!"

Roman growled low in his throat.

"Shut up, Roman. Don't make this situation any worse than it is," Aileen said.

Gage flew up and perched on top of a kitchen chair. Kevin's lion stood still and didn't growl or roar.

Sherm forced himself to stay in his human form.

Ari's liger grumbled. She lumbered out of the kitchen and headed toward the master bedroom.

Aileen and Sherm let out a sigh of relief.

Roman, Gage and Kevin shifted back.

"What the fuck?" Kevin asked. His eyes darted to his step-father's.

"Aileen, get Mr. Tran and Cama here. Something's not right," Roman said.

Sherm shut the kitchen door. He didn't realize he'd never shut it when he entered.

Mr. Butler crept down the stairs and looked around the corner before he stepped off the last stair. "Is the coast clear? I heard Roman's voice, so figured people were present."

Aileen grabbed him in a hug. "I told you to stay upstairs! This was a very dangerous situation."

He pecked her on the cheek.

Everyone's eyebrows raised, but no one uttered a word.

"I need a towel," Kevin said.

Mr. Butler darted into the pantry and retrieved one, and tossed it to Kevin.

He wrapped the towel around his waist and took off out the kitchen door to his room over the garage.

Roman and Gage mulled over what to do.

Gage huffed out an exasperated breath. "Come on, might as well go face the music. I'm not sitting around naked until she makes an appearance."

He and Roman headed to the master bedroom.

Mr. Butler gathered up the shredded clothing and brought it into the pantry to sort later.

Aileen called Cama. Sherm called Mr. Tran. They hadn't met yet, but they could pool their skills and get to the bottom of Ari's unusual behavior.

Ari was sprawled naked and face down on the bed when Roman and Gage opened the door.

"Honey?" Gage asked. "Do you want to talk, or do you want us to leave you alone?"

"Please leave me alone," she said without even looking at her partners.

Gage and Roman dressed quickly and left the room. They returned to the kitchen, which had been put back in order.

Phoebe came out of Eddie's bedroom, holding the little girl on her hip. She looked around and noticed Ari was missing. "Everything okay?"

"Thanks for removing Eddie from what could have been a disaster," Roman said. He kissed Eddie. "Your tiger kitten is very pretty."

"Is Mommy okay?" Eddie asked.

"Yes. She's sleeping," Gage said.

Mr. Butler and Aileen were reheating breakfast. They had put all the dishes into the dishwasher and had clean ones on the table.

They heard cars arrive, and Sherm opened the kitchen door and saw Mr. Tran and Cama parking their cars. He watched as they introduced themselves, then walked to where they saw Sherm.

"What happened?" Mr. Tran asked.

"I'm not sure. I arrived after Ari had already shifted to her liger and was getting ready to tear into Roman," Sherm said. "Aileen neutralized the situation."

They all walked to the kitchen door and entered. "Come, sit down," Roman said. "Have you had breakfast yet? Ours was interrupted, as you've no doubt heard."

Everyone settled at the table after getting their coffee. Mr. Butler and Aileen placed a plate of stacked pancakes, bowls of scrambled eggs, and fruit on the table. Mr. Butler returned to the toaster area and grabbed a plate of buttered toast, cut on the diagonal.

Kevin returned, fully dressed. He took his seat. "Where's Mom?"

"She's sleeping," Roman said.

Kevin let out a loud sigh. "Man, you were brave, Aunt Aileen! I would never, ever approach Mom in her liger form."

"I didn't want it to escalate. There would have been deep regrets," Aileen said.

They each gave their version of what happened, so that Mr. Tran and Cama could compare notes as to what caused everything to escalate out of control. After breakfast, Phoebe scooted

Eddie out of the room to her lessons. Kevin and Sherm walked over to the office building, which was significantly quieter with some of the renovation projects completed.

The two herbalists made lists of probable causes:

- Allergies
- Thyroid
- Hormone imbalance due to menopause
- Stress from not meeting her uncle
- The move from Reading to San Marcos
- Stress from all the renovations and the attempted kidnapping
- Something cropping up from her abduction, Roman's kidnapping, and Gage's accident

They listed everything, no matter how outrageous it sounded.

"It can't be menopause," Gage said. "Ari went through that a decade before we all met."

"That may be so, but I would think her physiology changed when she shifted for the first time in Italy," Mr. Tran said. "Maybe her body has shifted." He turned to Cama. "Don't these symptoms remind you of PMS?"

Cama's face crunched into a large frown as she tossed Mr. Tran's words around in her head. She nodded. "Yes. It definitely sounds like a roaring case of PMS."

Roman and Gage stared at them. They tried to comprehend the idea that Ari, in her middle seventies in human years, could remotely regenerate to the point of going through PMS and periods again.

Mr. Tran took a deep breath. To broach this subject was touchy, but he realized he had to throw this into the pot of possibilities. "The ONLY other prognosis I could offer is pregnancy."

No one was aware that Ari had walked into the room. "Pregnant?"

Roman and Gage flinched, then turned to face her, leery. "I can't be pregnant!" She looked wild-eyed. "In human years, I'm an old lady. A senior citizen. Decades past menopause."

Mr. Butler cleared his throat from where he was leaning on the kitchen island. "I could run to the drugstore and get a pregnancy test."

Aileen grabbed his hand. "Let's go!"

A half hour later, four unwrapped pregnancy tests were on the bathroom counter. Ari paced, staring at them. Roman and Gage stood off to the side, waiting for her to take any type of action at all.

"Do you need a glass of water?" Roman asked.

"No."

"Want us to leave?" Gage asked.

"No."

Finally, she hitched up her shirt, unbuttoned her crop pants, unzipped the zipper, and pulled down her pants and panties and sat on the toilet. She held out her hand. Gage hustled over to the counter and picked up the first strip and handed it to Ari.

Roman stood by with a paper towel. He placed it on the counter.

Gage handed Roman the strip and grabbed the next one. They had an assembly line going until the last test was on the paper towel.

Two pink lines lit up on the first strip. Then the next. All four test strips showed two pink lines. They stared at them in shock.

Roman picked up a discarded container and read the instructions again. He whispered. "You're pregnant."

Then, suddenly, Roman and Gage turned to each other and shouted with glee. "WE'RE GOING TO HAVE A BABY!"

Ari stood there, dumbfounded, staring at the pregnancy test strips on the counter. "I can't believe I'm pregnant."

She stared at her jubilant life partners in shock. Roman and Gage engulfed her in a tender embrace.

"This is the most incredible gift anyone has ever given to me," Roman said, tearing up.

"I never thought I'd experience being a father," Gage said reverently.

Everyone who sat in the living room waiting nervously overheard the announcement. When Roman, Ari, and Gage came out of the bedroom, they were greeted by congratulations in stereo.

Eddie ran up to Ari and kissed her stomach. "I'm going to have a little brother and a sister!"

"Whoa. It will be one or the other," Gage said.

"No, siree," Eddie said.

"We're having twins, Eddie?" Roman asked. "Are you sure?"

Eddie nodded. "I'll be the best big sister on the planet! I'll make sure my brother and sister are always safe!"

Ari sunk to the sofa. "Twins? Isn't pregnancy at my age enough of a surprise?"

Roman's cell rang. He looked at the screen and saw that Atsa was calling using FaceTime. "Hey, Atsa."

"I tried to call Ari's cell, but she didn't answer. Is she around?" Atsa asked. "I have a surprise for her."

"And she has a big surprise for you," Roman said. He handed the phone to Ari.

"Hi, Atsa. You first," Ari said, as she watched his features on the phone screen. "What's your surprise?"

"Ari, I'd like you to meet your father."

A handsome man joined Atsa on the screen. He had tears in his eyes.

"Hello, Ari," Kenneth Porter said. He had a gentle voice.

"Oh, my God!" Ari swallowed. Tears poured down her cheeks. "Dad? Is that really you?"

"I can't wait to meet you in person," he said.

Roman squeezed his face into the frame. "We'll send the jet. Can you get away in a few hours?"

He heard Atsa telling Kenneth, *that's Roman.*

"Yes!" Kenneth said.

"We'll take him to the airport. You coming into Four Corners?" Atsa asked.

Ari looked over at Roman. He nodded. Gage said something in the background. "Yes. Gage said Lonnie will be there in three hours."

"What's your surprise?" Atsa asked.

Ari smiled. "You'll have to wait until you get here."

They ended the call. Ari looked bewildered. "Can this day possibly get more exciting?"

Jason called. Kevin had blabbed the news about the baby. "Mom, is it true? You're having a baby? Kevin said there was a big fight this morning. Is everything okay? You didn't hurt Roman or Gage, did you?"

"I want you to charter a jet immediately and come home. Bring Janina," Ari said.

"What's wrong?" Jason asked, with more than a hint of panic in his voice.

"Nothing's wrong, Jase. Your grandfather—my father, is on his way here. Atsa found him. I want you to meet him," Ari said.

"You found my grandfather?" Jason sounded jubilant. "We'll be on the first jet out of here!"

As Jason was ending the call, Ari heard him call out for Marco.

Shortly after four-thirty that afternoon, the Navigator pulled up in the driveway, Lonnie at the wheel. The front door of the house burst open, and Ari, Roman, Gage, and Kevin plowed out. Ari stopped near the front of the car. She covered her mouth and nose with her hands, her eyes pooling with tears. She saw her father in the back seat across from Yiska. The car doors opened, and they piled out.

Kenneth Porter was a handsome man who looked to be in his mid-sixties. His sandy-colored hair was a little scraggly from his off-the-grid mountain living and reached to below his shoulders.

He and Ari rushed to each other and slammed into an embrace, both sobbing.

"Your mother never told me," Kenneth sobbed.

They pulled apart, each wiping their faces with their hands. They stared at each other for several long moments. Ari led him over to her men. "Dad, this is my youngest son, Kevin. Jason is flying in from Italy. He'll be here tomorrow with his girlfriend, Janina."

Kevin and his grandfather hugged. "Italy?" Kenneth asked.

"We have offices in Italy and Reading, Pennsylvania. Jason lives here," Kevin explained.

Ari motioned for Roman and Gage to approach. "These are my life partners, Roman Davenport and Gage Stryker."

They shook hands. Roman noticed Kenneth was a little reserved, judging his daughter's choices.

"I'm so glad to meet you, Mr. Porter," Roman said. He turned to Ari. "You have your father's eyes—that night sky blue."

"We just found out about you, Mr. Porter," Gage said. "Why don't we go inside? You and Ari have a lot of history to share."

Atsa and Yiska approached Roman and Gage. "What's the big surprise?" Atsa asked.

Gage made a zipper movement across his lips. "Ari will divulge when she calms down."

They all walked into the house. Ari led them to the living room, where Sherm sat with Eddie on his lap and Phoebe beside them, holding a thick book. Eddie squirmed out of Sherm's lap and ran across the floor toward Ari and Kenneth, shrieking.

"Grandpa!" she squealed with her arms outstretched.

Kenneth reached down and pulled Eddie up. He looked at Ari. "Your daughter?"

"Our adopted daughter," she said.

"My name is Edris, but you can call me Eddie," Eddie said—her standard spiel.

"How old are you?" Kenneth asked.

Eddie held up four fingers. "I'm four. Want to see what I'm studying?" She squirmed to get down.

"I'd love to see what you're learning," he said, with a huge grin.

Kenneth set her on the floor and she ran over to Phoebe, snatched the book out of her hands and returned to her new grandparent. She held up the book.

"Advanced Calculus and Linear Algebra?" Kenneth shot a questioning look at his daughter, then her partners.

"It started with geometry a few weeks ago," Roman said. "She practically sucked the book into her head. We're waiting for an appointment for academic testing."

"One day she was coloring—barely keeping between the lines; the next she picked up a geometry book and devoured it," Gage said.

"This is Phoebe, Eddie's tutor-slash-nanny," Ari said. "Everyone, sit down."

Mr. Butler and Aileen brought in a tray with glasses of iced tea.

"Kenneth? I'm Aileen O'Briain," Aileen said. Kenneth stood to face her. "Alanna's sister?" Aileen nodded, eyes sparkling with tears.

"Dad, I never even knew my mother's real name until my uncle Charles passed away a short time ago," Ari said. "I knew my mother as Susan Murphy. I knew I had an aunt, Aileen, but I never knew her last name, so I couldn't even search for her. My mother would never tell me about you."

Kenneth shook his head and sat down. "She was very troubled; could not accept the fact that shifters existed in the world. I loved her so much, but she disappeared when I was at work. Packed up her clothes and a few personal things, and that was that. Didn't even take the car. She took a cab to the airport and took off to parts unknown."

Aileen was visibly upset. "Charles and I watched her from a distance. We knew if we approached her, she'd take off again."

Ari stood. "Come look at Uncle Charles' office." She held her hand out to her father and led him to the office.

Kenneth looked at the pictures on the walls in wonder. Ari let out a sob. "I don't know why he didn't come forward when my mother died. I wish I had met him. I'm grateful that he told me about Aileen in his letter. She's the one who told me about you. So many wasted years with no family whatsoever."

"I don't know how your mother could have been so cruel, to keep me from you," Kenneth said. "You're happy with your life now? These two men?"

Ari's face bloomed with love. "Roman and Gage are my cornerstones. The loves of my life. I hope you can accept the fact that I have two life partners. We're bonded to each other as Tothars."

"Atsa and Yiska brought me up-to-date with your lives, your status, and all the hardships the three of you have experienced. I'm glad that's behind you, and you had the strength to make it through those bad times," Kenneth said. "Atsa said you're ferocious in your animal form."

Ari snorted out a laugh. They walked back into the living room, arm in arm. "I have to be ferocious with these guys."

Roman gauged the emotional atmosphere. "If you had been here for breakfast, you would have seen Ari as her liger."

Atsa and Yiska zeroed in on Ari.

"You shifted at the breakfast table?" Atsa asked, shocked. He looked at the faces around the room. "Did someone invade the property? What happened?"

Roman and Gage roared with laughter.

"I was a little hormonal," Ari explained. "I'm pregnant!"

CHAPTER TWENTY-FIVE

At two-fifteen in the morning, a cab pulled up to the house. Jason and Janina got out of the car. The driver popped the trunk, and they retrieved their luggage.

Jason paid the driver and gave the guy a handsome tip.

They approached the front door. Jason had his keys out when the door jerked open. Sherm stood there, barefoot, hair wild, wearing pajama pants, with his gun in hand.

Janina sucked in a breath, shocked.

"It's okay, it's just Sherm," Jason told her. He looked at Sherm. "What's up with the gun?"

"Too much training," Sherm said, with a sheepish grin. "I can hear every little sound now. This can be a good thing, but not so much in the middle of the night when there are animals out and about."

Sherm stepped back so that Jason and Janina could come into the house.

"Go back to bed," Jason said. "I hope my room is still available."

"Yeah. With you, it's a full house. See you at breakfast," Sherm said. He wandered down the hall to his room and quietly closed the door.

Jason picked up their rolling luggage so it wouldn't make a racket across the floor and wake anyone. He led Janina to his room.

🏛**ML**🏯

The next morning was a lively affair. Both Janina and Kenneth experienced what they were in for regarding the family dynamics. Roman and Gage doted on Ari in her new role as an expectant mother. Bantering around the table was loud and jovial.

They discovered that Kenneth was a retired programmer who dabbled in the occasional website development. The cabin in the mountains was not the rickety lean-to that Ari had envisioned. It was smaller than their house in the woods, but just as nice. Last night they had spent hours sharing histories and stories, sliding pictures across phone and iPad screens.

Kenneth was interested to understand Panther Industries and the Security Division.

Two questions were flung out at the breakfast table. The first was whether Kenneth would stay in the mountains or move to San Marcos. The second put Janina and Jason in the spotlight.

"Now that I have a daughter, two grandsons, a granddaughter, with two on the way, I don't want to be a great distance away," Kenneth said.

"The contractors should be finished with the apartments in the office building this coming week," Roman said. "Would you want to look at one?"

"Dad, we have an entire warehouse of furniture that Uncle Charles collected over the years," Ari said. "Leave your cabin intact for when you want to get away from the heat. Leave winter clothes there; bring everything else you want here."

"There's also the other apartment upstairs," Mr. Butler said.

"I don't know if I would be happy in an apartment," Kenneth said. "I may end up having to build something on your property."

"There's plenty of land to choose from," Gage said.

"You could always stay at your cabin, use FaceTime, and fly in when you wanted," Atsa said. "It's not that great a distance."

"I have a lot to think about," Kenneth said. "I definitely want to be settled by the time Ari gives birth."

"Janina," Ari said.

"Uh oh," Kevin said. "You're in the hot seat now, girl."

Janina's eyes widened. She swallowed an audible gulp as she met Ari's eyes. "Yes, ma'am?"

"Are you serious about my son?" Ari asked.

"Hon, that's not fair," Gage said.

"Mom!" Jason grabbed Janina's hand to calm her.

Ari stared Gage down. "There's nothing wrong with wanting to know where things are headed." She turned her focus back to

Janina. "I'm sorry if my thought processes are all whacked out. I don't mean to ask inappropriate questions. But a mother has a right to know what her children are up to, even if they are fully grown men."

"Ari, we need to find a GYN doctor, preferably a shifter," Aileen said.

"How's the database coming along?" Sherm asked.

"Will you all please stop trying to steer me away from my conversation," Ari said, as she screwed up her face in a threatening manner.

"You're not going to shift, are you?" Jason asked.

"I have no idea," Ari said.

"Mom, you're so cute when you can't get your way," Kevin said.

Ari harrumphed.

"Jason, are you thinking about moving to Italy?" Roman asked. He figured he'd head Ari off at the pass.

Jason squirmed now that he was in the hot seat. "No, I don't want to move to Italy. I'd miss out on family dinners, Sherm making jokes at our expense, my little sister, my brother, my new grandfather, Mom, you, and Gage. I like it here in San Marcos."

"What about you, Janina?" Gage asked, looking from Jason to Janina.

"Jason and I have discussed this," she said. "I have distant relatives in Lithuania, but my parents and grandparents are gone. I love the palazzo and the friends I've made there, but I love Jason. We want to get married eventually."

Ari jumped out of her chair and rushed to Janina. She threw her arms around the stunned girl. "That's wonderful!"

Jason huffed out in exasperation. "Honestly! Be right back." He returned in a couple of moments, dropped to one knee, opened a jeweler's box and presented it to Janina. "This isn't how I planned this, but what the hell... Janina, will you marry me?"

Janina scooted her chair back, hands clasped to her heart. "Oh, Jason—it's beautiful! Yes! I will marry you!"

He removed the yellow-gold band with a one-carat emerald-cut diamond in the center and princess-cut diamonds on each side. There were smaller, round diamonds along the band. He slipped it onto her finger. They grinned at each other. Janina flung her arms around his neck, then they kissed with enough heat to melt ice.

Everyone around the table clapped and offered their congratulations.

"What's your animal?" Aileen asked.

Janina blushed. "I'm a red fox. When we shift in the woods near the palazzo, Jason licks me all over!"

A procession walked over to the office building to see the apartments. Sherm stopped at the new reception center where Marcha and Big Bear were on duty.

"We need two badges," Sherm said. "One for Ari's father and one for Jason's fiancé."

Marcha typed in the information for the badge software. "Mr.

Porter," Big Bear said. "Would you stand here so I can take your picture?"

Kenneth stood where Big Bear indicated. The shifter adjusted the camera, snapped the picture, and checked the viability of the photo. It was a clean shot and looked good. He labeled the file.

Janina was next. She spelled her last name out loud: B-A- G-D-O-N-A-S. Then she stood in front of the camera.

Within a few minutes, Kenneth and Janina had badges on lanyards around their necks.

"Which apartments are available right now?" Roman asked Marcha.

She jumped on her computer, pulled up a spreadsheet and perused the criteria. "Apartment 603 was just painted yesterday, and all the appliances are in place. Number 525 is also ready."

"Let me have those keys," Roman said.

Marcha rolled over to the right and unlocked the lockbox that secured the keys. She perused the rows and grabbed the keys for the two apartments.

They all headed for the elevators. Everyone piled into the two elevators. They stopped on the fifth floor.

Apartment 525 faced the side of the building with a view of the parking lot and the woods. Stainless steel appliances were in the eat-in kitchen, along with a farmer's sink, plenty of cabinets, a pantry, and a half-bath. White plantation shutter blinds were on the windows.

There was room for two barstools at the kitchen island. The living room was a good size with plenty of wall area for a TV, bookcases, and pictures. There were two bedrooms, each with its own bathroom.

"Oh, I love this apartment," Janina said. "It's so modern and roomy."

"It could be yours," Ari said.

"Let's go look at the other one," Gage said.

They piled into the stairwell and climbed up to the sixth floor and found 603. The layout was different, with more square footage. The windows faced the woods, full-on.

"Oh! This is beautiful, also!" Janina said. She looked from Jason to Kenneth. "I would be happy in either of them. Which one do you like, Kenneth?"

Ari's heart went out to her future daughter-in-law. She was thoughtful and considerate. She knew right away that Jason was in good hands. "Dad, there will be more available next week."

"I would be comfortable with the one on the fifth floor," Kenneth said. "I like the ability to see the parking lot—who's coming to the building, as well as the serenity of the woods." He glanced over at Jason and Janina. "Besides, you two have a need for more area than I do at the moment."

"What do you think of this apartment, Jason?" Janina asked.

"I like it," he said. He glanced at his mother. "When can we move in?"

"We can go over to the warehouse and look at furniture," Ari said. "There's plenty to choose from, and you won't have to start hunting for furniture." She turned to her father. "What about you, Dad? Do you want to set something up temporarily until you sort out what you want to do, or do you want to stay in the house?"

Kenneth mulled it over. "Let's go see the furniture." He grinned at his daughter.

🦍ML🏞️

When Ari unlocked the door at the warehouse and ushered everyone inside, they stared in wonder at the enormous place packed with home furnishings.

"I can't believe it!" Sherm said. "Your uncle didn't get rid of anything, did he?"

She handed out sticky note pads and black markers. Her father received a blue sticky note pad, and Jason and Janina orange sticky note pads. "There's everything you could possibly want here, including table lamps, artwork for the wall, and I think I even saw a few statues and nic nacs. Put your initials on the notepads so Pablo knows where to deliver the stuff. Sherm, do you need anything, or want to swap something in your room?"

Sherm's mouth was hanging open. "Really? I can change things up?"

Ari plopped a green pad in Sherm's hand. Roman and Gage stuck their hands out. "Really?" Ari asked.

"I may find something I like better," Gage said.

Ari gave him a bright pink pad. She handed Roman a yellow pad. "There's no hurry. Take your time."

They were like kids in a candy shop. Pablo and his crew were smart to arrange everything according to specific items. All the desks were together, all the sofas, chairs, coffee tables—everything was so much easier to find and mull over for decision-making purposes.

After an hour and a half, everyone had their items labeled. They drove back to the house, and Mr. Butler served up iced tea and sandwiches. Ari retreated to her office and taped sticky notes on a piece of paper with names and locations, so that Pablo would know where to deliver the furniture.

Phoebe and Eddie were on their way outside, so Ari handed the paper off to them so they could track down Pablo.

🏛**ML**🏘

The rest of the week flew by. Kenneth returned to New Mexico with Atsa and Yiska. Jason and Janina returned to Italy. Aileen's furniture arrived.

Ari sat in her office and pulled up her San Marcos database. She sorted by profession and discovered there were several medical professionals among their people. Dr. Humberto Rosas was an OB-GYN. She jotted his information into her phone, and into her contacts, then she called and made an appointment.

Next up, she discovered a GP and a veterinarian. She made a note of them as well. She walked down the long hallway to Roman's office. During the renovations, they had a door cut into the wall so that Gage's and Roman's offices were easily accessible to each other.

She found Roman at his desk, sitting back with his feet propped on an open drawer while he read printed pages. She opened the connecting door and found Gage clacking away on the keyboard.

Ari stood in the doorway between the two offices. "I discovered three doctors in our San Marcos database." She told them she had an appointment with the OB-GYN for the following Wednesday at eleven in the morning.

Gage was out of his chair in a blink, then wrapped his arms around her. "This is so exciting! We'll go to all your doctor appointments with you."

Roman was on his feet and at her side. He snuggled into her neck and hair. "I can't wait to see our children. I'm so glad there's a shifter OB-GYN."

"We need to start thinking about names," Gage said. "What are we going to use for a last name?" Roman asked. "Davenport-Stryker?"

"I like the sound of that," Ari said.

Her men grinned, giddy with excitement at their new roles.

Ari left them to their chatter and returned to her office to tackle the O'Briain accounts. She was deep in the files when a tap on her office door made her raise her head. Pablo stood in the doorway, hat in hand.

"Ari, the golf cart I use every day won't start. I've looked at everything and can't see anything wrong with it," he said.

"Hold on, I'm pretty sure Tommy can fix it," Ari said. She picked up the phone and called Sherm and told him what the problem was. "Tommy and Sherm will meet you at the equipment building. Sherm says Tommy can fix anything."

Pablo thanked her and left. He walked over to the equipment building as Sherm and Tommy walked around the corner from the office building.

"What's wrong with it?" Sherm asked.

"Won't start," Pablo said.

"Where's it usually plugged in?" Tommy asked.

Pablo walked inside with Tommy and Sherm following. He pointed to the slot. "This is where the golf cart is housed to charge."

"Do you have a 120-volt tester?" Tommy asked.

Pablo walked over to several tool cabinets. "Everything you require will be in these cabinets." He pulled open the fourth drawer in the second cabinet and withdrew the volt tester and handed it off to Tommy.

"Better grab a couple of screwdrivers," Tommy said. Tommy tested the wall socket. It was working just fine.

Tommy walked over to the golf cart and flipped the seat up to expose the batteries. He checked each battery and discovered that a clamp was loose. He tightened the clamp, then walked to the back of the cart and unscrewed the six screws that secured the panel over the motor. He pressed the reset button.

Tommy flipped the seat down over the batteries, sat in the driver's seat and started the cart. "All set."

"What happened?" Pablo asked. "I didn't see anything wrong with anything."

"The clamp on the middle battery came loose. Once I tightened it, I reset the motor. These things take a beating, running all over the place, so things come loose," Tommy explained.

"Huh," Sherm said. "You're our go-to guy from now on."

ML

During dinner, Ari brought up the database of just the San Marcos area. She was excited to see so many professionals and service providers.

"I sure hope the GP is like Dr. Tanner," Roman said. "He's going to be hard to replace."

"We should invite Dr. Sterling to dinner," Gage said. "That way we can get to know her."

"I think it would be a good idea to invite the three of them, along with Mr. Tran and Cama. The doctors should have the benefit of meeting our herbalists," Ari said.

"Good idea," Aileen said. "I'm all for natural healing. I try to stay away from prescriptions and chemical treatments as much as possible."

"When would you like to have this dinner party?" Mr. Butler asked.

"Should we try for this weekend, or Tuesday evening?" Ari asked him.

"Let's shoot for Saturday," Mr. Butler said. "Friday nights for doctors might be wind-down time. Sunday may be filled with church services and getting the kids ready for the week. Saturday night is neutral."

"Okay. I'll put together an invitation. Local mail only takes one day, so there's plenty of time to plan and for them to RSVP," Ari said. "I think I'll ask them to specify whether they have food restrictions so we know how to plan."

Sherm brought up Tommy's successful repair job on the golf cart. "I've got to tell you, that kid really knows his way around not just a toolbox, but computers as well."

"How's Douglas doing?" Roman asked.

"Like Kevin, he's taken to things like a tadpole to water," Sherm said.

Kevin smirked.

Ari locked onto her son. "What exactly do you do now, son?"

"Mom, I work with cameras and a lot of electrical things," he said.

"If you were Pinocchio, your nose would be out the door," Ari said.

"This subject is off-limits, remember?" Roman said. "There's no point in trying to pull it out of Kevin, Sherm or Lonnie, Ari. What goes on in the security division is off-limits to you, for your own peace of mind."

She snorted. "If you think it's a comfort not knowing what Kevin does, you're highly mistaken. But I understand he's not my little boy any longer, and hopefully he isn't doing any Mission Impossible stunts."

Mr. Butler's eyes bounced from face to face while listening to the conversation. "At least Jason has a desk job, so you don't have to worry about him."

CHAPTER TWENTY-SIX

Dr. Humberto Rosas, his wife Francine, Dr. Amy Sterling, Dr. Duke Cavendish and his wife Gertie, fit into the dinner conversation around the immense table in the seldom-used dining room. Mr. Butler moved Eddie's little table and chairs into a corner so that Eddie and Lola Jean Cavendish could enjoy themselves. Phoebe was close-by at the end of the dining table, closest to the mini table.

Mr. Tran had moved into one of the largest office building apartments, while his son Douglas grabbed the last bedroom over the garage. The third bedroom in Mr. Tran's apartment held his herbal business. He and Cama had a lively conversation between themselves and the doctors about the treatments and various benefits to going natural.

Somewhere during the conversation, Dr. Sarantopoulos' name came up.

"He's just returned from Greece," Amy said.

"We have an appointment with him for Eddie's testing," Gage said. He, Roman, and Ari explained the whole reading test, the barometric pressure conversation, and where things went from there. They discussed Eddie's school placement issues and the decision to homeschool her.

"Phoebe, what's the latest news?" Roman asked.

"It's a challenge to keep pace with her learning skills. She absorbs everything. I'm pretty sure she could successfully perform brain surgery from what she's studied recently," Phoebe said.

The doctors raised eyebrows. The wives had little smirks on their faces. Everyone always thought their child was the brightest, so this display of how smart Eddie was made them think of their own children.

"Has she learned any languages yet?" Humberto asked.

"She's fluent in Spanish, French, Dutch, Italian, Greek, and Mandarin," Phoebe said.

"How old is she?" Gertie asked, changing her smirk to an expression of disbelief.

"She just turned four," Ari said.

"Ask her anything you learned in medical school," Roman suggested.

Dr. Rosas turned in his chair. "Eddie, have you studied blood types?"

She dazzled them with facts about the four blood types: A, B, AB, and O. Then she explained all about plasma, antibodies, and proteins. Roman stopped her when she started into a detailed explanation about alleles, genotypes, and phenotypes.

There was dead quiet around the table.

"Greg is going to love working with her," Amy said, with glee.

"We don't know where her intelligence comes from," Gage said. He explained about the attack that killed her mother and her father's betrayal. "We haven't looked closely at either side of her family. We couldn't find anyone on her mother's side, but her father's people are on the East Coast."

"I think you should dig deep and see what you can find," Duke said. He studied the girls at the little table. "For her vast intelligence, she seems content with Lola Jean, who is a normal five-year-old."

"She has two shifter girlfriends here that she plays with all the time," Ari said. "So, she seems to be able to fit herself into the surrounding circumstances, and she's happy to be included."

Roman tapped his lower lip. "I honestly don't think she's figured out she's smarter than anyone in this room."

🏭**ML**🏯

Ari, Roman and Gage showed up for her first doctor's appointment to check on her pregnancy and which trimester she was in. The front desk seemed to have an issue with the one woman in a two men relationship. Ari set them straight and informed them that both her life partners would be going through the door to the exam room.

When she had that ironed out, the nurse settled them into a room, handed Ari a soft cotton gown, and told her Dr. Rosas would be there shortly. Ari changed, sat on the end of the stainless-steel table with the white crinkly paper, and waited for the doctor.

Roman and Gage examined the table, the stirrups, the doctor's rolling stool, everything on the counters, and the posters on the walls. By the time they finished their thorough perusal, Dr. Rosas tapped on the door and entered with Dotty, his nurse.

"Hello, Ari!" Dr. Rosas held her hand, gently. He turned to the men. "Roman, Gage, are you ready to be fathers?"

"I've been reading up on the whole process and what to expect," Gage said.

"You might as well toss that out the window," Dr. Rosas said. "Every case is different. Especially with shifters."

Their eyes darted to Dotty, a human.

"It's okay," Dr. Rosas said. "Dotty has seen it all, which brings up another subject. I don't suggest you give birth in a hospital. There's always a teeny, tiny chance that you could have an animal birth. Or shift and give birth."

"Lord, I'll never, ever forget Mrs. Peters!" Dotty said.

Dr. Rosas laughed a huge belly laugh. "Poor Dotty. This was her first home shifter birth while assisting me. She was very green when it came to shifters. When Mrs. Peters shifted to her water buffalo and commenced to bring her calf into the world, I thought Dotty would faint dead away. But she soldiered on."

"I understand your animal is a liger, Ari?" Dotty asked.

"Yes, all seven-hundred-ninety-five pounds of me in my animal form," Ari said.

"Don't ever stand between her liger and whatever made her shift," Roman said. "As Tothars, my panther is twice the size of a normal cat, and Gage's eagle is twice the size of a standard bald eagle. We learned not to mess around when she shifts."

The exam went smoothly. Dr. Rosas determined Ari was at the end of her first trimester. He performed a sonogram, and they heard two distinct, healthy heartbeats. They stared at the screen in wonder at the two tiny fetuses.

"Eddie told us we were having a girl and a boy," Roman said.

Dr. Rosas stared at the screen. "Next time we should be able to get a better picture, provided they cooperate and show their genitalia. But with your daughter, I'd say that's like winning a bet."

Dotty wiped Ari's tummy and lowered the gown to cover her up.

Dr. Rosas took Ari's hand. "The last time you gave birth, you were one-hundred percent human. This pregnancy is going to be vastly different. Your animal may have needs yet-to-be-determined. So, if you crave a raw piece of meat at four in the morning, I suggest you dig in. Try to have someone with you if you get the urge to shift and run."

The doctor swung his eyes over to Roman and Gage. "There are going to be times when Ari may get extremely emotional. There are two choices. Either send warmth and love to her, along with holding her, or the second choice is to get the hell away from her and just plain shut up."

Gage was wide-eyed.

The room was so quiet, everyone heard Roman gulp.

"I've had to stitch up more than one husband over the past twenty-five years, so I'm dead serious. This is not a human pregnancy. I work with Duke sometimes when I need his veterinary experience. We'll have everything covered when the time comes for you to deliver."

Ari slid off the table.

"One more thing," Dr. Rosas said. "Due to too many unknowns because you are a shifter, and more so because of your Tothar heritage, you may not go the full nine months of a human pregnancy. Contact me immediately if there are any issues, no matter how trivial."

Dotty handed each of them a card with the doctor's personal information.

On the drive away from the doctor's office in downtown San Marcos, they took in what shops they could see while turning their heads right, left, then right again. Roman missed out on many of the sights, as he was the designated driver.

"Oh, look! There's an ice cream shop!" Ari pointed out.

Roman found parking, and they walked to the shop. Ari ordered a banana split with an extra scoop of ice cream and all the toppings, while Roman and Gage got ice cream cones. They stared at her as she devoured her sundae.

I've never seen her eat like this before, Gage sent.

You'd better pray you blocked her, Roman sent.

Gage glanced Ari's way as she scooped the last drop of melted butter pecan ice cream into her mouth. He let out a sigh of relief that she didn't pick up on his remark.

The day of Eddie's appointment with Dr. Sarantopoulos arrived. They all piled into the Mercedes, with Eddie in her child's seat, and arrived the requisite ten minutes early to fill in information. They divvied up the forms between the adults, even though Eddie thought she should be filling them out since it was her appointment.

"We don't have a lot of this information," Gage said.

"We'll explain it when we meet the doctor," Ari said.

The nurse called them and they were escorted to a room, which was not like a regular medical doctor's exam room. This room was more like a living room. They settled on the sofa with Eddie between Ari and Roman. Gage was on Ari's other side.

Dr. Sarantopoulos entered the room. He was a good-looking Greek with thick, black, wavy hair, wide shoulders, and an all-over athletic body. Ari placed him around fifty. Smile creases surrounded his dark eyes.

He approached the sofa and shook their hands, including Eddie's hand. "I understand you have a brilliant little young lady here."

"You must have talked to Amy," Roman said.

"She called to tell me she met you, and that I'd be seeing you today," the doctor said. "Why don't we get to know each other today, and I'll do some general assessments so I can determine what type of testing will benefit your daughter's education."

"That sounds good," Ari said.

For the next forty-five minutes, Dr. Sarantopoulos worked with Eddie. He presented her with some basic intelligence tests and had a lively dialog in Greek with the four-year-old. At the end of their session, he smiled widely at Ari, Roman and Gage.

"I'd like to set up a two-hour session for extensive testing, if that is agreeable with you," he said.

"Yes, we need to understand how best to prepare her for life. Being this smart, but too young to work or drive, will have great limitations on her immediate future," Roman said.

Dr. Sarantopoulos walked them to the front desk, where he shook their hands and set up the next appointment for them. Roman paid with his credit card.

That afternoon at the dinner table, Eddie was chattering away about the doctor and some of the problems he presented for her to solve. "I didn't want to say anything to him, but any little kid could have solved those problems."

"Honey, you're a lot smarter than most little kids your age," Gage said. "Dr. Sarantopoulos was trying to determine how smart you are, so he would have the right type of materials when we go back for the big two-hour test."

"Oh!" Eddie said. She continued eating her peas, mashed potatoes and meatloaf.

"So, it went well?" Phoebe asked.

"He's quite a nice guy," Roman said. "He'll be able to guide us on how to form her future."

"I think he and Amy Sterling are dating," Ari said.

"I sort of got that too," Gage said.

That night, Ari noted that while they slept in the same configuration, her men had started nothing in the romance department. It had been days since they had made love. She was getting frustrated. She climbed over Roman and got out of bed. Ari flopped down on one of the comfy, overstuffed leather sofas in the adjoining sitting room. Normally, she would reach for a glass of wine or a whisky, but, being pregnant, those options were no longer available. She almost let out a roar, but caught herself.

Roman plodded over to her, hair sticking out, his pajama pants low on his hips. He was in fine form, with his six-pack abs restored after his long recovery from his Italian experience in the old Tothar king's cell. He flopped down beside her and pulled her into his arms. "What's wrong? Can't sleep?"

She practically snarled at him with accusation. "Neither of you has even attempted to make love to me in over a week. I'm pregnant. I'm not stewing with some awful condition. I will not break with a little threesome."

Roman flinched. He backed off a generous distance. "We didn't know how you felt—if we should."

Her hormones lifted their ugly head, and all reasonableness left the room right when Gage staggered in and flopped down beside her.

"What's the matter? Why aren't you two in bed?" he asked, barely awake.

"I'm not even showing yet, and you two act as if I'm some two-ton Tessie that's no longer desirable!" Ari spewed, getting angrier by the minute.

Gage determined that this was one of those moments when they should retreat, not trying to hold or kiss her to make it better.

We'd better sleep in our offices, he sent to Roman.

Wow! I don't know what to make of this, Roman sent. *I thought she wouldn't be interested in sex.*

Best not to start anything right now, Gage sent. *You heard Dr. Rosas. She could shift at the wrong time.*

Roman took a chance and darted in for a kiss on her forehead. "We're going to our offices. We love you. You are the most beautiful woman in our universe, Ari. Get some rest."

The door snicked closed softly. Ari spread out on the leather sofa. She flung an arm over her eyes.

She wondered if she were being unreasonable. Ari wondered if things would return to normal.

She wondered what the new normal would look like.

After too many senseless questions racing through her mind, she got up and climbed into the bed. She fell into a deep sleep.

ML

Ari woke with a groan on her lips as teeth gently grazed her left nipple. Her clit pulsed with need. Hands lifted her hips, and a mouth latched onto her desperate bud. Then Gage's tongue slid up and down her slit, then darted inside her wet, hot core. He divided his efforts between her clit and her slit.

Roman tweaked her right nipple as he sucked on her left, his teeth scraping the pebbled nipple maddeningly slow.

Ari closed her eyes and shuddered. Roman abandoned her nipple and stretched up to capture her lips. His teeth tugged at her lower lip. His tongue licked the upper lip, then the lower before he plunged inside. She felt like she was being scorched with passion inside and out.

She broke her mouth away from Roman as her gut tightened and her clit throbbed. The orgasm that roared through her was intense. Her mouth froze in a little oh. No sound emerged as passion engulfed her. Finally, she sucked in a breath, and a gasp escaped her lips.

Before she caught another breath, Gage plunged inside her. Her heels dug into his butt, keeping him inside her. She matched his thrusts, passion igniting her higher and higher. She screamed out another orgasm just as he came with his own roar. When he thrust for the last time, he lowered his mouth to hers and kissed her like a starved man at a banquet. Then he moved to the side and slid off the bed.

Roman wiped Ari's nether region with a damp washcloth. Gage grabbed it and headed for the bathroom while Roman climbed on top of Ari and ravished her mouth with an erotic kiss. Her hands grabbed his hair, ran down the back of his head, across his shoulders, kneading his flesh.

His mouth traveled down her neck. He pulled her right nipple into his mouth with lips and teeth. He drove her crazy with his teeth scraping her tight, pebbled nipple. Then his mouth traveled further south. As his lips surrounded her clit, two fingers entered her dripping core.

She was a writhing, moaning mess of overactive hormones and great need. One minute her hands were in his hair, holding his head in place, and the next she was trying to pry his mouth off her. He sensed she was at her limit. He pulled himself up between her legs and plunged inside her.

Ari let out a blissful groan as Roman entered her. She grabbed his butt with both hands. Her hips matched his pace, his strength, as her mind just let go. She floated on the ecstasy. Her body hummed as her orgasm closed in. "I'm going to come! Come with me, Roman!"

Her orgasm boiled through her. She wailed as the intense pleasure shattered her. Roman arched as he came, pounding into her until every single drop of cum had pumped out of him. He forced himself not to collapse on top of her, using his arms to support his drained body.

Gage climbed onto the bed. Roman moved to his left, while Gage tucked a hand towel between Ari's legs.

"I need a nap," Gage said.

They giggled, snuggled into each other, and dropped off to sleep.

CHAPTER TWENTY-SEVEN

Eddie got along famously with Greg Sarantopoulos. Ari wasn't sure if Eddie was winning him over with her personality, or if he was drawing her in. Ari, Roman, and Gage were waiting in a room with a two-way mirror, while the doctor presented Eddie with materials.

After twenty minutes of watching, Gage pulled his laptop out of his bag and powered it up. Roman and Ari followed suit. They couldn't tell what tests Eddie was working on , so there didn't seem to be any point in staring through the glass.

Half an hour later, Ari's mind caught action through the mirror. She looked up to see Eddie and Dr. Sarantopoulos doing jumping jacks, then running in place. Roman and Gage caught her interest, geared toward the mirror, and smiled.

"That's a good way to break up the two hours," Gage said. He watched his adopted daughter give her very best. She was competitive. She looked so cute in her pink crop pants, white T-shirt with pink balloons, and pink sandals.

"I wonder what he's having her do in there," Ari said. "It seems as if there's some paperwork and computer work as well."

"We'll find out soon enough," Roman said. "She's practically halfway through the session."

The men worked on their laptops while Ari studied Eddie for a few more minutes. Then she dove back into the database she was reformatting.

Less than an hour later, the door opened to the room, and they were on their feet.

Eddie burst through the door and rammed into Roman's legs. He hoisted her up and gave her a smooch on the cheek and rubbed her back.

"All finished?" he asked.

"Uh huh. I'm going to school in Austin!" Eddie said.

"You are, huh?" Ari asked, tickling her.

"Eddie, why don't you take a look inside the toy box while I talk to your mommy and daddies," Dr. Sarantopoulos said.

"Okay!" Eddie dashed back into the testing room.

"Why don't we sit down for a chat," the doctor said.

"Uh oh," Gage said.

"Uh oh, indeed," Dr. Sarantopoulos said. "There's few testing applications that Eddie can't breeze through as if they were kindergarten work."

Ari, Gage, and Roman glanced at each other, then returned their focus to the doctor.

"You came to me for educational placement and recommendations. Your little girl will skip grade school, middle school, high school, and even undergraduate studies," he said.

"What?" Roman sputtered. "We thought she'd skip a few grades, but all of it?"

Dr. Sarantopoulos nodded, serious. "She's interested in the Texas McCombs IROM program, which focuses on training future researchers in the areas of decision science, information systems, operations management, and statistics. It's a five-year degree that I think she'll breeze through in a year or two."

After they regained their voices, Gage asked the doctor to explain what the program entailed.

"There's a major emphasis on business applications throughout the program," Dr. Sarantopoulos said.

Ari contemplated. "How do we even go about getting her into the program? She's only four years old!"

"I'll upload her scores and data online to a site that's used for the gifted children's programs around the country. Then I'll contact the dean," Dr. Sarantopoulos said.

"She can barely print. Forget about cursive," Roman said.

"But she knows how to type on a keyboard," the doctor said. "That's all she'll need, plus she absorbs what she learns—way, way beyond simply memorizing. Her brain sucks it in. I know this seems daunting, but believe me, she has a mind of her own. Adult students won't intimidate her. They're the ones who will be intimidated. She won't tolerate being looked down on either."

"Did you suggest this program to her?" Ari asked.

"No, she told me that's what she wanted. She said she's been looking at colleges with her nanny for the past few days," Dr. Sarantopoulos said.

"Well, okay then," Gage said, at a loss for words. "I guess you'll let us know what the dean says?"

Dr. Sarantopoulos held up a hand in the UT hook'em horns gesture. "Looks like you're going to have the youngest Texas Longhorn in the university's history. I hope you like the color orange."

The adventure continues.

BOOK 4: UNFORESEEN

Here are the highlights for Book 4 of the Bonded series.

Eddie's first day in the Texas McCombs IROM program started with Professor Akobar's accounting regulation and liability class. The professor could not believe he was having a high-level discussion with a four-year-old who was smarter than he was.

Roman, Ari and Gage regret that Eddie's scores were uploaded online when government SUVs arrive at the house in San Marcos, along with agents who want to *borrow* Eddie for an assignment. Sherm practically goes off on them.

Ari shifts to her liger... and doesn't shift back. Mr. Butler freaks out when the huge cat lumbers into the kitchen and sits in front of the refrigerator. He sneaks past Ari and grabs a steak out of the meat drawer and tosses it out the kitchen door into the yard for the big cat.

Roman goes running through the forest. He stumbles over an old grave with a cross.

Eddie discovers that Bem wo Taugh, the man who mows fields around the county, is a physicist who *dropped out* over a decade ago to live a simpler life.

Ari's father moves into the apartment on the fifth floor of the office building.

Aileen and Mr. Butler can't keep their eyes or hands off each other.

Gage risks getting between Ari and Kevin when she finds out some of Kevin's duties. Sherm defends the decision of keeping Ari out of the security business.

Leander and Trisha move to San Marcos. Jason and Janina move into the apartment. Lonnie moves out.

And so much more... just wait and read the book!

ABOUT THE AUTHOR

Dawn Greenfield Ireland is also known as D.E. Greenfield, DG Ireland. Dawn is an award-winning author of 22 novels, which include 5 series (cozy mystery, sci fi/fantasy, billionaire shapeshifters, and dystopian), and a stand-alone sci-fi romantic adventure.

Most of her 7 nonfiction books have won awards. Dawn has adapted a few of her screenplays into book format, and several of her books into TV series format. She also created over 50 themed notebooks.

She had two screenplays optioned, and she worked on a screenwriter-for-hire project. Dawn has a certificate from the Professional Program in Screenwriting from UCLA (2002), and a certificate from ScreenwritingU (2023).

Dawn writes full-time. She lives among dreams and fantasies with two cats and moving boxes. Her head is filled with stories. She doesn't suffer from writer's block.

Her business, Artistic Origins, has been around since 1995. Besides writing, she coaches writers, edits, formats, and publishes clients' books.

Her former day job as an award-winning technical writer played a major role in her fiction writing. She is detail-oriented, the organizational queen of the known universe, and never misses a deadline.

TO ALL MY READERS... if you discover bloopers in this book (or any of my books), PLEASE send me an email and tell me what the blooper is so I can fix it! dawn@degreenfield.com

facebook.com/dawn.ireland.18

x.com/dawnireland

instagram.com/dawngreenfieldIreland

goodreads.com/dawnireland

linkedin.com/in/dawnireland

www.ingramcontent.com/pod-product-compliance
Lightning Source LLC
Chambersburg PA
CBHW020356260626
47156CB00007B/2140